CW01501432

MURDER AT HAMBLEDON HALL

HALL

CLEOPATRA FOX MYSTERY, BOOK 10

C.J. ARCHER

WWW.CJARCHER.COM

Copyright © 2025 by C.J. Archer

Visit C.J. at www.cjarcher.com

All rights reserved.

No part of this book may be reproduced in any form or by any electronic or mechanical means, including information storage and retrieval systems, without written permission from the author, except for the use of brief quotations in a book review.

CHAPTER 1

BERKSHIRE, SEPTEMBER 1900

*T*he picnic on the lawn signaled an end to the crack of gunshots that had spoiled our morning. The extensive gardens of Hambledon Hall were peaceful once again, disturbed only by the movements of servants as they laid out refreshments and the gentle fluttering of ladies' fans. The shooting party of six gentlemen rejoined us at the same time as the children of our host and hostess arrived with their nanny, who firmly held the hands of her two excited charges. She appeared to be scolding them out of the corner of her mouth, but the children paid her no mind as they broke free and ran to their father, Lord Kershaw.

Lady Kershaw smiled at her husband as he ruffled the golden hair of their son. Her smile became tight as her gaze connected with the nanny's. The nanny dipped her head as she waited for her employer to send the children back to her. "She's new and is yet to earn their respect," Lady Kershaw said on a sigh. "I'm afraid they're a handful."

We ladies sat in the shade of the black-and-white-striped umbrellas, where tables and chairs had been set up. The food was laid out in a tent nearby. With the arrival of the gentlemen, we were merely waiting on a sign from Lady Kershaw to partake of the offerings.

Aunt Lilian stood before our hostess gave the signal, however. Having kept to her room all morning, she'd

1

appeared downstairs moments before we ventured outside. The twitching of her facial muscles and her enlarged pupils were evidence that she'd taken her tonic. The energizing effects of the cocaine would only last an hour before they wore off and she became irritable and fatigued. Her family knew all too well that it was best to avoid her company when that happened. Until then, she would be as restless as the children.

"Didn't you have a new nanny last year?" she asked Lady Kershaw.

Lady Kershaw watched the nanny usher the children to the tables of food and assist them with their selection from the vast spread. "She left three months ago."

"And the year before that, too?"

"They're so difficult to hold on to. I find it's the same for most of the young female staff. They simply don't want to be in service these days."

"How strange," my cousin Flossy said. "We don't have that trouble with our maids, do we, Mother?"

Aunt Lilian either didn't hear her or pretended not to, out of politeness to our hostess. Flossy seemed to realize too late that she may have offended Lady Kershaw. She was right in that the Mayfair Hotel had a large number of maids to service the guest rooms, and many of them stayed with us for years. But it wasn't polite to point this out after Lady Kershaw's comment. It implied there was a problem at Hambledon Hall that sent them packing. If it was only the female staff who didn't stay, it was likely the problem was a man.

I couldn't imagine the amiable Lord Kershaw being the cause, however. In his early forties, ten years older than his wife, my uncle's friend had warmly welcomed us to the three-day house party and seemed to have an open countenance. I'd chatted with him about all manner of topics, where most men his age wouldn't bother with a young female guest. I'd not felt uncomfortable for a moment during those conversations, or at any other time, nor had a I noticed him pay particular attention to the nanny or maids. We'd arrived only yesterday, so I didn't know him particularly well yet, but I prided myself on picking up certain cues from lecherous men, and I perceived none from him.

Perhaps the problem lay with one of the male staff. I made a mental note to warn Harmony and Aunt Lilian's maid to be careful.

With the children seated beside their nanny, Lady Kershaw rose and invited us to fill a plate. The game the men had shot would be served at dinner tonight, we'd been told, but there was still a variety of choices available for luncheon, from several different sandwiches to cold slices of meat, pies, cheeses and fruit.

My other cousin, Floyd, slipped in beside me, his plate already piled high. "The shooting was invigorating. You should try it, Cleo."

"Killing living things doesn't appeal to me."

"She says as she places a ham sandwich on her plate."

"I'm quite happy to eat what others kill out of necessity, but I don't want to make a sport of it, thank you. I hope you didn't shoot more than we need for dinner."

"Anything we shot that isn't served at Hambledon will be given to the villagers. It's a tradition that dates back to the time King Henry the Eighth stayed here and hunted game in the very same woods." He forked a slice of beef onto his plate. "We were supposed to continue this afternoon, but it's been called off."

"Why?"

"Don't know. Not enough birds, perhaps. Or perhaps it's so we can be sociable and play yet another round of croquet with the ladies."

"You could always plead a headache and retire if it bores you."

He glanced in his mother's direction. "Better not. One Bainbridge absence will be enough. Besides, I have a feeling Miss Browning will need guidance again, and I rather look forward to giving it to her."

"Floyd," I chided. "She's engaged to be married. Stop flirting with her."

"She's flirting with me! It's not my fault she likes me better than her dull fiancé."

"You've never met him."

"He's in banking, Cleo. He must be dull."

"I'm sure his family money makes him a great deal more

interesting than you think." I regretted it the moment I said it. Janet Browning's fiancé could be a wonderful man for all I knew, and it wasn't fair to presume she was marrying him for his money.

Lord Kershaw's niece was a year or two younger than me, and got along swimmingly with Flossy. Both lively, pretty girls, they turned heads wherever they went. They also seemed to find amusement in a great many things. What those things were, I wasn't entirely sure. They spent a lot of time giggling behind their fans.

Floyd rejoined the gentlemen reminiscing about the morning's shooting, while I sat at a table with the elderly Lady Elizabeth Wentworth, Lord Kershaw's aunt, and Mrs. Browning, his sister and Janet's mother. Mrs. Browning had placed a full plate in front of her aunt, but Lady Elizabeth only poked the contents with her fork as she inspected the selection. The hand holding the fork trembled.

"Wouldn't you prefer to sit with ladies your own age, Miss Fox?" she asked.

Just as she said it, Janet spilled a little claret on the table-cloth in her enthusiasm to signal to Floyd to join her and Flossy. Both girls giggled as a hovering footman swooped in and discreetly covered the spill with a cloth.

"I'd rather talk to you," I said. "I've been meaning to ask you about Hambledon Hall. How old is it?"

Lady Elizabeth's blue eyes lit up as she told me about the house she'd lived in since it was built fifty years ago, after the previous Tudor manor was torn down by her father. I'd not realized it was so new. The towers and battlements were purely for show, then. Hambledon Hall hadn't begun life as a fortified structure, despite appearances. The only shots that would have been fired in its vicinity were for sport.

"Some of the villagers call it a Gothic monstrosity, but I'm fond of the pile of stones," Lady Elizabeth said with a chuckle. "The old place was so drafty in comparison. Now it's full of life with the two children tearing along its halls. I'm fortunate to have lovely memories of both houses."

I placed her age at around eighty, so she would have well and truly been an adult when the current house was completed. She'd resided at either the previous or current Hambledon Hall her entire life. Having never married, she'd outlived her father and brother—the fourth and fifth earls of Kershaw—and was living with her nephew, the sixth, and his young wife. From what I could see, they doted on her.

Lord Kershaw's sister, Mrs. Browning, sat on her aunt's other side, her plate empty except for two slim ribbon sandwiches. "Did I overhear you mention oriel windows, Aunt Elizabeth? Miss Fox is a young lady. She doesn't want to talk about the style of windows in the gloomy old place."

Lady Elizabeth's hand fluttered to her mouth with a bird-like flap. "Oh dear, Miss Fox, I am sorry. I'm boring you, aren't I? I do tend to go on sometimes."

"Not at all," I said. "I asked about the Hall because I'm interested in architecture. In fact, a friend of mine will want to hear all about it when I return to London." I stopped myself before I let slip that my friend was a man. I didn't want to set tongues wagging.

From the way Lady Elizabeth's eyes sparkled, I wondered if she realized.

Lady Kershaw sat beside Mrs. Browning. The sisters-in-law couldn't look more different. The younger of the two, Lady Kershaw was short and full-figured whereas Mrs. Browning was tall and slim. Her ladyship's dark, almond-shaped eyes often brightened when she spoke and her apple cheeks turned pink after minor exertion. Like her husband, she'd welcomed me warmly into her home.

Mrs. Browning, however, peered down her nose at me from her great height through frosty blue eyes. I would have assumed that was how she treated everyone and not been offended, except that I was the *only* lady she looked at that way. Flossy suffered no such disdain. Given my father had been a mathematics professor of no particular lineage, and Flossy's father was related to nobility, albeit distantly, I didn't need to look hard for a reason for Mrs. Browning's prejudice. She might be the daughter of the late earl, but she had married a commoner, so I'd expected a measure of empathy from her, but she was snobbier than the rest of her family put together.

"I hear the shooting party was such a success they won't be continuing this afternoon," Lady Kershaw said. "They have enough birds."

Mrs. Browning made a scoffing noise. "There's never enough, Marion. Even if they'd shot a mountain of partridge, they'd want more." Her gaze slid to her husband, standing with some of the other gentlemen, a glass of beer in his hand. "That's men for you. Always eager to destroy unnecessarily."

Lady Kershaw looked uncomfortable at her sister-in-law's brutal assessment. She may outrank Mrs. Browning, but she tended to shrink in her presence. Even though she was the hostess, and the Brownings didn't reside at Hambledon Hall, she often deferred to Mrs. Browning before making a decision. Perhaps Lady Kershaw felt inferior because she'd come to the Hall only upon her marriage, whereas Mrs. Browning was born and raised here.

Lady Elizabeth asked to be excused. Lady Kershaw signaled to her husband to assist his aunt, but he was too intent on one of the outdoor servants emerging from the trees in the distance to notice. Instead, Uncle Ronald offered his arm. With him on her left side, and her walking stick in her right hand, Lady Elizabeth slowly made her way back to the house.

"I hope your aunt is all right," I said to Mrs. Browning. "She left very suddenly."

Mrs. Browning didn't respond. Like her brother, she was watching the outdoor servant as he strode across the lawn then disappeared around the side of the house in the direction of the outbuildings. Mr. Browning's hooded gaze also followed the figure. Once the servant was out of sight, Mr. Browning suddenly glanced at his wife.

With a regal jut of her chin, Mrs. Browning picked up her glass and pretended not to notice.

"Who is he?" I asked.

"Who?"

"That man you were looking at."

"I saw no one. Excuse me, Miss Fox. I must speak to my daughter." She took her glass with her but left behind the plate with the untouched sandwiches.

After luncheon, Lady Kershaw gave us a tour of the

garden, ending in the fernery. Plants of all varieties, shapes and sizes filled the room, many of them ferns and palms, but not all. Some had leaves as big as me reaching to the glass ceiling. A paved path meandered through the indoor oasis, past moss-covered rockeries and ponds where the silver bellies of fish flashed in the sunlight. I decided to return later with a book and sit on the bench seat sheltered by palm fronds.

A game of croquet came next, then afternoon tea, followed by a lull during which I found time to read in the fernery while the other ladies wrote letters. When the gong to dress for dinner sounded, I found my way to my room where Harmony had already laid out my evening gown, gloves, shoes, hair pieces, and jewelry. Her efficiency was born from boredom. After a triumphant stint as assistant to Floyd, organizing an important wedding reception at the Mayfair Hotel, she'd returned to maid's duties. Although she never complained, I sensed she missed the more interesting duties of the assistant's role. Uncle Ronald had promised her she would be allowed to organize future events but, as yet, the hotel had none booked.

She'd accompanied us to Hambledon Hall as lady's maid to Flossy and me. After I was ready, she'd go next door to help Flossy, but until then, we could talk. Of everyone at the Mayfair Hotel—my family and the rest of the staff—Harmony was the person with whom I felt most comfortable.

I remembered to warn her about my theory that a male member of staff could be causing the maids and nannies to leave prematurely. "I think someone is upsetting them, and I presume it's a man. Have you seen any of the men behaving terribly?"

"No, but your instincts are sharp, Cleo. Lady Bainbridge's maid and I were warned to stay away from the gamekeeper by Lady Kershaw's maid." She directed me to turn around with a wiggle of her finger, but I stood rooted to the spot.

I stared at her. "If the most senior female servant, aside from the housekeeper, thought the two visiting maids ought to be warned, why is the gamekeeper still working here? It's unacceptable."

"You misunderstand. I don't think he attacks anyone. He

simply tries to charm them out of their petticoats. He doesn't persist if he fails, but I think he has more successes than failures. A lot more. Then he tires of them and moves on, leaving behind a string of broken hearts. Some of them leave because of it."

"The maids and nannies resign from perfectly good positions because they're heartbroken?"

"Or maybe asked to resign because they're moping about and not doing their work properly."

This time when Harmony made a circling motion with her finger, I turned around. She proceeded to undo the buttons of my dress.

"Nannies are under the direct jurisdiction of the lady of the house, not the housekeeper," I said, half to myself. "So in their case, at least, they must be leaving of their own accord, because Lady Kershaw made it sound as though she wasn't dismissing them."

Harmony agreed but had more to say about the gamekeeper's continued employment. "His lordship should tell him to play away from the house, if he's not prepared to dismiss him."

"I suspect Lord Kershaw doesn't want to broach the topic. He's too nice."

I saw Harmony's lips pinch in the reflection of the dressing table mirror and decided to change the subject.

* * *

AFTER A HEARTY DINNER at which I overindulged in both pheasant and wine, I skipped breakfast altogether the following morning. Lady Kershaw had planned a game of tennis, but having never played, I preferred an activity in which I wouldn't make a fool of myself. Flossy had also complained that she wasn't very good at it, so I went in search of her after the breakfast hour to see if she wanted to go for a walk with me.

She wasn't in her room, but Harmony was, and informed me that Flossy had gone riding with Janet Browning.

I headed along the corridor that housed several guest bedrooms and small chambers, admiring the ornate plastered ceilings, rich carpets and heavily carved furniture. Hambledon Hall's opulence wasn't limited to the more public spaces of the dining room and reception rooms. Even the corridor on the guest wing had a beautifully plastered ceiling of leaves and plump pomegranates running its entire length. I came across a staircase I'd never seen before. It wasn't as grand as the double staircase in the entrance hall—which swept up two stories, highlighting a vaulted ceiling painted with an ecclesiastical scene resembling the works of Italian masters—but it was elegant nevertheless. The newel posts crowned with finials shaped like gargoyles were superbly Gothic.

My wanderings led me into another corridor I'd never seen, past closed doors. I realized I was quite lost. I paused, unable to decide whether I should try to retrace my steps or keep going, when I heard a sound coming from the only room with the door open. A maid must be inside. I'd ask her for directions.

I pushed the door open wider. "Excuse me, can you help —" I stopped abruptly when I saw it wasn't a maid at all. "Oh, sorry. I didn't mean to interrupt."

A man dressed in the clothes of an outdoor servant stood with an open book in hand beside a low bookshelf. The room was large, but so were most of the rooms in Hambledon Hall. The walls were covered with dark wood panels from the carpet to waist height, and paintings in gilt frames depicted bucolic country scenes. The wide mahogany desk near the window gave me the biggest clue that this was Lord Kershaw's study.

The man closed the book with a soft thud and slotted it back onto the shelf. "I was just waiting to have a word with his lordship, Miss."

I hadn't asked, but I supposed he felt the need to explain his presence in the study when his lordship wasn't there. While I couldn't be entirely certain, I was reasonably sure he was the same man Lord Kershaw and Mr. and Mrs. Browning had watched striding across the lawn the day before. Aged in his mid-forties, he had a strong build and square jaw. The flecks of gray in his thick dark hair added a dashing allure. I suspected this was the gamekeeper

Harmony had told me was causing the female staff to lose their hearts.

"Miss Fox," I said. "It's a pleasure to meet you, Mr…?"

"Shepherd." He smiled, his countenance friendly, albeit a little too warm considering we'd just met. "I've seen you around. Forgive me, but I was hoping we'd meet." He stepped closer.

I stepped back. His smile suddenly became slicker. I was even more sure he was the gamekeeper now, given his reputation. Why was he in Lord Kershaw's study? "I saw Lord Kershaw downstairs. Do you want me to tell him you're waiting here for him?"

He stepped closer again, and I stepped back once more. I bumped into the doorframe, having misjudged my position relative to the doorway. Mr. Shepherd's gaze heated. He stepped forward a third time, drawing very close. I pressed my spine into the doorframe and leveled my gaze with his.

His smile turned to a smirk as he brushed past me. "Seems he's forgotten our appointment. No matter. I'll talk to him later."

He strode off along the corridor. As I walked in the opposite direction, I tried to imagine myself in the position of a housemaid. Would I find Mr. Shepherd alluring enough to risk my position? I doubted it. Then again, no man compared to Harry Armitage. I could certainly no longer deny I had feelings for him, but that didn't mean I would do something about them. I was still determined not to marry anyone, even him.

Yet sometimes, in my more melancholy moments, I wondered what my life would be like without him in it.

It was these thoughts that occupied my mind as I left the house. I was so distracted that I didn't notice the carriage pulling away until I heard the crunch of gravel beneath its wheels. Lord Kershaw's jowly profile was clearly visible through the window. It would seem his lordship had indeed forgotten he was supposed to meet Mr. Shepherd in his study.

The walk through the woods was invigorating, and I enjoyed being alone in the fresh air with only my thoughts for company. It was easy to forget how vivid nature could be when living in London. The grass was a vibrant shade of green, and the earthiness filled my lungs. Wind rustled the leaves far above my head, and birds twittered musically, until the sound of two men arguing sent them fluttering away.

I headed toward the men, visible through the trees. I couldn't make out what they were saying, but it was clear they weren't getting along. I recognized the gamekeeper, Mr. Shepherd, but the other man had his back to me. With a gray cap covering his hair, I couldn't even tell if he was one of the gentlemen from our party.

Mr. Shepherd suddenly laughed at something the other fellow said. It was a cruel laugh, not at all as if he were sharing a joke. The other man responded by punching the gamekeeper in the stomach.

Mr. Shepherd bent over, clutching his middle, and the other fellow strode off, heading away from me.

I decided to leave, too. Mr. Shepherd seemed winded but otherwise unharmed.

Despite my intention to leave well enough alone, I couldn't help myself. I didn't head away from the clearing where I'd spotted the two men arguing. I circled it, hoping my path would join up with the path the other man had taken. Despite going in what I thought was the right direction, I found myself back where I started. The clearing was now empty, however.

After a lovely long walk, I decided to return to the house. The eastern tower was just visible through the trees when a gunshot rang out.

I froze. Should I hide? Run? Where had the shot come from?

Perhaps it was simply Mr. Shepherd shooting a rabbit.

I tugged on my jacket hem and continued on my way. My nerves remained taut, but I no longer thought I was going to be the next victim of a mad gunman. If Harmony were here, she'd tell me my imagination had been fueled by my experiences investigating murders and reading detective novels.

I emerged from the woods and saw a man dressed in black crouching on the driveway, alive, thankfully. It wasn't until he stood and shouted for help that I realized a crumpled body lay at his feet. From this distance, it was impossible to see who.

As I drew closer, however, I got the feeling I'd seen those clothes quite recently. One glance at the face, frozen in shock, confirmed it was Mr. Shepherd, the gamekeeper. He'd been shot in the chest. There was no gun in the vicinity, so it wasn't self-inflicted.

He'd been murdered.

CHAPTER 2

"*M*iss! Stay back! This isn't a sight for a young lady to witness." The bespectacled man dressed in black spoke quickly and with authority. I realized with a start that he wore a clerical collar, so he was probably the local vicar, come to call on the landed gentry of his parish.

Even though he was first on the scene, I dismissed him as a suspect. It was several minutes since I'd heard the gunshot. If he were the gunman, surely he would have fled. Besides, he looked very pale. He was more likely to faint than kill me next.

I bent to take a closer look at the body. Despite the horrid scene, I did my best to focus on the details. They might be important.

The bullet had entered Mr. Shepherd's chest, so if he'd been walking toward the house, the shot had been fired from there. If away, then the gunman had fired from the garden or one of the trees lining the long drive. I was no expert on bullet wounds, so I couldn't be sure what type of gun had been used.

I tucked my hand into Mr. Shepherd's outer jacket pocket.

"Miss! What are you doing?" the vicar cried. "That's sacrilege!"

"A clue to his murder could be in his pockets."

"M-murder! Good lord, I doubt it. It must have been an accident. This is Hambledon Hall!"

I wasn't sure what the house had to do with anything. Finding nothing in the pocket, I went to search another, but the vicar caught my wrist.

"I insist you step back, Miss. You're violating a dead man."

Others were coming now, so I obeyed. I didn't want to embarrass my uncle and aunt by being seen rummaging through a dead man's pockets.

Uncle Ronald was in the party of men approaching. Lord Kershaw was with him, as was Mr. Browning. The butler brought up the rear.

My gaze connected with my uncle's. His bullish features folded into a frown at the sight of me. He gave his head a slight shake, and I stepped back, a hand to my chest, pretending to be overwhelmed by my exposure to the gruesome sight. No one else seemed to be paying me any attention, however, so I dropped the act.

Lord Kershaw stood over the body. He scrubbed a hand over the back of his neck. "Dear God, no. Shepherd."

"I'm afraid he's dead," the vicar announced.

His lordship continued to stare down at the face of the gamekeeper. His own face gave no hint of his thoughts. Perhaps he was too shocked to feel anything yet.

"I heard a gunshot," Mr. Browning said. "I was in my room at the time and didn't see anything."

"Did you see anyone fleeing the scene, Reverend?" Uncle Ronald asked the vicar.

"No."

"You were here quickly," I pointed out.

The vicar stilled. It wasn't until that moment I realized how constant his movements had been. His thumb had rubbed across his gloved knuckles, over and over, and a muscle in his left cheek twitched, tugging the corner of his beard upward as if it were on a puppet string. The neatly trimmed beard made it difficult to guess his age, but I doubted he was older than mid-thirties. He was still extraordinarily pale, so perhaps that was his usual appearance and had nothing to do with what he'd witnessed.

"I was on the driveway," he said. "I assure you, I saw no one. I assume the gunman disappeared into the woods."

"I came from the woods," I said. "I didn't see or hear anyone running away. The only people I saw the entire time was Mr. Shepherd and another man, arguing."

The men peppered me with questions all at once.

I answered them one at a time. "I didn't see his face so I can't give a description of his appearance. All I can tell you is that he wore a gray cap." I'd never again disparage a witness for giving a poor account of what they'd seen. It was more difficult to recall details than I had realized.

"Must be a poacher," Lord Kershaw declared. "Shepherd had run-ins with them from time to time."

"Don't poachers usually operate at night?"

Uncle Ronald cleared his throat. "Cleopatra, perhaps you should check on your aunt. You know how delicate her nerves are."

I turned my attention to the house, but didn't leave the scene. I might not recall many details prior to the shooting, but I could take in as much as possible now. Given the position of the body—feet pointed toward the house—it was most likely the shot had been fired from there. Unless Mr. Shepherd had spun around after being hit and before falling to the ground, in which case the shot could have come from any direction.

Floyd approached, along with the other two gentlemen guests, plus Lady Kershaw and Mrs. Browning. The men mentioned hearing a gunshot and were full of questions. Uncle Ronald took it upon himself to intercept them before they got too close, but they all spotted the body despite his efforts. His tone was calm, but it didn't reassure Lady Kershaw and Mrs. Browning. They brushed past him.

Lady Kershaw gasped. "Is that…?"

Mrs. Browning pressed her fingers to her lips. After a moment, she walked away, back toward the house. Her husband's narrowed gaze tracked her.

"Is the local sergeant a good man?" Uncle Ronald asked.

Lord Kershaw circled an arm around his wife's waist and angled himself so that he blocked her view of the body. "Er, uh, yes, good enough." He directed the butler to send for the police.

I followed Mrs. Browning. Behind me, I heard Uncle Ronald sending the others on their way, too.

Floyd suddenly appeared at my side. "Don't, Cleo."

"Don't what?"

"I know that look. You're determined to find out who fired the fatal shot."

"I'm a detective, Floyd. It would be unprofessional to do nothing."

"There's no point. You heard them asking about the local plod. He's a good man, so Kershaw says. That's code for he'll do what he's told. Kershaw won't want a fuss made. He'll want this swept under the carpet as quickly and quietly as possible, and that means no one will be arrested. No doubt he'll convince everyone that it was simply a terrible accident."

"This isn't the Middle Ages. He can't dictate a police investigation."

Floyd snorted. "I didn't peg you as the naïve sort, Cousin."

I stopped and rounded on him. "Where were *you* when the shot was fired?"

"Excuse me?"

I arched my brows, waiting.

"Don't be petty, Cleo. Why would I shoot the game-keeper? Anyway, I was playing tennis." He indicated his sporting outfit of white pin-striped knickerbockers buttoned below the knees with high socks and a boater. He'd dispensed with the jacket, but his waistcoat matched the knickerbockers.

"Who was with you?" I asked.

"I'm not telling you that, because you're not inves-tigating."

The others joined us, so I didn't have the opportunity to press him. The two gentlemen also wore sporting clothes, as did Flossy, Lady Kershaw and Janet Browning. Mrs. Browning and Aunt Lilian wore elegant daytime outfits, suit-able for taking tea, but not for playing tennis. I'd question Flossy later about the other players, if Floyd remained obsti-nate. Hopefully I could eliminate them all as suspects if they were with her on the tennis court when the incident occurred. There were more staff than guests and family, however. If any of them had access to a gun, the list of suspects would be long.

Speaking of access to guns, my first task would be to check the armory.

Inside the house, we were met by Lady Elizabeth, cautiously making her way down the staircase. "Why all the commotion?"

Janet assisted her great-aunt down the final step. "It's the gamekeeper. He was shot."

Lady Elizabeth's breath hitched. "I heard the gunshot, but I presumed it was simply Mr. Shepherd shooting at a rabbit. Did he…? Was it…an accident?"

"Of course it was. It must have been." Janet patted her aunt's hand. "What else could it be?"

"I overheard them say a poacher was in the vicinity," Flossy said.

One of the gentlemen claimed a witness had seen blows exchanged between the gamekeeper and a trespasser. I didn't bother to tell them I was the witness and only one punch had been thrown.

"What happens now?" Lady Kershaw appealed to her sister-in-law. "Do we wait for the police to interview us?"

Mrs. Browning was quite composed by comparison, and looked comfortable taking charge. "We carry on as we were. It's an unfortunate incident, but we mustn't let it ruin the weekend. It's the final day, after all. The family and staff can mourn and pay their respects tomorrow. Perhaps you can have luncheon brought forward, Marion. That'll take everyone's mind off it. In the meantime, anyone for bridge?"

A look of relief passed over Lady Kershaw's face. "An excellent idea. I'll send word to the kitchen." She made eye contact with a footman who stepped forward to receive instructions.

Some of the party followed Mrs. Browning into the West Gallery and principal drawing room beyond, while others headed upstairs to change for lunch. I broke away while no one was looking and turned into the East Gallery. Thanks to the tour of Hambledon Hall by Lady Kershaw, I remembered the armory was located on the first floor of the bachelor's wing, accessed via a spiral staircase in the East Gallery.

I fished my lockpicking tool kit out of my pocket as I passed another set of stairs, then the smoking room and billiard room. To my surprise, Harmony stood outside the armory, a feather duster in hand.

She breathed a sigh of relief when she saw me. "It's you, Cleo. I thought you'd come up here."

I indicated the feather duster. "You're a lady's maid, not a parlor maid. No one will believe you're up here dusting."

"One maid looks a lot like any other to most." She tucked the duster under her arm. "I heard you were first at the scene."

"Second. The vicar claims he was walking toward the house when he heard the gunshot. I'm glad you're here. You can keep watch while I pick the armory door lock."

"You fetched your tools already?"

I unfolded the tool kit and removed a pair of slender picks. "I carry them with me everywhere, nowadays." I crouched and set to the task. "How long have you been waiting for me?"

Harmony checked the watch she kept in the pocket of her skirt. "Seven minutes. The shot was fired ten minutes ago, and no one passed me while I waited here."

"So the murderer had three minutes in which to return a gun after firing it from a window, assuming it is in here. That's not long in a house this size. This wing is quite separate."

"Are you sure it's murder?"

"Unless I hear a good explanation for why it's not, I'm treating it as suspicious."

"Was the shot fired from the direction of the house?"

"I can't be certain. The body was in front of the house, at the point where the long drive opens up. It's an exposed area." The lock clicked and I pushed the door open. "If someone took a gun from here, it's my guess they still have it and will return it later, when things have settled down, mostly likely during the night."

The armory housed new guns as well as antiques, including shotguns that were used for hunting and by the previous day's shooting party. There was other military para-phernalia, too, including dozens of swords and knives

18

displayed on the wall, and a shirt of chain mail that an ancestor had worn in battle. The more decorative pieces were on display either on the wall, or behind glass in cabinets.

"There are so many," Harmony said, wonder in her voice.

"Lord Kershaw is a collector, as was his father and grandfather before him. He inherited most of these. When Lady Kershaw gave me a tour of the house, he was already in here with all the gentlemen."

"I don't understand why all the guns are stored here," Harmony said. "Even the ones used for hunting."

"They're safer in the house than an outbuilding."

Harmony studied a pair of dueling pistols, their bone handles etched with the Kershaw crest. She opened the glass door of the display cabinet and picked one up. "Do these old ones still work?"

"I don't know." I was more interested in the modern guns, stored in two cupboards. Neither cupboard door was locked, but none of the guns were missing. *Drat.* I'd been so sure the murder weapon had been taken from the armory.

"Cleo." Harmony sounded ominous. "Was that space empty when you came in here on your tour?"

I followed her gaze to the wooden display pegs sticking out from the wall. "No. Those were holding an antique rifle."

"It must be the murder weapon. Now all we have to do is wait and watch to see who returns it."

That would have been a good plan, except we'd stand out like elephants. While the bachelor's wing wasn't strictly off-limits to women, there was no reason for us to be there. We'd look suspicious.

"I have another task for you," I told her. "Find out where the servants were when the shot was fired and who was with them. Take a note of any who can't be accounted for or were alone at that time."

"What will you do?"

"The same thing, but with the guests and family."

* * *

WE ATE a light luncheon on the terrace. The casual arrangement allowed me to move among the other guests and listen in to conversations. Lady Kershaw put an end to my endeavors before I'd truly begun, however. She made a point of introducing me to the vicar, Reverend Pritchard.

"I know you have already met, but I don't think that should count," she said, smiling. "This is a more appropriate place to make new acquaintances. Or, if I may be forward, new *friends*."

I caught her exchanging a sly look with Aunt Lilian and inwardly groaned.

If Reverend Pritchard noticed, he was polite enough not to say. "I want to apologize for earlier, Miss Fox. I don't think we started on the right foot."

"I agree with Lady Kershaw. That encounter should be set aside. The circumstances were…extenuating."

"Reverend Pritchard was invited to join us for shooting and dinner yesterday," Lady Kershaw went on, "but unfortunately, he was detained elsewhere."

"Duty called." The vicar pressed one finger to the bridge of his glasses as he glanced around at the party. His gaze settled on one of the gentlemen chatting to Floyd.

Lady Kershaw encouraged me with a nod then excused herself, leaving me alone with someone who may or may not have killed the gamekeeper. "Did you know Mr. Shepherd?" I asked.

"Who? Oh. Yes, the er… No, not really. I met him only once."

"He wasn't a regular churchgoer?"

"Not in my time, but I've only served this parish for six months."

"Where were you before that?"

"Cornwall."

"You don't have a Cornish accent." When he didn't respond, I added, "Whereabouts in Cornwall?"

"A small village. A mere speck on the map." He gave me the sort of smile I suspected he gave an annoying parishioner he was forced to converse with after a service. "Tell me about yourself, Miss Fox. You're the niece of Lady Bainbridge, I hear."

Despite giving me his undivided attention, I got the

distinct impression he wasn't interested in a word I said. I was relieved when Floyd joined us.

"Excuse me, Reverend, do you mind if I borrow my cousin for a moment?" Floyd asked.

The vicar stepped away with a bow and sipped from his wineglass. He was alone for barely a moment before Lady Kershaw swooped in. She seemed to have recovered from her earlier uncertainty over the correct protocol following the untimely death of one's gamekeeper, and was once again immersing herself in her hostess duties.

"I thought you might need rescuing," Floyd said to me.

"You thought correctly, although you do surprise me. I was sure you'd want me to become good *friends* with him by the end of luncheon."

"The vicar?" He snorted. "He's not your type. If that's my mother's reason for forcing an introduction, then I apologize. She's not in her right mind at the moment."

I saw an opening for a deeper conversation about his mother's health. "You need to do something about that."

"Me?"

"Talk to her. Tell her to get a new doctor, at the very least."

He shook his head. "It's up to my father to talk to her, not me." He eyed the table of food. "Do you think it's too soon for a second helping?"

We both added cucumber sandwiches to our plates. "Do you find this all very odd?" I whispered. "A man has died and everyone is carrying on as normal. Not only that, but I believe the police have already left."

"They have."

"Why didn't the sergeant speak to me about the argument I overheard in the woods? I gather Lord Kershaw will try to place the blame on that man, so I expected to be questioned about it, if only to add weight to his theory."

"His lordship passed on your account. You didn't see his face, he wore a cap, you couldn't hear their words, but you sensed they were heated…" He waved a sandwich in the air before taking a bite. "There's nothing more to it, is there?"

He was right, there wasn't, but I would have liked the opportunity to give my version.

Through a combination of eavesdropping and asking

discreet questions, by the time the servants came to clear away the plates and glasses, I'd learned that the only people unaccounted for at the time of the gunshot were Lord and Lady Kershaw, Mr. and Mrs. Browning, Janet Browning, and Lady Elizabeth. The rest were either playing tennis or walking in the garden with one or more witnesses. Hopefully Harmony had similar success with the staff, which would leave us with a limited pool of suspects.

* * *

DESPITE LADY KERSHAW'S EFFORTS, the mood at Hambledon Hall was strange. It didn't feel right to continue as we were. Playing sports and parlor games required a liveliness that no one felt comfortable expressing, even those of us who didn't know Mr. Shepherd. Yet the air was not heavy with mourning, either. Lord and Lady Kershaw seemed unaffected by the gamekeeper's passing, and the footmen and butler maintained typically blank expressions as they carried out their duties.

It wasn't until most of the guests had dispersed to their rooms after lunch finished that I saw Lord and Lady Kershaw having a terse discussion at the end of the terrace. I couldn't hear the words exchanged, but it was obvious from their faces and the way they held themselves that all wasn't well. Her lips formed a thin line, while he scrubbed one forefinger so vigorously, I worried he'd remove skin.

When we met in my bedroom, Harmony reported the mood was similar below stairs. "The only person mourning him is one of the young maids. The housekeeper sent her to her room, because she won't stop crying. The rest seem unaffected."

"Are they pleased, do you think? Relieved?"

"It's difficult to say. They're not giving much away in front of the visiting maids and valets. They exchange glances with each other from time to time, but it's not clear what message they're conveying among themselves. I think they're still coming to terms with the fact he's actually gone. I got the impression Mr. Shepherd was quite the fixture at Hambledon."

"He has worked here for years, apparently. His father was the gamekeeper before him, so he grew up on the estate."

"Lord Kershaw would have known him since childhood," she pointed out.

"As would his sister, Mrs. Browning. His aunt, Lady Elizabeth, would have known him since he was born. If Shepherd's murder is the result of a long-held grudge, then they should be our prime suspects."

Harmony arched her brows at me. "Lady Elizabeth seems rather doddery. I doubt she could hold a gun steady."

I agreed it wasn't likely. "The shot was spot on. It probably killed him instantly. Such accuracy requires a steady hand and good eye."

"And experience. I suspect it would require years of practice."

She had a point. While the women hadn't participated in the shooting the day before, it didn't rule them out. I'd have to discover whether Lady Kershaw, Mrs. Browning and Janet had any skill with firearms.

We spent some time searching the woods for the missing antique rifle. Finding it before it was returned to the armory would be a great help in narrowing down the list of suspects. Most had come from the house after hearing the gunshot, but the Reverend Pritchard had approached from along the driveway. There was also the fellow in the gray cap we'd seen earlier. If the rifle had been stashed behind a bush or tree, either one must surely be the murderer.

While we searched, Harmony informed me that the only staff member unaccounted for at the time of the gunshot was the butler. "Everyone else was with at least one other member of staff who can vouch for them. The butler was in his room, napping, according to gossip. His room is on the top floor."

"The top floor? He descended quickly to be among the first group to emerge from the house. And napping in the middle of the day you say?"

"I gather he likes a nip of his lordship's brandy, and its effects catch up to him. He's getting on a bit."

I poked at a bush with a stick, but there was nothing hidden beneath it. "How long has he worked at Hambledon Hall?"

"More than thirty years. He started here as a footman and worked his way up. He's certainly a suspect, although I don't know why he would want to kill the gamekeeper." She planted her hands on her hips and looked around at all the trees. "There's too much ground to cover, and you have to return to the house to change for the excursion to the river."

Lady Kershaw had decided we ladies should go for a drive while the gentlemen played billiards. Aunt Lilian had already declined, claiming she had a raging headache. "I'm not going. I'll say I want to stay with my aunt."

Harmony's eyes brightened. "You have a plan, don't you? Are you going to watch the armory to see who returns the missing rifle? That'll be difficult with the men in the billiard room nearby."

"I'll ask Floyd to keep one eye on the armory door while he's playing. I'll do something else. Something that involves you."

"Then I like your idea already. Where are we going?"

"To the gamekeeper's cottage. He lived alone, so it should be empty. I doubt the police will have bothered looking there, if the sergeant has already made up his mind about the culprit."

* * *

HARMONY and I were prepared to climb through a window at the gamekeeper's cottage if necessary, however the lock on the door gave me no trouble. Surrounded by the woods on the Hambledon estate, it was cool inside. Built from the same grim, dark stone as the main house, the cottage would be a miserable place in the depths of winter.

Harmony picked up a photograph from a side table. "What are we looking for?"

"Anything that gives us a sense of the man, and why someone wanted him dead."

She showed me the photograph. "I presume the couple in this are his parents."

It would seem so, going by the way he rested his hand on the seated woman's shoulder. At her other side stood an older man dressed in his Sunday best. "Shepherd appears to be aged in his mid-twenties when this was taken."

Harmony returned the photograph to the table. Beside it was another photograph of Shepherd's parents, taken many years before the other. He wasn't in it, and I guessed they were aged in their thirties. A teenage girl stood between them, her fair hair tied in ribbons.

"I wonder who she is," Harmony said.

She went to pick up the framed photograph, but I caught her hand. "Someone has studied it recently and placed it back down, but they didn't place it precisely in the same spot." I pointed out the dust pattern. There was a clean space where the frame had been previously positioned.

Had they studied it before or after Shepherd's death?

We walked around the ground floor of the cottage. The parlor was neat, with nothing out of place, but it needed a thorough clean. The novels hadn't been removed from the bookshelf for some time, if the layer of undisturbed dust was anything to go by, and a mustiness wafted from the carpet.

In stark contrast to the parlor, the kitchen lacked dust, but the gamekeeper wasn't one for cleaning his dirty dishes. Flies buzzed around plates and cups piled up in the tub.

I pinched my nose and inspected the food scraps. "There's mold on some of these. He hasn't washed up for days."

"Pig," Harmony said with a wrinkle of her nose. "How can anyone live like this?"

"I think he lived in this room, and rarely ventured into the parlor except to pass through. There are signs of habitation in here and none in there."

"Signs of a putrid life."

She walked out of the kitchen, but I took my time looking around. I found a used train ticket from London that had fallen on the floor under the table, and a newspaper opened to the racing pages. A bunch of keys on an iron ring sat amidst odds and ends in a drawer. Another drawer was used for paperwork, including correspondence from a bank, betting slips, and some private correspondence addressed to Mrs. Mabel Shepherd, the last of which was dated a month earlier. It wasn't much, but I did learn his first name was Esmond. If this was the sum of Esmond Shepherd's life, it was rather sad. As far as I could tell, he didn't have any hobbies except horseracing, and he had no friends or family who wrote to him. Perhaps Harmony found more belongings upstairs.

I joined her in one of the two bedrooms. "Anything?"

She dangled a gold watch from its chain. "This was in the bedside drawer."

"It looks expensive."

"And new. It's in pristine condition. There are no engraved initials or other identifying markings, but there's also no reason to assume it didn't belong to him. It wasn't hidden."

"What else have you found?" I asked.

She returned the watch to the drawer. "There are some good clothes in the trunk. They also look new, and they're not the sort of suits worn by a gamekeeper."

The trunk was the only storage for clothing in the room. Two well-made jackets lay flat on top of folded trousers, waistcoats and shirts underneath. One of the jackets was made from dark gray wool, the other cotton, suitable for summer. I checked pockets as I inspected each item but found nothing. Not even a ball of lint. He may not have even worn them yet.

"They're more suited for a city gentleman," I said. "There's no tweed, nothing sturdy for a winter spent outdoors. These are the sorts of suits Floyd would wear day to day."

"Precisely. Why would a gamekeeper purchase them? And where did he get the money?"

"He likes to bet on horses, so perhaps he had a good win." I closed the trunk lid. "No new hats?"

"Under the bed in hatboxes, along with a great deal of dust."

I knelt and peered under the bed. The dust had been disturbed where Harmony had pulled each hatbox out to inspect the contents. "Is there any sign he brought women up here?"

"It's cleaner than the kitchen, so he may have. I didn't find anything pointing to a specific woman, though."

I stood and dusted off my gloved hands. "You said one of the maids was upset by his death. Just the one?"

Harmony nodded. "According to Lady Kershaw's maid, the girl was Shepherd's latest. She was new, the previous girl having left when she was set aside by Shepherd."

"So he went straight from one to the other. Charming."

"Lady Kershaw's maid rolled her eyes when she told me. I got the impression she thought the previous girl was pathetic, or perhaps stupid for letting her feelings for Shepherd ruin a perfectly good position here."

"You sound as though you do, too."

Harmony gave it some thought before answering. "Not pathetic, but I do think she shouldn't have become so upset when he moved on to another. Lady Kershaw's maid says she warns all the new girls about him, but some just don't listen. They only have themselves to blame when he tires of them, if you ask me."

"He's a cad. Or *was*. It's not the fault of the girls for being naïve. Some are quite young, and not as worldly as you or I."

To my surprise, Harmony chuckled. "You're not worldly, Cleo. You're wise and sensible, but that's not the same thing."

I supposed she was right. I'd always lived a comfortable life, protected by people who loved me, although I was cautious by nature when it came to trusting strangers, something that saved me from men like Shepherd. An innocent country girl who'd been thrust into the world too soon might not have any defenses against charming rogues.

"I may not be worldly," I said, "but I wouldn't fall for Shepherd any more than you would."

"That we can agree on." Harmony wiped her hand down my skirt. "You're covered in dust."

"Shepherd didn't like doing housework."

I continued to look around the rather bare bedroom, but found nothing that pointed to a reason why he would have been killed.

We left the cottage and locked the door. Before returning to the house, we walked around the perimeter of the building. We'd found no sign that he kept guns on the premises, or evidence of secrets buried beneath mounds of earth that had been recently turned over.

"What now?" Harmony asked as we headed back through the woods to the main house.

We emerged onto the driveway where the long shadows cast by the trees lining it hinted at the lateness of the hour. "The ladies will be back soon. I have to change for afternoon tea. Then we both need to talk to as many witnesses as possible, as subtly as possible. We leave tomorrow morning, so this could be our last opportunity to find the killer."

"You could ask to extend your stay. I'm sure Lady Kershaw wouldn't mind. She seems to like you."

"I'd rather return to London."

She smiled silkily.

"Why are you smiling like that? Never mind. I don't want to know." I lengthened my strides.

Harmony easily caught up. "I think you want to return to London as soon as possible because you miss a certain tall, dark and handsome private detective."

"I don't miss Harry. I miss London. It's galleries and museums, the parks, my friends and the hotel. Anyway, I'm not the only one who wants to return. I believe *you* want to return because you miss a certain cook."

"I do miss Victor and, yes, I would like to see him." Her ready agreement rather took the wind out of my sails. She couldn't be teased. "Just like I know *you* miss Harry. The sooner you admit you like him, the happier you'll be, Cleo."

We parted ways so that she could enter the house via the service entrance while I went through the front door. Her words left me reeling. Was I unhappy? I didn't think so. Not when I was in London, anyway. But I hadn't been completely happy here in Berkshire. Despite all the distractions the country house party had to offer, I'd felt somewhat lackluster since leaving London. I was mature enough to admit that it was because Harry wasn't here, too.

Tomorrow, I could see him again. The question was, should I?

CHAPTER 3

*A*s an only child, I'd been spared the teasing and competitiveness of siblings, but I'd also missed out on the special bond unique to brothers and sisters. Moving into the same building with my two cousins as adults had been a little like having siblings, although I could never attain the deep understanding Floyd and Flossy shared. It placed our relationship into a different category altogether. I was neither sibling nor friend, yet they respected me more than they respected each other, and when they teased me it lacked the bitterness that edged their own interactions.

Floyd still found it necessary to treat me as if I needed protecting, however. I put that down to his upbringing, in a family where men ruled and women were raised to be decorative. It was quite different to how I was brought up. Different, too, to how Harry was raised, first by an independent mother who worked as a teacher at an all-girls school, and then by a couple who were a team of equals. Based on what I'd observed, the behaviors of adults laid the foundations for the lifelong values of the children they raised.

Floyd's protectiveness came to the fore when I asked him if he'd seen anyone return a rifle to the armory. He flatly refused to answer the question. "The police know who fired the fatal shot, so you can stop investigating, Cleo." He strode along the corridor toward his room.

I picked up my skirts and followed. "Who is it?"

"A poacher. Apparently, you saw him arguing with Shepherd in the woods."

"I never saw that man's face, and there was no indication he was a poacher. Besides, the police haven't spoken to me directly. How can they arrest someone based on a complete lack of evidence?"

Floyd stopped at his bedroom door. "They didn't arrest him. He stayed at an inn in the village last night, but has already fled. He must have scarpered after shooting Shepherd. Before you ask, he didn't leave a home address. The inn doesn't note that information when their guests check in."

He went to open the door, but I placed a hand to it, keeping it shut. "A poacher stayed at a village inn," I said flatly. "Really, Floyd? You believe any of this?"

He shrugged. "It's none of my business, and none of yours, Cleo. If they want to blame an anonymous fellow nobody can locate, what does it matter to me?"

I leaned in and lowered my voice. "It matters if the murderer is under the same roof as you."

He barked a laugh. "He's not coming for me next. Or you."

"He? So you saw a *man* return the rifle to the armory?"

He sighed before finally giving in. "I didn't see anyone. Nobody came or went from the armory while we played billiards. I asked Kershaw if I could take another look at some old pistols in his collection and he obliged. The empty space on the wall was still empty—much to Kershaw's consternation, I might add."

"He didn't know the gun was missing until that moment?"

"It seems not, going by his reaction. He quickly covered up his shock, however, and didn't mention it to me."

"That's odd."

Floyd opened the door and entered.

I followed. "Lord Kershaw's shock would imply *he* didn't take it. If only we'd found it when we searched the woods."

"We?"

"Harmony and I."

"Don't drag her into this. Father won't think twice about dismissing her if she causes trouble with the Kershaws, and I don't want to lose her. I'll never find another assistant who makes me look so good." He removed his tie and undid his collar. "You're wasting your time, anyway. If you do find the missing rifle, the police won't test it if they want to continue to blame the poacher."

"I don't follow."

"It would mean the poacher got into the locked armory on the first floor of the house without being seen, and that's impossible. It doesn't fit with the theory they're pushing." He scrunched up the tie and tossed it onto the bed. "I'm sure the rifle will be returned to its place on the wall quietly, before anyone else discovers it went missing."

"Yes, I understand that, but what do you mean by test it? I didn't think bullets could be matched to a gun anymore, not since they began making them by machine."

"I don't know. I'm not a ballistics expert." He suddenly rounded on me. "No, Cleo."

"No what?"

"You're thinking about a gun expert, and that's leading you to consider calling on Armitage. Well, don't. He might be magnificent in your view, and the view of every woman under the sun, but he can't be an expert on everything."

"His father would know about matching bullets to guns."

Floyd sighed.

"Thank you for the information, but I must dash. I need to dress for dinner. I don't want to be late. I have suspects to observe."

I closed the door on his protests that the Kershaw family and guests weren't suspects.

* * *

WE DINED on more partridge from the shoot at the final dinner of the weekend party. I was pleased to be seated beside Mr. Browning. Of all the guests, I knew him the least, having had few opportunities to speak to him. It wasn't that I'd avoided him, or he me, it was more that we found ourselves in different conversations with different people. I doubted we had much in common.

By the time the soup course finished, I knew that to be correct. He enjoyed blood sports—the literal ones, like shooting and boxing, and the metaphorical one of politics. None of those interested me.

I thought a bloody murder might be up his alley, so asked him for his opinion of Esmond Shepherd's death. "It looked to me like a rifle bullet must have done it. It certainly wasn't a shotgun. Do you agree?"

His thick gray moustache and beard moved rather vigorously, but they almost covered his lips, so I wasn't sure if he was disgusted, horrified or trying not to laugh. "I'd heard you were…unconventional, Miss Fox, but that is a more unconventional topic of conversation than I'm used to having with a young lady at dinner."

His response didn't shed any more light on his opinion of my question, so I decided to take a different path. "I heard you bagged quite a number of birds yesterday. How impressive."

"I've always been a good shot, even though I came to the sport later in life."

"Oh?"

"I'd never shot a bird until I married into this family."

"Remarkable. I suppose it does help to practice from a young age. I presume his lordship is very good."

Mr. Browning had shoveled a forkful of partridge between the moustache and beard so could only nod in answer.

"Does Mrs. Browning usually join the shooting? And Lady Kershaw?"

He dabbed at his moustache with a napkin, wiping off the gravy stuck to it. "My brother-in-law indulges them, but they didn't want your cousin and aunt to feel left out this time. They each would have bagged more than Floyd if they'd participated." He grunted a laugh. "It's a miracle he didn't shoot himself in the foot."

"He hasn't had much practice. If he did, I'm sure he'd be as excellent a shot as you. He enjoys all sports."

He glared at Floyd, chatting to Mrs. Browning on the other side of the table. "Seems to me his favorite sport is flirting with the ladies." He stabbed his fork into the partridge and sawed off a slice with his knife.

At that moment, Mrs. Browning said something to Floyd then pointedly turned away. The look of disdain on her face made her seem even more regal. Floyd suddenly glanced in her husband's direction, then swallowed heavily.

Mr. Browning grunted again, this time in satisfaction. "Looks like he's not as good at flirting as I thought." He forked the partridge into his mouth. Before he swallowed, he turned away from me just as pointedly as his wife had turned away from Floyd.

My gaze connected with Floyd's across the table. I arched my brows. He merely shrugged, and struck up a conversation with Janet Browning, seated on his other side.

I hoped he wasn't trying to flirt with the daughter after failing with the mother.

I was about to engage Lord Kershaw in conversation when I noticed Lady Kershaw's gaze lingering on the mantel-piece. I frowned. Something about the mantel's decorations was amiss, but it took me a moment to realize the two ornate silver candlesticks that had stood at either end were missing. Their absence left two rather large empty spaces. I tried to think when I'd last seen them. They were there the previous night, I was sure.

I asked Lord Kershaw about the candlesticks.

He glanced at the mantelpiece, then at his wife. "I presume Renton was polishing them and forgot to put them back."

"That seems careless," I said.

He tucked into his food. With the mention of Renton, I hoped to draw out Lord Kershaw's opinion on the butler, but he didn't nibble at the bait I dangled.

"I'm sorry if our lack of shooting skill stopped your wife and sister from joining your party yesterday," I said. "I hear they're quite good shots."

His lordship glanced past me to his brother-in-law. "They're probably a little relieved they had an excuse not to participate, to be honest. My wife loathes the sport, and my sister would prefer to gossip. She admires your aunt greatly."

I doubted that. While they interacted politely enough, it

was clear that Aunt Lilian's true friend was Lady Kershaw. Even though she was closer in age to Mrs. Browning, she seemed to prefer the younger woman's company.

I decided to ask his lordship about Esmond Shepherd. Although I'd been shut down by Mr. Browning, I hoped Lord Kershaw would indulge me, even if he found my topic of conversation vulgar. "I know it's not the done thing to bring it up, but I wanted to tell you how dreadfully sorry I am about your gamekeeper."

Lord Kershaw's knife and fork stilled before he continued cutting a boiled potato. "Thank you, Miss Fox. That's kind of you. It's been a shock. Sergeant Honeyman assures me the poacher has left the area, so you don't need to worry. The man's argument was with Shepherd, and Shepherd alone."

I decided not to poke that particular hive. Lord Kershaw wouldn't deviate from the official line. Instead, I poured on more sympathy in an attempt to lull him into lowering his defenses. "It's no wonder Mr. Shepherd's death has hit you so hard. He's been with you a long time, I believe."

"Forever, and his father before him and his grandfather before that. Not that I ever knew his grandfather, mind. I'm not *that* old." He chuckled.

I pretended not to find it odd that he was chuckling after his long-term employee had been killed that very day. "Did he have any family who'll mourn him?"

"We were his family. The other staff, too."

"No parents still living? Siblings?"

"His mother died not long ago, but her death was to be expected. She was older than my aunt." He nodded at Lady Elizabeth. "Mrs. Shepherd was proof that clean country air is good for the constitution."

"Indeed. What about siblings? Did Mr. Shepherd have any? It's just that I thought I overheard one of the servants say there was a sister."

"There was, but she died before he was even born."

That must be the young girl in the second photograph, the one that had been moved. "Did the police look through Mr. Shepherd's cottage?"

He picked up his wine. "I suppose." He sipped.

He may be trying to shut down my questions, but I wasn't

giving up yet. "You must have had a special rapport with the outdoor staff, as you're clearly a man who enjoys nature."

He looked up sharply. "What?"

I indicated the greenish tinge on his finger. Without his gloves, I'd spotted it immediately.

He placed his knife and fork together on the plate and tucked his finger under his thumb. "I picked up a leaf and crushed it to release the lovely smell. Lemon, I think it was. Or perhaps peppery. Anyway, the thing stained my skin, and no amount of scrubbing gets rid of it."

I didn't know of any plant or leaf that could stain skin that exact shade of green, but I was no botanist.

"I'm surprised the vicar didn't see the poacher leave the vicinity," I said. "He was quite close by when it happened."

"Reverend Pritchard can be somewhat vague. Always losing his place in the sermon. It wouldn't surprise me if the poacher ran right past him and he took no notice, but it's more likely the man escaped through the woods. Not past you, of course, Miss Fox. I doubt you are vague." He chuckled again.

"I believe Reverend Pritchard is new to your parish."

"Previous vicar died. Heart gave out. We're fortunate Pritchard could come so quickly."

"Why did he want to leave his position in Cornwall?"

"I don't know. You'd have to ask him." He went to sip his wine, only to pause and lower the glass without drinking. "Do you know, that's a good question. It's unusual for a vicar to be available immediately to move to another parish. Usually, the church's administrative wheels move slowly. I wonder if he left under a cloud and had to be moved on in a hurry."

Now, that was interesting. "Do you know what parish he moved from in Cornwall?"

"He has never mentioned it. Whenever the topic comes up, he says the place is so small we would never have heard of it, then he changes the subject. Odd."

Indeed.

* * *

C.J. ARCHER

I ASKED Lady Kershaw about the silver candlesticks when we ladies left the men in the dining room to smoke their cigars and drink port. "They're such fine pieces," I said. "I hope one of the maids didn't damage them while dusting."

"Oh, no, nothing like that." She smiled brightly. "Renton took them away to polish and forgot to put them back."

It was the same answer Lord Kershaw had given me, however in her case, I felt as though it were a lie. I'd hoped to question her about Renton's penchant for sipping his lordship's brandy when no one was looking, and perhaps she'd then inform me that Mr. Shepherd had discovered the butler's secret, thereby giving him a motive to murder the gamekeeper. Now I was having second thoughts. There was no diplomatic way to ask such a thing.

I considered how best to phrase it for so long that Lady Elizabeth filled the void by suggesting we play bridge. "Come and join my table, Miss Fox. You seem sharp, and I do enjoy a good game."

Lady Kershaw was eager to oblige, as were my aunt and the younger ladies. Mrs. Browning also agreed to join in. "You're very persuasive, Aunt Elizabeth," she said.

"If I don't do something, I'm in danger of nodding off in the corner." Lady Elizabeth laughed, having done exactly that after dinner the night before.

Lady Kershaw instructed the footmen to set up the card tables and arrange the chairs. "This is just the distraction we all need after such a trying day."

Mrs. Browning looked askance at her sister-in-law. "Do you mean from that episode on the drive? Good lord, Marion, he may have been here for as long as the dirt, but we hardly knew him. We don't *need* to be distracted from anything."

Janet Browning looked like she'd jump out of her skin if she didn't impart her gossip soon. "I heard he was quite the favorite among the maids, if you know what I mean." She giggled.

Lady Kershaw smothered a gasp, and Lady Elizabeth frowned at her great-niece. Janet's giggles died. She looked like she'd burst into tears, but managed to mumble an apology as she sat down heavily.

Her mother briskly accepted a deck of cards from the footman. If it weren't for the extra firm jut of her chin, I'd say she looked as composed as ever. Like many ladies born into nobility, she oozed confidence even in prickly social situations. Her daughter hadn't yet acquired the skill, but I suspected she would with her mother as teacher. Lady Kershaw also wasn't quite as adept at brushing over a faux pas. She had a good pedigree, but she wasn't of the same class as Lord Kershaw and his family. She'd risen quite high when she married him.

His sister's marriage had not been as beneficial, but she'd lost none of her noble bearing because of it. According to Aunt Lilian, Mrs. Browning had fallen in love and married young. Having got to know Mr. Browning a little better, I presumed a handsome man had once existed beneath all that grizzly facial hair, and his character hadn't been quite so bullish in his youth in order to attract a young wellborn bride.

I felt sorry for Lady Kershaw, having the stiff and judgmental Mrs. Browning as her sister-in-law, but at least her husband's aunt was kind to her. The two women exchanged little smiles across the card table.

* * *

AFTER EXCHANGING farewells and promises to write, we were driven away from Hambledon Hall in Lord Kershaw's carriages. The rail journey to London was mercifully quick, and not long after the locomotive steamed out of the station, Frank, the doorman of the Mayfair Hotel, welcomed us home as we alighted from carriages in front of the hotel.

He was all smiles for the Bainbridge family, who greeted him warmly. Even Aunt Lilian managed a polite smile, even though she'd been morosely silent since leaving Hambledon Hall.

I stopped to speak to him. "You'll never believe what happened, Frank."

Once the door closed behind my family, Frank abandoned his attempt at cheerfulness. His features settled into their regular downturned pattern. "Whatever it is, it can't be worse than what happened here."

My heart dropped. "Is everyone all right?"

"A maid has been dismissed, Goliath feels responsible, and several other staff are upset."

"What did she do?"

"She was caught sneaking around the male staff quarters at the residence hall."

"It is a dismissible offence," I reminded him. "I'm quite sure the rule has existed since the hotel began."

"It's never been *enforced* before. No one has ever been let go for breaking it."

Most of the younger staff lived nearby in a lodging house owned by the hotel. Without the accommodation, they wouldn't have been able to afford to live so close to their place of work. London's rents were unaffordable for workers on a low wage. The rent may be free, but it still came with a price. They had to maintain what my uncle deemed 'a respectable character' even after their shifts ended. For most, the rule didn't pose a problem.

"I presume Goliath feels responsible because the dismissed maid was visiting his room," I said.

Frank stepped away as the door opened and a guest emerged. He wished the gentleman a pleasant day by name.

Once he was out of earshot, I asked, "Are the other staff upset because they liked the maid?"

"She was liked well enough, but the reason they're upset is because Mrs. Short has forbidden *all* staff from relationship entanglements, even respectable ones. Do you know how many couples there are? I can name at least seven, all of them serious. One couple is even married! What are they supposed to do? Get a divorce so they can keep their jobs?"

"Now you're being silly."

"There's Harmony and Victor, Donny and the tall redheaded maid, Felicity and that waiter—"

I put up my hand to stop him rattling off every couple. "Does Mrs. Short have the authority to make that decision?" As housekeeper, she managed the maids, but waitstaff were under the jurisdiction of Mr. Chapman, the steward, and the cooks were under the *chef de cuisine*, Mrs. Poole. Front of house staff reported directly to the assistant manager, Peter Leyland, while Mr. Hobart, the hotel manager, oversaw the entire cohort. Surely it was his decision to make a blanket rule of no fraternizing, not Mrs. Short's.

Frank shrugged. "Mr. Hobart hasn't overruled her yet. I reckon he was waiting for Sir Ronald to return to gauge his thoughts. If you ask me, Miss Fox, it's bad. This is a new century, and the young folk don't want to be restricted by old rules set by old people. We'll lose staff over this, you just watch."

I ventured inside, a little concerned that Frank might not be overreacting, for once.

The foyer was an inviting place, with its large displays of flowers filling enormous vases, and the potted palm trees adding a hint of the tropics. While not as densely packed as the fernery at Hambledon Hall, the greenery provided an exotic touch to an otherwise very English hotel.

There was no sign of Frank's doom and gloom in the foyer. It was peaceful. September in London was empty of the sort of people who could afford a room at the Mayfair. According to Flossy, September was the month for spending time with family and friends at country manors. According to Floyd, it was when those who didn't own a country estate took themselves off to Germany, Austria, or France for a rejuvenating holiday at a health spa. Apparently, Monaco was popular for those who liked to gamble, as well as for husband-hunting ladies whose reputations weren't pristine enough for the ever-vigilant mothers of eligible bachelors back in England.

Mr. Hobart walked beside Uncle Ronald, heading to the corridor that housed the senior staff offices. Aunt Lilian and my cousins had already disappeared into the lift. I joined Peter at the check-in desk. He and the clerk appeared to be going over the reservations book, but I caught a snippet of their conversation, and it wasn't about the guests.

"Frank tells me the sky is falling," I said. "I hoped you could give me the more accurate picture."

Peter smiled. "Welcome back, Miss Fox. How was Berkshire?"

"Lovely, until the…" I glanced at the check-in clerk. "Never mind. Is the situation here causing a problem?"

Peter rounded the counter and invited me to walk with

him. "Frank isn't overstating the tension for once. Mrs. Short's new rule of no fraternizing is causing problems with some of the staff."

"For just the seven couples already in relationships, or everyone?"

"All of the staff are agitated. They think the rule is grossly unfair."

"Are they agitating to the point of going on strike?"

"Not yet."

We'd recently had trouble with the mews staff striking when a motorized vehicle took up space in the coach house. No one wanted to endure that again. If the entire staff went on strike, it would be disastrous.

I'd not taken much notice of our direction, until we found ourselves in the staff parlor, tucked away behind the lift and stairs, with access from the service rooms at the rear of the hotel. It was late morning, a time when most of the maids were cleaning rooms, but the waiters had little to do. The cooks would be preparing for lunch in the kitchen, so I was surprised to see Victor there with Goliath, the hotel's porter. Victor wasn't dressed in chef's whites however, so he mustn't be on duty.

"I'm on the dinner shift," he told me when I asked. "I organized with Harmony to meet in here when she returned. How was the three-day-long party? How many birds died for the gentlemen's sport?"

Goliath frowned at him. "I didn't know you were anti-shooting."

"Only when it's for the amusement of toffs. Sorry, Miss Fox, but I don't think it's necessary."

I assured him he didn't offend me. "I agree with you, although I should point out that everything that was shot was eaten by our party or given to the villagers. Every *bird*, that is."

Only Victor noticed my clarification. He leaned forward, elbows resting on his knees, and opened his mouth to speak. Harmony's arrival had him forgetting all about me, however. He rose and smiled at her. Victor rarely smiled, so it was rather lovely to see. It wasn't lost on Harmony, either, who smiled sweetly back at him.

He offered her a chair. "Welcome home. Tea? Biscuit?"

"Yes, please, to both," she said as she sat. "I came here directly and was stopped at least a half dozen times by someone wanting to tell me about Mrs. Short's new rule. Can someone elaborate?"

Peter told her what he'd told me. Goliath grunted at several points, letting everyone know his thoughts. Harmony, however, kept hers to herself. She accepted the teacup from Victor, eyeing him the entire time from beneath her dark lashes.

I accepted a teacup, too. "I'm sure Uncle Ronald will over-rule Mrs. Short. Perhaps your sweetheart will even be allowed to return to work, Goliath. Don't worry yet."

Goliath's boulder-sized shoulders slumped as he crossed his arms over his chest. "She's not talking to me anymore, and I really liked her."

"I'm sure she'll talk to you again if she really likes you, too," I said gently.

Peter hadn't sat, and he now headed for the door. He paused before opening it and pointed at Harmony and Victor. "You two need to be careful."

Victor shook his head. "Some rules are meant to be broken. This is one of them."

Harmony stayed quiet. While she wasn't necessarily a stickler for rules to the point of following foolish ones, she didn't like rocking boats. It was even more important for her to follow the rules now, with the promotion carrot dangling in front of her.

Victor noticed her silence. "Harmony? Is something wrong?"

"Hmmm? Ah, yes. In a way. The gamekeeper at Hambledon Hall was shot dead. Cleo saw the body and has begun an investigation."

They all stared at me, open-mouthed. Peter returned and sat down. "Were you first on the scene, Miss Fox?"

"Second," I said. "The vicar was first. He'd been walking toward the house along the drive when he heard the gunshot. I was emerging from the woods nearby."

"Is he a suspect?"

"He has to be," Victor said, matter of fact. "Being first on the scene places him in the vicinity. What type of gun did the killer use?"

"A rifle," I said. "It hasn't been found, but there is one missing from the armory. And yes, Reverend Pritchard is a suspect."

Goliath looked at each of us in turn, a frown of incredulity scoring his forehead. "But he's a man of the cloth! Vicars don't kill people. They save their souls."

Victor rolled his eyes. "And fairies exist, as do unicorns and pots of gold at the end of rainbows."

Goliath gave him a withering glare. "If Frank were here, he'd agree with me. We might not agree on much, but he's a churchgoer, like myself."

"I hope the vicar isn't guilty," I reassured him before they started an ecclesiastical argument. "But he must be considered, until he's ruled out altogether."

I told them how Reverend Pritchard had avoided giving proper answers to my questions about his former parish, then moved on to describe the other suspects. The butler was the only member of staff on the list. Everyone else who couldn't be accounted for at the time of the murder were members of Lord Kershaw's family.

"Of course, the shot could have come from *outside* the house," I said. "The police believe a poacher did it. A poacher who has since disappeared."

"I hear doubt in your voice," Peter said.

"There's no evidence pointing to the poacher's guilt."

"And the local sergeant is in Lord Kershaw's pocket," Harmony added. "He won't investigate further."

Victor agreed that seemed unlikely. "So, Kershaw is making the sergeant sweep it under the carpet to protect himself or one of his family. His lordship sounds guilty to me."

"He could simply be attempting to suppress scandal," I pointed out. "He won't want word reaching his friends or important people."

"You sound like you're defending him."

"He's a good man."

"Good men have secrets to hide, too."

He was right. I needed to keep an open mind, or I'd find

myself making poor judgments. It was good having outside opinions to keep me focused. There was one other person who could give an outsider's opinion of the facts. Someone whose opinion I valued and had relied upon while conducting numerous investigations.

Someone I'd already decided to consult when I realized I needed to understand the science of ballistics.

CHAPTER 4

The office of Harry Armitage's private detective agency was located in a narrow Soho street among an eclectic array of shops and flats. Compared to the busier thoroughfares nearby, it felt somewhat eerie with its ramshackle buildings and sheets of newspaper drifting in the breeze. I'd been there so often, however, that I wasn't worried to walk down it. In fact, I rather liked its ambience.

The door painted with the sign ARMITAGE AND ASSOCIATES: PRIVATE DETECTIVES was squeezed between a barber and the Roma Café, the latter owned by Luigi, a man of Italian descent who served excellent coffee and pasta. The door led to a set of stairs, at the top of which was another door that opened up to Harry's office. When I found the lower door locked, I ventured into the café.

The two leathery old men occupying stools at the counter looked up from their cups. Each bobbed their head in a nod before turning back to their coffees and resuming their conversation in rapid Italian.

Luigi flipped a green, white and red striped cloth over his shoulder and welcomed me with a smile. "Harry thought you would stop by today." He reached under the counter and removed a key. "He left this for you and said to wait for him. He won't be long."

It was rather presumptuous of Harry to assume I'd visit on the very day I returned from my long weekend away.

Luigi's smile widened as he dangled the key in front of me. "I'll make a coffee to take with you. Or do you want muddy English water?"

"No to tea, yes to coffee, thank you."

I took the cup upstairs and sat on Harry's chair behind his desk. It was the perfect opportunity to take a peek at his papers and see what cases he had. It was easy to work out his system since he was very organized. There were three ongoing investigations—a missing pet, a missing wife, and missing money. His handwritten notes summarized his initial thoughts then went on to detail his progress. It was clear that his limited time and resources were directed at the latter two cases, not the first.

A confident knock on the door preceded the entry of an elegant middle-aged woman, dressed in black lace and wearing a large hat decorated with enough black feathers to cover an entire crow.

She strode up to the desk, looked down her beaked nose at me, then sat on the chair. "I'd like to leave a message for Mr. Armitage." When I didn't pick up a pen to write, she added, "Please."

"I'm not his assistant, but I'll pass on your message." To appease her, I took a pen from the inkstand and opened the inkpot lid.

"Please advise Mr. Armitage that my Percy returned home this morning."

"You must be the owner of the missing Pekingese." According to Harry's notes on the file, he hadn't yet begun his investigation into the dog's disappearance, but he'd made a number of suggestions to the owner, Mrs. Grantley-Owen, including simply to wait and see if her pet returned home of its own accord. "I'll let Mr. Armitage know. I'm sure he'll be very pleased."

"Tell him that I'd like to know which one of my neighbors seemed the most likely dognapper, in his opinion."

I scanned Harry's notes again, but there was nothing about speaking to neighbors, although it was on Harry's list of things to do. "Are you sure one of the neighbors took your dog?"

"Who else could have?"

"Perhaps Percy ran away, and returned when he got hungry."

She shot to her feet. "Nonsense! My Percy would never leave me. He was dognapped by a neighbor, I'm sure of it. It was they who complained about Percy's barking, so one of them *must* have taken him. Mr. Armitage told me he would threaten them all to shake out the truth."

That didn't sound like Harry.

Mrs. Grantley-Owen removed a banknote from her bag and placed it on the desk. "His fee. Tell Mr. Armitage I'll inform all of my friends what an excellent investigator he is." She marched out of the office and closed the door.

I sat back with a laugh. Harry's instincts had been right. The dog had simply returned home when he was hungry, but if Mrs. Grantley-Owen thought Harry had something to do with it, then it wasn't my place to disabuse her of the notion.

A few minutes later, Harry arrived. He didn't look surprised to see me, so must have been warned by Luigi. "Hello, Cleo. I see you've made yourself comfortable."

The sight of him always affected me in some way, usually good, but this time my heart quickened out of all proportion to the length of our absence. I'd seen him a mere week ago, when we finished our investigation into the murder on the Brighton Express.

"Hello, Harry." I rose and rounded the desk. "It was rather arrogant of you to presume I'd visit today."

He smiled as he removed his hat and hung it on the stand near the door. "You call it arrogance, I call it knowing you very well."

"Are you suggesting that I can't stay away after a short absence?"

His smile widened. It was all the answer I required.

"As I said, *arrogant* since you couldn't possibly have predicted there'd be a murder and I'd need—"

"Murder!" His smile vanished. He lifted his hands, as if to place them on my shoulders, but he lowered them to his sides and settled for frowning fiercely instead. "Cleo, are you all right?"

"I'm fine. The gamekeeper, however, was shot on the

driveway; the murder weapon hasn't been found. I thought you might know about the science of ballistics."

"I don't know much. Not enough to pay me for my knowledge." He picked up the banknote Mrs. Grantley-Owen had placed on the desk. "I'll always help you for free anyway, Cleo. You've supported me enough by allowing me to take the glory when you solve a case." The more he spoke, the more his voice softened. By the end, I was left in no doubt of his feelings for me, simply by the velvety purr.

I tried very hard not to let his tone affect me, but I found I couldn't meet his gaze, not if I wanted to keep the meeting on a professional footing. Something I'd planned to do, but my resolve was cracking with every thud of my heart. "That arrangement suits me, too, since the journalists won't give up without a name and my uncle would explode if *my* name was mentioned as the investigating detective. Anyway, that's not from me. Percy the Pekingese returned home. Mrs. Grantley-Owen dropped by to pay you."

He opened the file and picked up the pen, only to put it back. "I see you've already made the required note, but I'd like to point out that I didn't threaten anyone. I hadn't got around to beginning the investigation properly."

"I thought so, but couldn't be sure. I know how much you care about animals, and I have seen you be rather threatening when you're angry."

He tucked the money into his pocket and closed the file. "Tell me about the murder."

I began with the moment I heard the gunshot, then told him everything I'd discovered since Esmond Shepherd's murder and finished with a list of my suspects. "So you see, I need to know what sort of gun fired the bullet that killed him, and if there is a way to know if the bullet was fired from a specific gun."

"I can't answer that, but my father probably could. As for the type of gun that was used, was there an exit wound?"

"There wasn't any blood pooling underneath the body, so I assume not."

"Then the bullet is still inside. What did the entry wound look like?"

"Neat and rather small."

"Shotguns produce irregular entries, so we can rule that out. I'd also rule out pistols if you're sure the shot was fired from a distance. That leaves a rifle." He reached for the telephone on the desk. "Nothing I just said seems to be news to you."

"I was reasonably sure it would be a rifle, but I wanted another opinion. I'd still like you to check with your father about ballistics."

"Do you want Scotland Yard to advise the local sergeant on testing? You made it sound like he'll follow Lord Kershaw's wishes and blame the missing man who may or may not be a poacher."

"He'll most likely continue to push that angle, so I doubt he'd tell me anything about the bullet, but even so, I'd like to know more about ballistics."

His eyes gleamed. "Interesting."

"What is?"

"That I was right, and you came here to see me, not discuss your case. None of this is news to you and knowing about ballistics won't help if you can't get access to the bullet or potential murder weapons to perform comparison tests. So, I stand by my initial opinion. You can't stay away from me, Cleo. You're thinking up excuses just to visit."

I folded my arms. "And I stand by my initial opinion that you're arrogant."

He suddenly grinned, reminding me in a most delightful way that he had the loveliest dimples. "Whatever your reason for coming, I'm glad you did. Even without a murder to discuss, your company is very welcome."

He picked up the telephone receiver and asked the operator to put him through to his father's number. After a brief conversation with the former Scotland Yard detective inspector, Harry hung up.

"My parents have invited you to dinner."

I narrowed my gaze. "Tonight? Oh, I…uh…I'm not sure…"

"Stop panicking, Cleo. You don't have to if you don't want to."

"I *do* want to."

I liked his father and, after a rocky start, his mother had been much nicer on my last visit. It was her change of tune that worried me. When she resented me for getting Harry dismissed from his position at the hotel, it was another reason why Harry and I couldn't be together. But with that barrier removed, the only remaining reason for us not to act on our feelings was my conviction that I'd never marry. Yet my resolve was being whittled away little by little as I came to understand what Harry meant to me, and how much I missed him when we were apart.

He was right about everything—I came to his office because I wanted to see him; I'd missed him in the week since last seeing him; and I was panicking about all of it.

"Good," he said. "Fortunately, the invitation wasn't for tonight. It was for any night of your choosing." He tossed me a triumphant look.

I cleared my throat. "I'll be in touch about a date. Thank you for your assistance."

"Any time." He opened the door for me. "How will you proceed?"

"I'll find out more about my suspects. I only knew them for three days, but my family have known them for years. I'll ask for their opinions, without rousing their suspicions, of course. This is definitely not the sort of case Uncle Ronald would approve of me taking."

"I've been thinking about that." He hesitated, only continuing after I prompted him. His next words came out in a rush, as if he wanted to get them out before he changed his mind. "Perhaps you should let him know you're investigating murders. It's not fair that you have to hide the excellent work you do."

I thought about it for a moment before dismissing it. "He's too unpredictable. He might throw me out. I have no doubt that he loves me and would regret his decision once he calmed down, but he'd be too proud to retract it. Of all people, you know that."

Harry's gaze turned smoky. "You wouldn't be alone, Cleo. I'd take care of you."

It no longer seemed like such a terrible notion to be taken care of by Harry if my relationship with my family broke down. Indeed, the idea of moving into Harry's flat thrilled me.

With that realization came another—I didn't want my relationship with my family to break down. The Bainbridges were important to me. I didn't want to lose a single family member, including my stubborn, overbearing uncle.

"Thank you, Harry, but I enjoy living in a luxury hotel."

He grunted. I wasn't sure if he took my words as the joke they were intended to be, or if he felt offended.

"Speaking of my uncle, do you think he'd overrule any of the senior staff if they did something he disagreed with?"

"He wouldn't hesitate."

It was the same opinion I held, but it was good to get Harry's thoughts.

"I assume Uncle Alfred hasn't done anything controversial," he said, referring to Mr. Hobart, his father's brother. "Controversy is not his style. And Chapman has been employed long enough to know not to implement changes without Sir Ronald's approval first. So that leaves Mrs. Poole or Mrs. Short. I don't know either woman, since both were employed after I left, but based on your past assessments, my guess is the housekeeper waded into waters she shouldn't have."

"Now you're just showing off. You are correct, Detective Armitage. She dismissed one of the maids after the girl was seen in the men's quarters at the residence hall."

"That rule has been in place as long as I can recall. It's not new. All staff are aware of it and have been taking the necessary precautions for as long as I can remember."

I arched my brows. "Necessary precautions?"

"They're always careful not to be caught. It's only when they're caught that action has to be taken. I'm afraid the maid wasn't careful enough."

"I presume *you* knew how to avoid being caught sneaking into or out of a room?"

He crossed his arms. "I never had a relationship with a maid. It wouldn't be appropriate. Even when I started at the bottom, I was aware that my uncle was the manager."

"I never said you were visiting a maid's room in the residence hall. I was referring to the merry widows staying at the hotel."

His lips curved with his mischievous smile.

My face heated, which he found amusing, going by the widening smile. The devil.

I cleared my throat. "Mrs. Short has forbidden the staff from having any kind of relationship, even those being conducted properly and openly."

"That's an overreaction. The maid's dismissal should have been enough. I imagine the staff are upset."

"Furious. That's why I'm hoping Uncle Ronald will retract her rule."

"He might not realize how upset they are, but I'm sure you can diplomatically inform him. If anyone can handle him, it's you."

Once upon a time, that wasn't the case at all, but I'd grown used to my uncle's moods these last few months. I think he even respected my opinion, more than he respected the opinions of his own children. I thanked Harry, feeling confident about both the investigation and my relationship with Uncle Ronald.

He opened the door wider. "Let me know when you're free and I'll arrange dinner with my parents."

"I'll see you then."

"If not before."

I couldn't come up with a witty response, so I left him sporting a mysterious smile that I couldn't decipher.

* * *

I TOOK afternoon tea with Flossy and Floyd in Flossy's sitting room. My cousins and I each had our own suite on the hotel's fourth floor. The suites each comprised a bedroom, sitting room and bathroom. Although not as large as my uncle and aunt's suite, they provided ample space for one person living alone. With the staff at my beck and call, and a speaking tube through which I could order whatever I wanted from the kitchen, I was fortunate indeed to be living in a luxury hotel. My good fortune meant I could take on investigations where I knew I wouldn't receive a fee. Few other investigators were in

C.J. ARCHER

a position to forgo a fee for the sake of seeing justice served. Like Harry, they had to put food on the table and pay rent. I could afford to take cases *gratis*.

The investigation into the murder of Esmond Shepherd would be one such case. Lord Kershaw wouldn't pay me to poke my nose into his family's affairs. My nosiness began with asking my cousins for their opinion of the extended Kershaw family.

"Wentworth," Floyd corrected me. "The family name is Wentworth. Kershaw is the title."

Seated beside his sister on the sofa, it was quite obvious they didn't resemble each other. I was often mistaken for Floyd's sister and Flossy our cousin. He and I had the same shade of light brown hair and green eyes with a slender build, whereas Flossy was all luscious curves, with strawberry-blonde hair, and a pug nose sprinkled with freckles. Despite their many differences, they did have one thing in common. They were both dreadful snobs.

Floyd had already realized why I'd asked him to join us in Flossy's suite. I expected him to thwart all my attempts at getting answers, but I tried anyway. "So Lady Elizabeth Wentworth is the *previous* Lord Kershaw's sister. Her father was the current lord's grandfather. She must know all the family secrets."

"She's elderly," he snapped. "Leave her alone, Cleo. She didn't murder the gamekeeper."

Flossy gasped. "Why would anyone think that sweet old lady is a murderer! Honestly, Floyd, you do say the vilest things sometimes. Cleo simply wants to get to know our parents' friends better."

"If that were true, she'd ask these questions *before* visiting them, not after." He pointed his teacup at me. "Our dear cousin is investigating the murder of the gamekeeper, and she thinks one of the Wentworths did it."

Flossy gasped. "Cleo!"

"Hopefully I can prove they *didn't* do it," I said.

Floyd looked skeptical.

"I think that's a good idea," Flossy said. "To prove they didn't do it, I mean. It won't be long before news of the gamekeeper's death reaches London, and some cruel people will blame the family, particularly if they learn Lord Kershaw influenced the police investigation. I think Cleo should get involved to prove the family is innocent."

"Thank you, Flossy. In that case, may I have your opinions on the family members? With a view to eliminating them, you understand."

I saw Floyd's lips pinch out of the corner of my eye. Unlike his sister, he was worried I might discover that one of Lord Kershaw's family was a murderer. Flossy was under the impression they were all innocent. Did he know something that she didn't?

"Let me see." Flossy put down her teacup and got up to pace the floor. "As I said, Lady Elizabeth is a sweet old thing and quite doddery. Her hands shake, so she can't have shot anyone, even if she knew how to handle a gun. Her nephew, Lord Kershaw is the true embodiment of a gentleman. He's kind to everyone. I can't imagine he had a bad thought about his gamekeeper. If he did, he'd just dismiss him. He wouldn't need to kill him."

It was a good point. Even Floyd seemed to think so. He no longer looked annoyed, but nodded along.

"His wife is also very sweet. I know there's a large age gap between Lord and Lady Kershaw, but neither seems to mind. They married for love."

"They may be in love *now*," Floyd countered, "but I think it was arranged, so I remember Mother once saying."

"What about Lord Kershaw's sister and brother-in-law, the Brownings?" I asked.

Flossy wrinkled her nose. "I don't like either of them. He ignored me most of the weekend, and I overheard her call me fat."

Poor Flossy. That must have been awful to hear. I wasn't surprised at Mrs. Browning's rudeness. I'd seen her cast a disgusted look at Flossy when she placed a second slice of cake on her plate one afternoon tea. Her standoffishness toward me didn't bother me in the least, but Flossy's skin wasn't as thick as mine.

"I like their daughter, though," she went on. "Janet's marvelous company. We've always gotten along well when we've met at Hambledon Hall."

"Is she excited to marry?" I asked.

"Oh, yes. She'll be coming to London soon for her next dress fitting, and to select decorations and have invitations made… It's all such fun."

"And her future husband?" I prompted.

Flossy shrugged. "She didn't say much about him."

"What do you know about Esmond Shepherd?" I asked.

"Nothing, other than he was the gamekeeper," Flossy said. "I never met him."

"I spoke to him at the shoot," Floyd said. "He was capable, which is understandable considering he learned everything from his father, the previous gamekeeper."

"How were the family's interactions with him?" At their blank looks, I added, "Were they formal? Friendly? Tense?"

Floyd shrugged, which could have meant he knew something and wasn't going to tell me, or he'd noticed nothing out of the ordinary.

"I never saw him interact with the family," Flossy said.

"Did Janet Browning mention him?"

Flossy wrinkled her nose again. "No. Why would she?"

My gaze connected with Floyd's. He gave a slight shake of his head. I decided to ignore him. While Flossy could be silly at times, she wasn't naïve. She was aware that not all men were gentlemen. Besides, awareness would give her a measure of protection against such men, too.

"Esmond Shepherd was a terrible scoundrel," I told her. "He made a habit of seducing the young housemaids, then discarding them when he grew tired of them. I wondered if he ever looked beyond the staff and at the family for his… diversion."

Flossy's gasp filled the room. "Cleo! How could you suggest such a thing?"

"I'm sorry, but I had to ask. To eliminate Janet and her parents as suspects, you understand."

My explanation appeased her a little. "I see. I suppose. Well, you can strike them off your list if that's the reason for his murder. I never once saw Janet look at him, look for him, nor mention his name. She didn't seem particularly upset after he died, either."

I could vouch for that last observation myself. In the hours after the murder, I'd watched everyone closely. No one had been distressed. No one had acted happy or relieved, either. It was possible most were pretending, but not Janet. Like Flossy, Janet seemed to be the sort of girl who wore her emotions for everyone to see. If Shepherd had seduced her, and her father had shot him in retaliation, she would have displayed *something*. Yet she'd been indifferent.

I asked a few more questions about the gamekeeper, but neither could offer any insights about Esmond Shepherd and his history with the Wentworth family. If I wanted to know more, I needed to ask someone who'd been visiting Hambledon Hall for decades.

I finished my tea and thanked my cousins for their help.

Floyd followed me to the door. He opened it for me. "What will you do if you discover the murderer is one of Lord Kershaw's family?"

"Do you think one of them did it?"

"No."

"Then the question is moot, isn't it?"

Not satisfied with my answer, he followed me all the way to Uncle Ronald's office. "He won't like that you're investigating a murder, let alone adding the entire Wentworth family to your list of suspects."

"I'll interrogate him so subtly he won't realize he's being interrogated."

"Like you did with Flossy and me? Ha! Good luck, Cleo. You're going to need it."

I hesitated, my fist poised to knock. How could I phrase my questions so as not to raise Uncle Ronald's suspicions, let alone his ire?

The door suddenly opened from the other side, and my uncle almost walked into my fist. "Cleopatra, I was just on my way to find you. I want to talk to you."

I froze. How did he know I was investigating? Had I not been discreet enough?

Floyd sidled closer to me. For all his teasing, he could be supportive when he wanted to be. I knew he'd always be there for me when I needed him most. But if I wanted my uncle to respect my decision to be a private detective, I had to stand on my own two feet.

CHAPTER 5

I put on a smile and brightly asked my uncle what he wanted to talk to me about. Perhaps a little charm would disarm him enough to soften that stern expression on his face.

"I want to discuss business with you," he barked.

I released a pent-up breath. That was an unexpected answer. He must be referring to the current staffing problem.

It was a welcome topic for me, but not Floyd. He stiffened. He was keenly aware that his father sometimes listened to my opinions about the hotel more than his own. Although my connection to the staff probably made me a better choice to help resolve the fraternization issue, I didn't want to step on my cousin's toes.

"I'm sure Floyd has some good ideas for calming the situation down." I tried to encourage Floyd to step in without saying anything, but he gave me a vacant look.

I sighed. It seemed he didn't know anything about the dismissed maid.

Uncle Ronald moved aside and indicated I should enter his office. "It's not hotel business. It's detective business."

Floyd looked sharply at his father. "Are you going to engage her to investigate the incident at Hambledon? Why?"

"Kershaw is an old friend. He doesn't deserve to have his name dragged through the mud simply because the fellow was an employee and he died on the estate. But you know how cruel gossip can be. Until the murderer is found, a cloud will hang over Kershaw's head. I know the local sergeant is placing the blame on a poacher, but rumors will continue to swirl. That's where Cleopatra comes in. Find the murderer, ensure there's enough evidence to convict him, and work with the authorities to see that he's arrested."

"Is that all?" Floyd said lightly. "Should be a doddle, Cleo. I'll leave you to it." He sauntered off down the corridor.

Uncle Ronald closed the door and sat in his chair behind the desk, while I sat opposite.

"Perhaps you could employ Harry Armitage," I said. "I don't know if you've read the newspapers lately, but he has solved a number of high-profile murders. He's very good."

Uncle Ronald gathered a stack of papers from his desk and shuffled them. "He's too expensive."

"I wasn't aware his fees had gone up."

"I don't know what his fees are, but they're more than yours. You're free." He returned the papers to the same position they'd occupied before he moved them. "Besides, I don't want to encourage Armitage's detective endeavors."

"Why not?"

He waved off my question. Before I could ask again, he said, "I want you to investigate *discreetly*, Cleopatra. I don't want anyone thinking you've got mannish tendencies."

"Mannish?"

"Investigating murders is hardly a feminine pastime."

"It's not a pastime, and perhaps it's not seen as feminine because women are discouraged from doing it."

He dismissed my protest with another casual wave, as if it were of no more concern to him than an irritating fly at a picnic. "Before you begin, there are some things you should know."

I'd been prepared to continue my protests, but the prospect of learning something pertinent this early in the investigation had me leaning forward instead. "Any information you can provide about Esmond Shepherd will be welcome."

"I don't know much about him. He's always been there, every time I've visited Hambledon Hall, which is almost every year since I can remember. I never liked him, even when we were children."

"Why not?"

"He looked down on me, because he was always a better shot, a better rider, a better hunter, even though he was younger than me by a few years. Naturally, he was better at sports. His father was the bloody gamekeeper! He lived and breathed the outdoors since he was a baby. Damned fellow liked to rub my nose in it. Sorry for the language, but Shepherd riles me, even in death. At least he didn't die on Kershaw's driveway on purpose."

Considerate of him. "I heard he was a bit of a bounder, breaking hearts without a care. Did you see evidence of that?"

"The women always liked him. They thought he was handsome. He knew it, too. That was partly why he was so unbearable, if you ask me."

"Was Lord Kershaw jealous of Shepherd when they were younger?"

Uncle Ronald made a throaty scoffing sound that made his jowls wobble. "Of course not. Shepherd is—was—older, but Kershaw didn't look up to the fellow. He was just the gamekeeper's son."

"Could Cicely Browning have lost her heart to Esmond Shepherd before she married Mr. Browning?"

He snorted. "Don't be absurd." But even as he said it, I could see him trying to recall. "She may have found him handsome, but that's all. She wouldn't… They never…" He cleared his throat. "Hambledon Hall was burgled recently. A number of items were stolen. Did you know that, Cleopatra?"

"I was aware of silver candlesticks missing from the dining room mantelpiece."

"A number of other items were taken, not just candlesticks."

"All silver?"

"I believe so. Shepherd may have taken them."

"Wouldn't it be more likely that a member of the indoor staff stole them, not the gamekeeper?"

Uncle Ronald settled back in his chair and clasped his hands over his stomach. "Shepherd could come and go from the house. He may have entered while no one was looking and squirreled the candlesticks and other things away."

I recalled seeing Esmond Shepherd in Lord Kershaw's office, reading a book. None of the staff had told him he couldn't be there, so I assumed he had full access, as Uncle Ronald said. "I'll see if I can link Shepherd to the thefts."

He looked pleased with my answer. "My theory is that he and his partner in crime had a disagreement, which would be the argument you saw in the woods. Then the partner killed Shepherd in anger and disappeared with the stolen goods."

"It sounds plausible."

"Good. Good." He twiddled his thumbs.

"Is there something else, Uncle? Do you have other suspicions?"

"It's probably nothing."

I waited.

He finally gave in. "You may have noticed we didn't go into the village during our stay."

I had, but I didn't know that was unusual. "Were Lord and Lady Kershaw deliberately avoiding it?"

"I believe so. The villagers have been somewhat restless lately, and our hosts wouldn't want their guests to witness that. The villagers aren't happy with Kershaw, you see. Apparently it has something to do with blocking a path they've always used. It's on his land, so he has every right, but it's been available for the public's use for centuries."

"Why did Kershaw block it now?"

"I don't know. The thing is, it was the gamekeeper's job to keep trespassers off the land. That's interesting, don't you agree?"

What I found interesting was the timing. The path that was open for centuries closes recently, items that have been in the house for years were stolen recently, and the gamekeeper who worked there for decades was murdered recently. Perhaps I didn't need to dig into the gamekeeper's past for answers.

Uncle Ronald checked the time on his pocket watch. "I'll let you get on with it, Cleopatra." He opened a leather-bound ledger and ran his finger down one of the columns. "If you need to visit the village, take Floyd with you, or Miss Cotton.

Not Florence, and your aunt isn't up to it. I'm sure I don't need to tell you to be discreet."

"I'll be as subtle as possible." I stood, only to sit again. "Uncle, are you aware of the rule Mrs. Short initiated during our absence?"

"She mentioned she has forbidden the staff from fraternizing after catching one of the maids in the male dormitory," he said without looking up from the ledger. "I'm in full agreement. We can't have girls like that working here."

I bit down on my rising temper and bit back the first retort that sprang to mind. Uncle Ronald required delicate managing, or he was likely to close his mind to other possibilities altogether. "I quite agree. We want respectable women and men representing the hotel. But the maid in question was in a *relationship* with one of the male staff members."

"That's irrelevant. If her beau had been caught in the female quarters, then he would have been dismissed instead. Don't accuse me of treating the women differently to the men, Cleopatra."

"I wasn't. My point is that Mrs. Short may have gone too far. She has forbidden more than fraternizing. She has put a stop to relationships between staff members altogether, whether they reside in the residence hall or not. There are a number of couples who are romantically involved. One couple is even married."

"That's different, naturally. I've decided that Mrs. Short's rule may be a good idea. Relationships between young people often come to nothing, and when they do, it leads to tension. I don't want that here. I want a harmonious environment for all employees."

"It's good of you to care for your staff."

"A harmonious workplace leads to better efficiency," he clarified.

I should have known that was where his priorities lay. "And the couples already in relationships?"

"You're right, Cleopatra. That must be addressed. I'll let Mrs. Short sort it out."

"Are you sure she's the right person to do that, Uncle?" I was afraid the housekeeper would ruffle more feathers, not smooth them.

"She can be rather heavy-handed, but there's no one else. Hobart is busy with more important tasks, and Leyland doesn't yet have the respect of the staff who've been here longer than him."

He was right about Peter. He'd been employed at the front desk for a few years before becoming assistant manager, but his promotion to that role was relatively recent, and he was still considered more of an equal by the staff, not their superior.

"The task would have been handled by Armitage." My uncle's lips flattened, not in anger but disappointment. It seemed his opinion of Harry was softening as more time passed since he dismissed him. Given the angry words exchanged at the time, it was pleasing—albeit unexpected—to see my uncle's change of heart. "Thank you for bringing it to my attention, Cleopatra. Now, if you don't mind…"

There was a knock at the door, and my uncle's assistant arrived, armed with more ledgers.

I saw myself out and headed back to my suite. Somehow, I'd made the situation with the staff worse.

* * *

THERE WAS one other person I could ask for an opinion about the residents of Hambledon Hall, past and present, but avoiding Aunt Lilian had become necessary of late. Her addiction to the cocaine in her tonic made her unbearable. She was snappy and irritable, and sometimes even cruel. I'd seen her maid leave the suite in tears, and waiters hurriedly close the door after delivering food from the kitchen. Her husband and children kept their distance, when possible, and tiptoed around her when not.

I felt guilty for avoiding her. She needed help, particularly from those who loved her and wanted the kindhearted woman she used to be to return. The problem was, until she admitted she needed help, she wouldn't seek it out, or accept it when it was offered.

Before he left for the day, Mr. Hobart sent a note to my suite to say that Harry had telephoned and invited me to afternoon tea the following day at his parents' house. The message didn't ask for me to return the call. Harry assumed I'd go.

He knew me well.

Over breakfast the following morning, Harmony and I drew up a list of suspects and planned our trip to Morcombe, the village near Hambledon Hall. I then spent the morning at the British Library, reading as much as I could find on the history of the Kershaw family and the estate. The story of King Henry the Eighth hunting there appeared to be true, although the title of Kershaw hadn't been created then. Indeed, the Wentworth family at the time were minor lords and quite insignificant, but the king coveted their woods for hunting. It wasn't until the mid-eighteenth century that the first earl of Kershaw was created, but he and his descendants continued to live in the drafty old building, as Lady Elizabeth called it, until her father replaced the small manor with the current grand Gothic revival one.

I wished the old Hall still stood, so I could imagine what it would have been like to tread the same floorboards as one of the most famous monarchs. The newer house didn't have the history behind it, but it had certainly been comfortable with its modern layout and amenities.

I also learned how the estate had changed over the centuries. The woods used to cover three-quarters of it but many stands of trees had been cut down to allow more space for the farming of sheep. When wool prices plummeted, crops were planted instead. I suspected a path at the estate's northern edge that was marked as a bridleway in a seven-teenth century map was the contentious one my uncle mentioned. It was located nearer the village and provided access between Hambledon Hall and the neighboring estate to the north. It was the fastest route between the two grand houses on the estates without making it necessary to return to the village. If a shopkeeper from Morcombe had to deliver goods to both estates, he could make one delivery after the other in short order. However, without access to that path, he had to return to the village in between, adding a considerable amount of time to the journey. From what I could find or, rather, *couldn't* find, the bridleway was never legally made a public right of way. Did that mean Lord Kershaw was within his rights to stop the villagers using it? Or did the centuries of use by the villagers give them some legal standing to keep accessing it?

I skipped luncheon altogether, then took the train to Ealing in the mid-afternoon. Harry had lived in the semi-detached house with the Hobarts, the couple who adopted him aged thirteen, until he moved into the Mayfair Hotel when he became assistant manager several years later. He briefly moved in with his parents again after his dismissal from that job, until he got back on his feet. He lived in a flat in Soho now, but still visited them often.

Both of Harry's parents welcomed me, although Mrs. Hobart's reception was a little stiffer than her husband's. At least she wasn't as outwardly rude as she had been in our early encounters, after she'd learned of my role in Harry's dismissal.

This time, they weren't alone in the parlor. Harry introduced me to his aunt, Mrs. Ann Hobart. Married to Alfred Hobart, the hotel manager, she lived next door to her brother-in-law and his wife.

She greeted me with eyes that twinkled with her smile and patted the seat beside her on the sofa. "Come sit with me, Miss Fox. I've been wanting to meet you for some time. My Alfred mentions you quite often."

"Oh dear," I said, smiling back. "Should I be worried?"

She giggled like a schoolgirl. "Not at all. He says you're great company for Miss Bainbridge, and have been a good influence on Mr. Bainbridge. Apparently, he was quite wild last year, but seems to have settled down lately."

My gaze flicked to Harry as he sat opposite. He'd been a better influence on Floyd than I had. He'd extracted Floyd from a sticky situation some months back. Floyd's behavior had improved since then, although he would never be an angel.

The two Mrs. Hobarts excused themselves to make the tea. I offered to help, but Harry's aunt said I should stay in the parlor. She said it with a light tone then followed it with a speaking glance at Harry.

His cheeks pinked ever so slightly. "Ballistics," he blurted out.

I cleared my throat as I felt a blush coming on. "Yes. The science of matching bullets to guns. Obviously you know what it is, Inspector, but perhaps you could enlighten me."

Detective Inspector Hobart—as I still called him, despite his retirement from Scotland Yard—waited until the two sisters-in-law had left before telling me about the advancements in ballistics since the advent of machine-made guns. After he waded through the science, he concluded that although small differences in bullet markings probably existed, not even the most powerful microscopes could detect them.

"No expert is prepared to swear in court that a particular bullet came from a particular gun," he said. "They used to, when bullets and gun barrels were handmade, but it's an area of manufacturing that has actually set the science back."

"The science will catch up when microscopes become more sophisticated," Harry said. "One day."

It was a long way to come to hear a few short sentences that could have been told to me over the telephone, but I didn't mind. There was one more thing I wanted to ask D.I. Hobart. I told him about the bridleway marked on the old map.

"I believe the current Lord Kershaw has revoked the right for the public to use it," I said. "If the right was never actually given, can he simply do as he pleases? It doesn't seem fair if the villagers have been using it for centuries."

"I don't know a lot about country laws. Not a lot of need for that kind of knowledge at Scotland Yard. But I think that if the villagers can prove they've been using the path for a long period of time without interruption, there'd be a case to have Lord Kershaw's decision overturned by the courts."

"The proof would have to be documented," Harry added. "No judge will overrule a landowner of Kershaw's caliber based on the testimony of a few elderly locals who've lived in the area all their lives."

I refrained from discussing it further as the two Mrs. Hobarts returned. I didn't want to talk about the rather upsetting topic of murder in front of Ann Hobart. While I knew Harry's mother didn't mind, having been married to a policeman for so long, I didn't want the twinkle in his aunt's eye to disappear.

We talked about other topics while they poured tea and sliced up the lemon cake. It gave me an opportunity to get to know them all better. Usually, our conversations were of a gruesome nature, but now I got to see how they interacted as a family. They were clearly all fond of Harry. If he accepted every slice of cake and refill of his cup offered to him, he would have to be rolled out of the house, but he politely declined with his usual charm. It seemed the two childless couples had raised him together. As a lonely thirteen-year-old who'd spent some time living on the streets, they'd given him just what he needed.

I wasn't sure why the conversation turned to gardening, but when it did, it triggered a memory of something Lord Kershaw had said. That led to further questions I needed to add to my list.

I hadn't realized my concentration drifted until Harry spoke up. "Go on, Cleo. Out with it."

"Out with what?"

"You haven't been listening to a word I've said."

"That's because you were talking about how the Eiffel Tower was made."

"I was talking about Philadelphia City Hall's tower."

I glanced around at the three Hobarts, hoping I hadn't offended any of them by suggesting Harry's conversation was dull. While his mother scrutinized me over the rim of her teacup, and his father looked oblivious, his aunt smiled at me.

"I found myself drifting off, too, Miss Fox," she said. "I don't share Harry's enthusiasm for science and mathematics. Sorry, Harry dear."

That gave me the opening I needed to broach the topic that was occupying my mind. "I was thinking about science just now, actually. Forgive me, but my current case is somewhat complicated and there's a particular point I wanted Harry's expertise on."

His aunt's smile brightened even more. "I'm not surprised. He is very clever."

His mother's gaze softened a little, and his father stopped

giving his cake so much attention and regarded me with interest. It seemed I'd said the perfect thing.

"You read a great deal of science books when you were young," I began. "What do you know of botany?"

Harry laughed softly. "I've lived in the city my entire life, so very little. My interest has always been in engineering. Mother and Aunt both like gardening, though."

"We do!" Ann Hobart declared. "We would love to be able to assist you in your investigation, Miss Fox."

Harry's mother put down her cup. All vestiges of stern scrutiny and stiffness were gone. She was as eager to help me as her sister-in-law. "What would you like to know?"

"The leaf or stem of a plant can stain the gardener's skin, I presume."

"If the gardener is foolish enough not to wear gloves."

I indicated the side of my right forefinger where Lord Kershaw had tried and failed to rub off the discoloration. "One of the suspects had a stain here, but it was an unusual shade of green."

"Unusual how?" Harry's aunt asked.

I looked around the room in an attempt to find a match but couldn't. "It was similar to teal, but softer."

"The leaves of many succulents are teal."

"She said it was softer," the other Mrs. Hobart pointed out.

"I've seen succulents," I said. "That's not the right color."

"Was there a hint of mint?"

"Not quite."

"Aqua?"

D.I. Hobart pulled out a handkerchief on which his initials were stitched in the corner. "Is this it?"

His wife rolled her eyes. "That's olive green. It's very different to teal."

D.I. Hobart looked to Harry. Harry shrugged. His father shrugged, too, and pocketed the handkerchief.

"I can picture it, but I can't describe it," I said. "It's not the color of any plant I've seen before."

"Is there a greenhouse on the estate?" D.I. Hobart asked.

"There's a fernery filled with interesting plants, most of which I'd not seen before. The stain must have come from one of them. I'll try to take another look, although I'm not sure how. I'm making some inquiries in the village tomorrow, but didn't have plans to call at the house. I don't want anyone from Hambledon Hall to know I'm in the area."

Ann Hobart suddenly brightened. "You should take Harry with you. For protection against the murderer, obviously, as well as his help."

"Aunt," Harry chided. "Cleo doesn't need my help. Although you do have a point about protection." He arched his brows at me. "I can be free tomorrow, if I move a few appointments around."

"It's not appropriate," his mother said tightly. "She's a young, unwed lady."

Her sister-in-law rolled her eyes. "Pishposh. No one concerns themselves with that these days, as long as they stay in public areas."

"They do when the young lady in question is a Bainbridge."

"I'm a Fox," I stated. "And Harry's company would be welcome." It just slipped out before I could stop myself. "Although Harmony has already agreed to join me."

"Then I'm superfluous," Harry said with a smile that had begun when I said his company would be welcome.

I quickly turned to his father, catching D.I. Hobart unawares. He'd been watching his son with the sort of scrutiny I'd seen him give witnesses. "I have one more question before I go. How difficult is it for a thief to sell stolen silverware? Distinctive silverware, I should add."

"Not easy for an opportunistic amateur. The thief would have to know a fence connected to an underground criminal network, or someone local who knows how to melt it down."

That's what I'd thought. "Do you think D.S. Forrester could make inquiries with the Morcombe police about known thieves in the area?"

"I'll ask him."

"Oh, I didn't mean for you to lift a finger. I don't want to put you out. I can call on Monty at Scotland Yard."

"Monty!" Harry's aunt cried. When she realized how loud she sounded, she softened her voice. "You must be great friends to be on a first name basis, Miss Fox."

I wasn't, but D.S. Forrester had asked me to call him that, and he called me Cleo. It was quite obvious to me why he insisted, although I'd never given him reason to hope there could be anything other than friendship between us, and nor would I.

"Stephen?" Harry's aunt prompted. "Could *you* speak to your contacts at the Yard? Miss Fox has enough to do already."

"Hmmm?" At his sister-in-law's glare, D.I. Hobart added, "Yes, of course."

I knew what they were doing, and why. I expected Harry's mother to overrule them, or at least attempt to encourage me in the direction of Monty and therefore away from her son, but she sat in silence. It was both unsettling and pleasing. I wasn't sure whether it made me happy or worried. It certainly twisted my insides into knots.

When I made a move to leave, Harry's aunt suggested he return on the train with me for company. We said our good-byes, and I thanked them all for the afternoon tea and assistance. As I left, I realized I'd quite enjoyed myself. It was nice to call on Harry's parents and not have his mother glare at me for the duration, and his aunt was very amiable.

"Do you think the thefts are related to the murder?" Harry asked as we walked to the station.

"It's too soon to tell. Hopefully my visit to the village tomorrow will provide answers, although I doubt it. If I do find a suspect for the thefts, they're unlikely to admit they stole the Kershaws' candlesticks simply because I ask nicely."

We fell into a comfortable silence. My thoughts were occupied with potential questions to ask in Morcombe and I thought Harry's mind was similarly engaged. I was wrong.

"You'll be gone all day," he said.

"Yes."

"What excuse did you give your family this time?"

"None. Uncle Ronald not only approves of me investigating the murder, he's actively encouraging me. He's convinced Lord Kershaw and his family are innocent and wants me to prove it."

"That's a nice change from his previous attitude to your

investigating. But what happens if you discover one of them is a murderer?"

"I'll cross that hurdle when I come to it."

He opened his mouth to say something, only to close it again. He adjusted his hat in an attempt to cover his change of mind.

"Go on, Harry. You know you can be honest with me, even if it's something you think I won't want to hear. I want your honesty. Always."

His pace slowed, then he finally stopped. "It's not your reaction that concerns me. I'm a little ashamed to be thinking it, let alone saying it."

"I don't understand."

He tapped the toe of his shoe against an uneven section of pavement. "I was going to tell you to be careful, and not upset Sir Ronald."

"You mean, if I do find out Lord Kershaw or one of his family murdered the gamekeeper, you want me to keep it to myself?"

His lips flattened. "Ordinarily, I want justice to be served, no matter who the guilty party is. Highborn or low, it's all the same to me. Perpetrators of crime should pay." He drew in a breath and released it slowly. "It pains me that I even want to warn you. But, Cleo, I really don't want you to upset your uncle. I know how vindictive he can be when he thinks someone has disobeyed him."

I lifted my hand to reach for his, but let it fall to my side again before we touched. I didn't know what to say. Harry had a strong sense of justice, so to even think of letting a murderer go meant he felt strongly that it was the right thing to do. "Don't worry," I assured him. "If it comes to it, I'll manage Uncle Ronald. He can't blame me altogether if it turns out his friend is guilty."

"It's not just you. I've somehow found myself back in his good books—well, almost—and I'd like to stay there."

This time I did reach out and take his hand. "It's not your investigation, so you wouldn't be tainted by my decision. Anyway, I'm quite sure you *are* back in his good books, Harry, and I'm quite sure the reason is because he wants to re-hire you at some point."

His eyes widened. "I miss the hotel sometimes, but I'd never consider working there again. Never." He squeezed my hand. "Don't worry on my account. If you need my help, I'll give it. If Harmony has to work tomorrow, then telephone me. I'll come with you to the village. If you're placed in Sir Ronald's bad books, then I'll be there with you."

"Let's hope the entire Wentworth family is innocent." I released his hand and we continued on. "You can't come tomorrow. You have a lot of work to do on your own cases."

"Nothing urgent. It can all be rearranged with a few telephone calls."

"You need an assistant."

"Want to apply for the position?"

I laughed, but sobered when he didn't join in. "I can't be your assistant, Harry. You'd be my superior and you know that arrangement won't work."

"You would never be inferior to anyone, Cleo. If you came to work with me, you'd be running the entire operation within weeks, and I'd be the one answering the telephone for you."

"Now there's an interesting thought. Will it get my name on the door? Fox and Armitage: Private Detectives."

"Sounds awful. It doesn't have a good ring to it at all."

"All right, I concede. Armitage and Fox, since that's alphabetical order."

He continued on, a crooked tilt of his lips his only response.

CHAPTER 6

*B*efore dining with Uncle Ronald and my cousins in the hotel restaurant, Harmony joined me in my suite to help me dress and arrange my hair. She brought some exciting news with her.

"I've been assigned to work with Mr. Hobart tomorrow."

I swiveled in the chair to look at her. "On your day off?"

"I'll be given Friday off instead. Turn around so I can fix this."

She pulled a face as she plucked out one of the tortoise-shell combs. I'd arranged my hair myself that morning. Most ladies had their maids redo their hair before each social engagement, but I only bothered for formal occasions. Usually I just did it once a day and left it.

"What will you be doing for Mr. Hobart?" I asked her reflection in the dressing table mirror.

"Going through his old notes and files and archiving anything that's no longer relevant and updating those that are."

I pulled a face. "Sounds tedious."

"Not at all. I discovered while assisting Mr. Bainbridge to organize the wedding reception that I enjoy making processes more efficient. Besides, cleaning out old files will be better than cleaning out guests' rooms."

I couldn't argue with that. I also knew she should take on extra administrative tasks when offered. It would show her willingness to step into a more permanent role. "I'll miss your company tomorrow, but I'll manage alone."

She dragged the brush through my hair, stroking it vigorously all the way through to the end at the middle of my back. "You won't be alone. I told Mr. Hobart I was supposed to help you, so he suggested Harry go in my stead. He telephoned him then and there, and Harry agreed. He'll meet you at the station."

I blinked at her in the mirror, but she was focused on my hair, not my face. I couldn't tell if there was a conspiracy or not, let alone if she was one of the conspirators.

"I think you should take a man with you, anyway," she went on. "As much as it galls me to admit, you'll probably get answers more easily from male witnesses if you do. I discovered the hard way that country men don't have much respect for women."

I swiveled in my chair to face her, earning a scowl as my hair slipped through her fingers. "Which man treated you disrespectfully?"

"The butler, for one. He didn't deign to even address me. The other maids said it wasn't personal. He didn't talk to any of them unless he absolutely had to. They said he even spoke down to the housekeeper. Apparently, Mr. Browning is disrespectful to them, too. I had nothing to do with him, but the maids said he can be rude and revolting, particularly when he's drunk. They loathe it when he stays at Hambledon. Poor Mrs. Browning, forced into a marriage with an oaf." She shook her head as she signaled for me to face the mirror again. "She's such an elegant, noble lady."

"Don't pity her too much," I said. "I found her to be rude and condescending."

"Most toffs are. Present company excepted."

I frowned at her reflection.

"I don't think of you as a toff, Cleo, but others do. You're related to toffs, so you sometimes get lumped in with them around here." When she saw that I didn't like what she'd said, she gave my shoulders an affectionate squeeze. "Don't pout. It'll create lines on your face. Besides, those of us who know you, know you're modest and fair. Now, how would you like me to do your hair?"

* * *

It was mid-morning by the time Harry and I called at the Red Lion Inn in Morcombe. With its bricks painted white and a red-tiled roof, the inn exemplified the quaintness of the village itself. Ivy-leaved geraniums spilled over the edge of the two hanging baskets flanking the door, while the leaves of the Virginia creeper growing up the facade were already turning a vibrant crimson.

Inside wasn't as light and bright as the outside, but it felt cozy with the large fireplace and well-worn leather seats. Harry removed his hat at the door so that he wouldn't have to duck beneath the low wooden beams. He set it down on the counter and ordered us a half-pint of ale each.

The publican gave me a look down his bulbous nose as if to say I shouldn't be in the area where the men drank, but he'd allow it this time. Perhaps I was overly sensitive, having been told to move to the women's room in pubs before, but that was how it came across to me.

Harry paid for the ales and added a generous tip, which didn't go unnoticed.

The publican's frown deepened as he waited for Harry to speak. The frown turned to wide-eyed curiosity when I spoke up instead.

"A man stayed in one of your rooms recently. He was tall-ish, but not as tall as my friend here, and wore a gray cap."

The publican straightened, a sign that he knew the man, despite my vague description. "He bolted on the afternoon of the incident at Hambledon. Collected his things and cleared off without so much as a farewell."

"That's unfortunate for you. I hope the police find him and make him pay you what he owes."

"He paid up front for two nights and left after just one. He also left what he owed for lunch on the dresser."

That was intriguing, and somewhat unexpected. If the man was a poacher or ne'er-do-well traveler, as Lord Kershaw and the police suggested, he wouldn't bother with payment. "Can you describe him more fully?"

He leaned his elbows on the counter. "About thirty, curly brown hair, slim build. My wife delivered a tray to his room at lunch. She said he was polite, spoke like a Londoner, and was neat." He straightened. "You reckon the lodger killed the gamekeeper over at Hambledon and you want to find him."

I saluted him with my tankard before taking a sip.

"You're wasting your time. The man's well and truly gone."

"We'd still like to try. Is there anything else you can tell us about him? Did he mention where he'd come from or where he was going? Or what his business was here in Morcombe?"

The publican picked up a cloth and wiped down the counter. "No. He kept to himself. Why would he go blurting out his business if he came here to poach on Kershaw land?"

"That's if he was a poacher."

The publican's hand stilled. He glanced at me then past me, at a patron drinking alone in a booth. Harry followed his gaze, then angled himself so he could keep an eye on the patron. He leaned one elbow on the counter and nodded a greeting at the man.

The man nodded back. It was difficult to determine his age. He had few lines on his face, but the black beard obscured most of it, and a gray cap covered his head so I couldn't tell if his hair was thinning or graying. "Sergeant says he was a poacher," he said. "Lord Kershaw says he was, too. Are you saying something different, Miss…?"

"I'm keeping an open mind."

I didn't want to give him my name. Even though I'd not visited the village during my stay at Hambledon Hall, there was a chance my name had been bandied about in Morcombe as a guest of the Kershaws. I'd worn a simple outfit of navy blue skirt and jacket for today's outing in the hope of fitting in.

"You're wasting your time," the man said, repeating the publican's words.

"Even so, I'd like to at least *try* to find him," I said.

"I mean, if you're hoping his lordship will pay you for the time you spend investigating, he won't. He won't even thank you."

Before I made an amateurish mistake and told him we didn't expect payment, Harry cut in. "Why do you say that?"

The patron shrugged broad shoulders. "Blame the man no

one can find and that's the end of it. But don't blame him, and the investigation will have to continue. That means Kershaw's family and guests will suffer the indignity of having their business aired in public. Kershaw won't want the attention."

It was interesting that we weren't the only ones to come to that conclusion already.

Harry took his tankard and approached the booth. "My name is Harry Armitage. May we?"

The man indicated we could sit opposite. "Martin Faine."

Harry invited me to slide onto the bench seat first then he sat beside me. "Do you work nearby?"

Mr. Faine hesitated. "I work here and there, laboring, farm work, fixing things. Sometimes I'm a beater at the larger shooting parties up at Hambledon, but I wasn't helping out on the weekend."

"Have you lived in Morcombe a while?"

"All my life."

"So you know the family up at Hambledon Hall well."

Mr. Faine nodded in the direction of the publican. "I'm not the only one. Anyone who has lived here their whole life knows all about the Wentworth family."

Harry signaled for the publican to pour another drink for Mr. Faine. "Is Kershaw a good man?"

"I used to think so, until he blocked the bridleway." He tapped his finger on the table beside his empty tankard. "He's got no right. Folk from 'round here have been using it for centuries. Ask anyone. The deliverymen need it, the mailman…"

The publican deposited another tankard on the table. "The ramblers who come here from London for the day, too. I reckon that's why Kershaw put a fence across it, to deter strangers, but he won't admit it. I need those tourists in here, having a pie and a pint after their ramble. Lucky for us, Faine here is leading the fight to reopen it."

Mr. Faine picked up the tankard. "Just protecting our rights. It's the law that if a road or path has been used for years then it can't be taken away by the landowner." He tapped his finger on the table again. "That bridleway has been used since the day King Henry the Eighth came here to hunt."

The publican scoffed as he walked back to the counter. "That's just a story."

Mr. Faine became indignant. "A *true* story." He addressed Harry and me, once again tapping his finger on the table. "When King Henry stayed at the old Hall, he fell in love with one of the maids. She was a local Morcombe girl, and a real beauty. You may think a lowly maid should be pleased to attract the attention of a king, but this girl was in love with a groom from the neighboring estate, and the king was old and fat by that time. That didn't slow him down. He was relentless in his pursuit of her. When the groom found out, he decided to whisk her away to safety in the middle of the night and hide her until after the king left. He used an old poacher's track through the woods that crosses both properties. It was hard going on account of the track wasn't used anymore after the Hambledon gamekeeper's cottage was built close to it. The groom forged on, though, until he finally reached the house. He went into the servants' quarters, where he saw the king entering his betrothed's room. He knew if he laid a finger on the king, he'd be killed instantly if he was caught. So, he caused a commotion in the dark which startled the king. Old Henry abandoned his plan to seduce the maid. The groom then rescued his betrothed and together they fled back along the same track. The groom hid her in the stables of the neighboring estate for a night and a day until the king left. The lady of Hambledon Hall at that time—Kershaw's ancestor—was so happy the honor of her maid was saved, she asked her husband to allow the locals to use the path whenever they wanted. So you see, the bridleway has significance to the area. It's not just a path used for convenience. It represents the triumph of a lowly groom over a king. It's importance to the good folk of Morcombe can't be overstated."

The publican snorted. "Don't listen to Faine. The story is bollocks."

"It ain't!"

"The king wouldn't go to a maid's room for a start. He'd have her brought to his own chambers. And if he was old and fat, as the story goes, he won't be hunting beasts or maids. *And* are you trying to say no one looked for the maid after she disappeared? The groom's the first person they'd turn to."

Mr. Faine sniffed. "The staff at both houses and the villagers protected him. They weren't going to turn over one of their own." He swiped up his tankard, all the while glaring at the publican. "That's what we do in Morcombe. You wouldn't know. You're a newcomer."

"I've lived here forty-three years!"

"Is there any documentation stating the public was granted the right to use it?" Harry asked.

"If there is, it's probably in the house and his lordship won't give it up."

"What reason does Lord Kershaw give for blocking the bridleway now?" I asked.

Mr. Faine shrugged. "He doesn't give one. He doesn't have to discuss his plans with us. He's the important man in the big house and we're just lowly folk from the village. One thing I do know is, his father would never have blocked the bridleway. Now, *he* was a good man."

The publican nodded agreement. "Maybe now Shepherd's gone it will be reopened."

Mr. Faine had been about to take a sip of his ale but lowered it again and glared at the publican. "What's it to do with him? It was his lordship's decision to block it, not the gamekeeper's. Shepherd may have worked for him, but he was on our side in here." Mr. Faine tapped his chest.

The publican rubbed his chin. "I don't know. I don't want to speak ill of the dead, but Shepherd wasn't liked by some."

"Who?" I asked.

The publican must have realized he could cause a great deal of trouble to friends, neighbors, and customers, so he turned his back to us, pretending not to have heard my question.

Mr. Faine answered for him. "He had a reputation as a womanizer. Some husbands didn't like him because their wives swooned in his presence."

I couldn't be sure, but I thought I heard the publican grunt. "If he had a reputation, why didn't Lord Kershaw stop him?" I asked. "The actions of his staff reflect on him. He should have threatened to dismiss Mr. Shepherd if he didn't mend his ways."

Grunts came from both Mr. Faine and the publican this time.

Harry and I exchanged glances. "Are you suggesting Kershaw wouldn't try to curtail his gamekeeper's behavior?" Harry asked. "Why not?"

"Don't know," Mr. Faine said. "Lord Kershaw has always overlooked Shepherd's indiscretions. So did the previous lord."

"He died five years ago, didn't he?" I asked, feigning ignorance.

"That he did, and his wife a few years before him." He leaned forward and lowered his voice. "The old folk around here have a theory that Lord Kershaw's grandfather had a liaison with Esmond Shepherd's mother, Mabel, and Esmond's sister Susannah was the result." He winked at Harry.

"What happened to Susannah?" I asked.

"Died of a fever back in the fifties. She being the fourth Lord Kershaw's daughter explains why the fifth and now the sixth have always treated the Shepherds well. There's a strong connection between the two families."

"What about the rest of the Wentworth family?" I asked. "How well do you know them, Mr. Faine?"

"I've never met the current Lady Kershaw, but I haven't heard a bad word about her. Same with the aunt, Lady Elizabeth. She's respected around here. She used to come into the village a lot, until old age made her unsteady. Real lively and friendly she was in her younger days. She got involved in village life, helping at the annual fair and delivering care baskets to the needy. She didn't come into Morcombe as much when she had to take care of her elderly parents, but after they died, she resumed her duties in the village with good cheer. Shame she can't get out much anymore," he added wistfully.

"What about the Brownings? You must have known Mrs. Browning from before she married. Was she as respected as her brother, his lordship?"

"I never had anything to do with her. None of us did.

When she was a girl, she was always accompanied by her mother or aunt. They never let her out of their sight. Then she married young and moved away. Not far, mind, but she only ever comes back to Hambledon occasionally and rarely into Morcombe. None of us really knows her, or her husband and daughter."

Harry and I thanked Mr. Faine and the publican and rose to leave. I stopped before exiting the inn, however, and approached Mr. Faine's booth again. "Do you know if the women of the family ever participate in the shooting parties?"

He blinked in surprise. "No, I—" He cut himself off and scratched his beard. "I remember now. I used to help out on the estate sometimes when I was younger. Mrs. Browning was allowed to join in the shooting parties. She was a good shot, even as a girl. I hear her husband doesn't think women should participate in shooting or hunting, so he forbids her to join in now. He's probably worried she'll bag more birds than him." He chuckled.

I expected Mr. Faine to connect my question to the shooting of the gamekeeper, but if he did, he didn't point out that Mrs. Browning should be considered a suspect because of her skill.

"What do you think?" Harry asked as we walked along Morcombe's High Street.

"I think we haven't narrowed down our list of suspects. In fact, we've added one. Mr. Faine wears a gray cap. He could have been the man I saw arguing with Shepherd near the gamekeeper's cottage. I never saw that person's face."

"Gray caps are common. Besides, the publican confirmed that a man wearing a gray cap left the inn in a hurry after the murder. That's suspicious behavior."

"A poacher settling his account when he could have just left without leaving a trace? It doesn't fit, Harry."

"Perhaps he's not a poacher. His quick departure is suspicious, you have to admit."

I did admit it. I also doubted he was a poacher. The question was, *why* had he come to Morcombe? And was he the man I saw arguing with Shepherd in the woods? There was only one thing I knew for certain after speaking to the publican and Mr. Faine.

"Sergeant Honeyman is placing the blame on a man he has no intention of finding," I said. "And it's more than likely that Lord Kershaw is encouraging him."

My uncle's wish that I would exonerate his lordship once and for all looked more and more unlikely to come to fruition. If it didn't, I had a difficult decision to make.

CHAPTER 7

*W*e didn't need to ask directions to the church. Its bell tower rose higher than all the buildings in the village. It looked interesting, with its arches and buttresses, and I thought Harry might start talking about Medieval architecture, but he simply suggested we search for Reverend Pritchard in the vicarage first. The housekeeper there told us he wasn't at home, however, and to look for him in the church.

"He'll be praying, most like," she said with a heavy dose of pride in her voice. "Always praying, is our Reverend Pritchard. Very devout, he is."

I rather thought that was the point of vicars. "I've heard the same thing from a number of sources. It's why we've come to speak to him. We'd like his blessing for…" I cleared my throat, in an attempt to give myself time in which to think of something. Something *else*, that is. But I couldn't, so I continued with the only explanation that had come to mind. "…for our marriage."

"Oh, how wonderful! Congratulations to you both." She pressed a hand to her bosom and gave us a wistful look. "What a lovely couple you make, and if I may say so, Miss, you'll be a lovely bride."

"She will indeed," Harry said smoothly. "I feel very blessed already, but divine approval can't hurt. My fiancée remembers Reverend Pritchard from when she lived in Cornwall, and we decided to seek him out. It was a surprise to find him here in Berkshire, wasn't it, my love?"

I wasn't sure whether it was him calling me his love, or the softening of his gaze as he looked at me, or both, but I suddenly flushed. I touched my cheek with the back of my hand. "Goodness, the sun is warm today."

The housekeeper chuckled. "Would you like to come in for refreshments?"

Harry and I declined.

"It'll be cooler in the church," she went on. "I'm sure Reverend Pritchard will be happy to bless you on the spot, particularly as you knew him from his last position. Where did you say that was again?"

"Cornwall," I said.

"Yes, but where *exactly* in Cornwall?" Her interest in the precise location renewed my own interest. I could understand the vicar not wanting to tell me, a stranger he met over a dead body, but I'd expected him to mention where he'd come from to his housekeeper.

"It's a small village," I said, repeating what Reverend Pritchard had said. "A mere speck on the map. Thank you for your—"

"It's just that you don't have a Cornish accent." The housekeeper leaned closer, turning her ear to me as if that would help her hear the nuances of my speech pattern.

"I was there only briefly."

"Yes, of course, of course. Reverend Pritchard mustn't have been there very long either, as he also doesn't have a Cornish accent. Is he originally from London, do you know?"

"I'm not sure." I'd not really detected any specific accent when the vicar spoke. That in itself was intriguing. But I'd not talked to him for long. The housekeeper, however, would have had many conversations with him. "What do *you* think?" I asked.

She twisted her mouth to the side as she thought. "Sometimes, I think I detect a London one. We get a lot of city folk coming here, so I've heard a variety of accents, and I'm quite sure I've heard a hint or two in his, but when I asked him, he said he has never lived there. Well. Never mind. He doesn't have to tell the likes of us where he's from, does he? That's between him and God, as is the reason for him leaving his former parish." She leaned forward a little, unable to hide her interest in my reaction.

"You don't know *why* he left?" I asked, innocently.

"No. Do you?"

"No."

"I'm sure there isn't a particular reason." Her cheerful smile returned. "God sent him to Morcombe knowing we needed him after our last vicar passed away suddenly."

That was one answer for the vicar's expedited transfer. A less spiritual one was that he'd been quickly moved out of his former parish because of something he'd done. We needed to know where he moved from so we could learn the answer and decide whether it was related to the murder.

The housekeeper hadn't exaggerated when she said the vicar was a devout man. We found him alone in the church, prostrated on the cold stone floor in front of the altar. We couldn't hear his whispers, but he must have been in deep prayer to have not heard our footsteps.

I was reluctant to disturb him, but Harry cleared his throat. "Excuse us, Reverend."

The vicar stood so quickly that his glasses fell off. He caught them and replaced them. He blinked at Harry. "Oh. Hello. I'm sorry, I was just…" He indicated the floor without taking his gaze off Harry.

"Do you remember me, Reverend?" I asked. "Miss Fox. I was a guest at Hambledon Hall over the weekend."

"Of course, I remember. Miss Fox, what a pleasure to see you again. Are you on your way to the Hall with your friend?"

"This is Mr. Harry Armitage," I said, ignoring his question for the moment. "He's a private detective."

Reverend Pritchard's face fell. "Private detective?"

Harry shook the vicar's hand. "I'm trying to locate the man suspected of murdering the gamekeeper from Hambledon Hall."

"Ohhh. I'm not sure how I can help. I know nothing about him."

I was grateful Harry followed my lead and didn't tell him I was also a private detective. Uncle Ronald wanted me to investigate discreetly. It was also a good idea to let everyone think Harry was looking for the missing poacher and not an alternative suspect. It would put people at ease, and hopefully that would lead them to lower their guard and divulge a clue.

"You were first to reach the body," Harry said. "Did you see anyone in the vicinity just before the gunshot? Anyone at all, even if it wasn't the missing poacher?"

The vicar pressed a finger to the bridge of his glasses. "How will that help you find him?"

"It helps me picture the scene. It's simply a part of my process. It doesn't mean anything more than that."

Reverend Pritchard seemed to believe him and relaxed a little. "The first person I saw was the already deceased Mr. Shepherd, then Miss Fox arrived. She emerged from the woods. If anyone saw someone, it would be her. The shot came from that direction."

"Are you sure?"

"It must have. The poacher would hardly be in the house."

"Did you see the moment Mr. Shepherd was struck by the bullet?"

"No. He was already on the ground when I came upon him."

"Did you hear anything? Voices, rustling leaves, footsteps perhaps?"

The vicar shook his head. "I didn't even hear Miss Fox approach. I'm afraid I'm a dreadful witness, Mr. Armitage. I am sorry."

Harry rushed to reassure him. "It's quite common not to notice the small details. It must have been traumatic for you to see one of your parishioners moments after he died."

"Mr. Shepherd wasn't a parishioner, as such. He never came to church. Actually, that's not entirely true. He came once, but not for the Sunday service. But yes, it was a shock seeing him lying there. I haven't been able to get the image of his face out of my mind since."

"You look pale, Reverend. Would you like to sit down?" Harry indicated the nearest pew.

The vicar gave a self-conscious laugh. "I assure you, I'm stronger than I look."

Harry seemed to have finished with his questions, but I felt as though we could learn more from the vicar. It would be a shame to take over from Harry, though. He had Reverend Pritchard's full attention and seemed to have his trust, too. My intrusion might risk what he'd gained. But Harry asked no more questions, so it was up to me.

"What do you think of Lord Kershaw and his family?"

Reverend Pritchard looked from Harry to me and back again. When Harry gave an encouraging nod, he finally answered. "Both Lord and Lady Kershaw are very kind, and Lady Elizabeth, too. Indeed, I've had more to do with his lordship's aunt than his wife. She never misses a parish council meeting."

"And the Brownings? How well do you know them?"

Again, he glanced at Harry before answering. "I don't, really. I've met them from time to time at the house, but they've never been to one of my services. I presume they attend church where they live."

"Do you know the Hambledon Hall servants?"

He bristled. "I'm a little familiar with those who attend Sunday service. Some don't, and I'm not sure why his lordship doesn't force them. I wouldn't want an ungodly person working for me, but that's my opinion." He looked as though he was going to say more, but stopped himself. "Miss Fox, why are you here?"

"I, uh…"

"I assume Lord Kershaw employed Mr. Armitage to find the poacher, but that doesn't require your presence."

While I was scrambling for a suitable answer, Harry offered one. "I asked her to join me. I thought having a friend of Lady Kershaw's accompany me might give my inquiries more weight."

Reverend Pritchard didn't look like he believed him, but he made no comment.

"Just one more question," Harry went on. "Your accent… I can't quite place it. Miss Fox said you're from Cornwall, but you don't sound Cornish."

"I'm from here and there, most recently from Cornwall. Now, if you don't mind, my housekeeper will have my lunch ready and she loathes it when I'm late." He indicated we should walk ahead of him.

Outside, the sky was clear and blue. The church grounds were lovely with large trees providing shade over the section of graveyard where the old headstones leaned in a southerly direction, like sunflowers seeking the sun. We parted ways with Reverend Pritchard in front of the vicarage and continued on into the heart of the village.

Harry's long strides meant he quickly drew ahead of me. Realizing I'd been left behind, he turned to face me, and slowly walked backwards. His features softened as his gaze unashamedly admired me.

My face heated again. "What are you doing, Harry?"

His attention turned to the church behind me. "Admiring the view." At my arch look, he added, "The buttresses and so forth."

"Buttresses?"

"And so forth."

He turned around again as I drew alongside him. We stopped at the window of an establishment with a sign out the front advertising homemade lemonade and scones, claiming they were 'perfect after a ramble in the Berkshire countryside.' Through the window we could see four ladies seated at two tables covered with yellow-and-white-check-ered tablecloths. There were no gentlemen, but it looked respectable enough for an unwed couple to enjoy a light lunch together.

"Shall we go in?" Harry opened the door for me.

Based on the sign, I'd expected the four ladies enjoying refreshments to be ramblers, but none wore sturdy walking boots. Indeed, I suspected they were local women as they seemed to know one another. Even though they sat at two tables, they'd been having one conversation amongst them-selves. It was somewhat heated, going by the stern looks on their faces and the way they fell silent upon our entry.

The one wearing a white apron stood and invited us to choose a table. "Lovely day for it."

I presumed 'it' was walking in the countryside. "A very pleasant day. What a beautiful village you have here, and so close to London."

The woman took our order then set to work behind the counter preparing our sandwiches. She was the youngest of the four. I guessed her age to be about fifty, while two others must be at least sixty, and the fourth at least seventy. They were perfect for our needs.

While the proprietress made our lunch, Harry introduced himself as a private investigator searching for the man the police claimed murdered Esmond Shepherd. After some initial fluttering of fans and exchange of glances, they all wanted to give their opinion. I suspected they'd been discussing the very topic moments before we arrived and were keen to pass on their thoughts to someone who wanted to actually solve the crime.

A woman who introduced herself as Mrs. Clayborn was the first to openly question Sergeant Honeyman's conclusion. "Hopeless Honeyman, that's what we call him. He always chooses the easier path, if he can. Usually, Lord Kershaw tells him to smarten up if the sergeant's laziness becomes too obvious, but this time, his lordship is letting him get away it."

"For the sake of appearances," Mrs. Smith, the eldest of the quartet added. Unlike the other three, she wore black from neck to toe, with a white lace cap covering her white hair. She reminded me of a picture I'd seen in the newspaper of the aging queen, who sported a similarly authoritative air about her, even in a black-and-white photograph. "Make no mistake, Lord Kershaw is a good man. He's simply trying to avoid scandal. The London papers would love nothing more than to come here and pester the folk up at the Hall." She shook a finger at Harry. "It's a good thing you and your assistant are taking on this investigation, but you need to widen your net. Don't just search for the missing man."

Neither Harry nor I corrected her assumption that I was his assistant. As with the witnesses at the Red Lion, I'd not given my name. I didn't want them associating me with the guests who'd stayed for the weekend. It might curb their enthusiasm for gossip if they knew I had a personal connection.

"You don't think the poacher did it?" Harry asked.

Two of the women scoffed, Mrs. Smith rolled her eyes, but it was Mrs. Clayborn who answered. "Is he even a poacher?

Why would a poacher, who isn't from around here, come to *this* village, and stay at the inn? It doesn't make sense. We think Sergeant Honeyman is using him as an escape goat."

"Scapegoat," the proprietress corrected her as she set down a plate of sandwiches in front of Harry and me. "We all think it's too neat, and if Mr. Conan Doyle has taught us anything, it's that murder is never neat."

I hid my smile by biting into a sandwich. As a lover of detective novels myself, I understood why these ladies were so keen to share their thoughts with us.

"Pointing the finger at the poacher raises a number of other questions," Mrs. Clayborn went on. "Why does Lord Kershaw want him blamed? Is he covering up for a member of his family?"

Mrs. Smith didn't like that idea. She shook her head vehemently. "They're good people. They're not murderers."

I suspected this was the point they'd reached in their heated conversation when we'd walked in.

Mrs. Clayborn picked up her teacup. "I'm just saying that no one should be ruled out. Not until all doubts are banished. Hopefully, Mr. Armitage can do that. I'm a good judge of character, and I can tell he's got the right stuff to see this through to the end, even if *some* in this village want the so-called poacher blamed." She gave Harry a firm nod, and it felt as though he'd just been given a stamp of approval by the queen herself.

He regarded the women with an earnest expression, his bright eyes clearly revealing his interest in what each of them had to say. He wanted them to know he was taking them seriously and valued their opinions. According to my grandmother, women were often ignored once they lost their youthful looks, something which had galled her. Having a young, handsome man like Harry giving these ladies his full attention was the best way to loosen their tongues. Harmony and I would have had to work harder to achieve the same result, but he was doing it without having to say much at all. The thing was, I knew Harry well enough to know he wasn't feigning interest. He genuinely thought they could offer valuable insights.

"Do you have a theory, Mrs. Clayborn?" he asked.

MURDER AT HAMBLEDON HALL

"Unfortunately not. Without knowing who was where at the time the shot was fired, there are simply too many suspects."

Fortunately, that was one thing I'd managed to achieve while I was staying at Hambledon Hall.

"Do you know of any grudges against Esmond Shepherd?" Harry prompted. "Anyone who had a disagreement with him?"

Mrs. Clayborn leaned forward. "He did upset a number of men. A lot of women liked him, you see. He could be charming to the young, pretty ones." She rolled her eyes. "Silly flibbertigibbets, the lot of them, but that's young maids for you."

The other women nodded, so I doubted any of them was the recipient of the gamekeeper's attentions.

"It didn't upset any husbands," the proprietress clarified. "He chased after *unmarried* girls, and mostly only Hambledon housemaids."

"And the nannies," Mrs. Clayborn added. "I never understood why his lordship didn't put a stop to it. They must have gone through dozens of girls over the years, all leaving in tears because Mr. Shepherd lost interest in them."

"You know why his lordship didn't," the proprietress chided, hand on hip. "Don't pretend innocence, Mrs. Clayborn."

Mrs. Clayborn's lips pinched before she relented with a sigh. "I suppose Mr. Armitage should know, even if it's not relevant. It will help him get a better picture of the victim."

Mrs. Smith scoffed. "That old rumor? It's not true."

"It might be true," Mrs. Clayborn said snippily.

"I think it's true," said the proprietress.

"So do I," added the fourth woman, speaking up for the first time.

"What rumor?" Harry asked. "Why do you think Lord Kershaw never dismissed Esmond Shepherd for his behavior toward the female staff?"

Mrs. Clayborn's lips pinched again. "The rumor is that Lord Kershaw's grandfather got Esmond Shepherd's mother pregnant. Apparently, Susannah Shepherd was the fourth earl's daughter. That close tie between the families meant the current Lord Kershaw didn't want to dismiss Esmond Shepherd, Susannah's younger brother. She died years ago, aged just twenty-one, poor thing."

It was the same rumor Mr. Faine had told us. Mrs. Clayborn clearly also believed it, as did the proprietress of the teashop and the fourth woman, who both nodded along as if it were a certainty.

The oldest woman, Mrs. Smith, shook her head vehemently. "No. I don't believe it for a moment, and I never have. I think it's time to put that nasty rumor to bed, once and for all."

"Why don't you believe it?" Mrs. Clayborn asked with genuine curiosity. She and the other women seemed to respect the older woman's opinion.

Mrs. Smith settled her bulk in the chair, pleased she had everyone's attention. "For one thing, I'm the only one here who remembers the fourth Lord Kershaw well, and he was a stiff, upright man. An affair of the heart wasn't in his nature. He was also quite a bit older than Mabel Shepherd, who was happily married at the time, may I point out. That's not all," she added crisply. "I clearly remember seeing them in the same vicinity from time to time, and there was no spark between them. Lovers are easy to spot. They share certain signals without knowing it. But I saw no sign they'd shared even a moment of intimacy."

"They could have been good actors," Mrs. Clayborn said.

Mrs. Smith barreled on, undeterred. "Do you remember how upset William Shepherd was when Susannah died?"

"It was over forty years ago!" the proprietress cried. "I was just a girl then."

"I remember how devastated he and Mabel were. Inconsolable. If Susannah wasn't *his* daughter, he wouldn't have been as upset as that."

"He raised her," Mrs. Clayborn pointed out. "That must account for something."

Harry and I had both been raised by people who were not our parents, albeit only for a few years, not our entire lives. But it meant we'd witnessed firsthand that it was possible to feel all the deep emotions that went along with parenthood despite not being the natural parent. I found myself nodding along to Mrs. Clayborn's response for that very reason.

"Mabel Shepherd died recently, didn't she?" I asked.

"A month ago," Mrs. Smith said. "It's a good thing she wasn't alive to see her youngest die before his time. She'd already buried Susannah, and she doted on Esmond. It would have been a tragedy."

Once again, I tried to think how the rumors surrounding Susannah's father's identity could have a bearing on the murder of her brother, but I couldn't see a connection. The scandal was hardly news. Everyone in the village seemed to have heard it. Besides, it happened years ago. All the parties involved were deceased. Indeed, there was only one person alive who could know the truth.

"Lady Elizabeth Wentworth and Mabel Shepherd were a similar age, is that right?" I asked.

The three younger women turned to Mrs. Smith. "Mabel was the older by a few years," she said. "Perhaps five or so."

"Did they get along?"

She frowned at my question. "As well as the wife of the gamekeeper and daughter of the earl could. I never heard them exchange cross words, or even glares. They appeared friendly enough."

"Both were kind, good women," Mrs. Clayborn added. "Lady Elizabeth still is, although she doesn't get into the village much lately."

"She comes to parish council meetings," the fourth woman noted.

"She took tea here a few weeks ago," the proprietress said with a healthy dose of pride in her voice. "She used to come in more, but not lately. If you want to find out about her family's past, Mr. Armitage, you should talk to her."

Mrs. Smith gasped in horror. "They can't ask Lady Elizabeth if her father was also Susannah Shepherd's father!"

The proprietress planted her hand on her hip again. "I wasn't suggesting they should. I just think that if anyone here remembers anything from back then, it's her. Her mind's still sharp. She's a kind soul, too. She won't turn such a nice young man as Mr. Armitage away from the Hall, as long as he's respectful." This she said to Harry with an arch of her brows, as if it were a question.

"Of course, we would be respectful," he assured her. "Lady Elizabeth sounds like someone I'd like to meet, anyway. She seems interesting."

"Oh, she is. Spirited, too. Or she used to be."

"Why did she never marry?" I asked.

The women all looked at one another, but no one had an answer.

"It was fortunate she didn't," Mrs. Smith said. "She was needed at the Hall to take care of her parents in their dotage. Her brother, the next heir and father of the current Lord Kershaw, was back and forth to London a lot at that time, so she was all they had."

I would have liked to call at Hambledon Hall next to speak to Lady Elizabeth about her recollections of the past, but dismissed the idea. Uncle Ronald wouldn't want me interrogating Lord Kershaw's family. Besides, as Mrs. Smith said, we couldn't simply ask the difficult questions that needed to be asked.

Harry finished the last sandwich finger and wiped his hands on the napkin. "You mentioned Lord Kershaw is a good man."

"He is," Mrs. Clayborn said.

"We've heard he blocked the bridleway that runs through his property, so the public can't use it."

Three of the women regarded one another with varying degrees of frustration and annoyance, while Mrs. Smith puffed out her chest and huffed, her matronly authority on full display.

"Don't get all het up about it," she told them. "None of you have walked that path in years."

The proprietress snatched up our empty plate, all the while glaring at Mrs. Smith. "That's not the point. Others use it and should be allowed to continue to use it. We need the ramblers coming through Morcombe. They're good for business."

"I don't disagree with you, but don't go telling Mr. Armitage that Lord Kershaw is a monster for blocking it. I'm sure it was an oversight, and it will be reopened to the public soon. Mr. Faine is making it all much worse than it needs to be by carrying on. He's a troublemaker, that one."

The proprietress huffed as she strode to the counter. "Ordinarily, I would agree with you about Martin Faine. He *is* a troublemaker. But this time he has a point. If his lordship planned for the bridleway to be closed temporarily, why not let us know? He didn't. He put a fence across it. My George takes twice as long to do his deliveries now."

Mrs. Smith sighed. "I just don't want Mr. Armitage thinking Lord Kershaw is an overbearing, greedy landlord. He isn't. He's a good man."

"I'm sure he is," Harry quickly cut in. "Everyone I've spoken to in the village only has kind words about him and his family. Or I should say, they have kind words about his wife and aunt. His sister and brother-in-law seem less well-liked."

The proprietress placed the plate down hard on the counter. "That's right! They were there when the gamekeeper died. Perhaps one of them did it."

"I wouldn't put it past that Mr. Browning," Mrs. Clayborn said. "Such a horrid man. I've never liked him. What kind of grown man wants to marry a fourteen-year-old girl?"

"Fourteen!" I blurted out.

Mrs. Smith cast a frosty look at her friend. "Mrs. Browning wasn't fourteen when they married. They waited until she was seventeen."

"And he was twenty-seven. Make of that what you will, Mr. Armitage." Mrs. Clayborn returned Mrs. Smith's frosty glare with an even frostier one of her own.

Mrs. Smith ignored her and addressed Harry and me. "Lady Cicely Wentworth, as Mrs. Browning was called then, was rather quiet as a child. Shy girls can often become attached to older men. They offer a sense of security."

The proprietress and Mrs. Clayborn spoke over the top of each other in their eagerness to disagree with Mrs. Smith. "Mr. Browning was as horrid then as he is now," the proprietress declared with a wrinkle of her nose, while Mrs. Clayborn pointed out that Cicely had a secure older man in her life already—her father.

Mrs. Smith didn't have a response to that.

"If Mr. Browning is so horrid," I said, "why did Cicely's parents consent to the marriage, particularly when he's a commoner?"

Mrs. Smith shrugged. "Perhaps they allowed her to choose her own husband. Some of their ilk do. Or perhaps she urged them to agree to it. What you're all forgetting is that some young girls simply *want* to get married. They have idealized notions of what marriage will be like and don't care overmuch about the man as long as he is offering to take them away from a dreary life. If a young Lady Cicely found living at Hambledon Hall stifling, then she may very well have seen Mr. Browning as a way out. They've led quite interesting married lives, living overseas and in London, throwing parties for important people… Being married to him brought little Cicely out of her shell. She has blossomed."

She wasn't describing the woman I'd met at Hambledon Hall a few days earlier. Mrs. Browning had been condescending to me when she deigned to talk to me, not a blossom in any sense of the word. I suspected these women didn't know Cicely Browning very well and were simply idealizing the life she'd gone on to lead after her marriage.

Harry paid the proprietress more than we owed for lunch. The women had been very helpful, their insights into the two families and village life invaluable. I left the teashop worrying we'd forgotten to ask something and said as much to Harry as we walked back to the station.

"Don't worry," he said. "We can always come back."

We might need to seek out Mrs. Smith and her friends again, because I couldn't help thinking that knowing the past would help us solve the murder. Or perhaps I was getting caught up in the salacious nature of the rumors and scandals. Either way, I wanted to unravel the mysteries of the Wentworth family, despite my uncle's wishes.

There was one other thing I knew for certain—I wasn't ready to leave yet. I wanted to make one more stop before we caught the train back to London.

CHAPTER 8

*G*etting to Esmond Shepherd's cottage without being seen wasn't as easy as I had thought it would be. Avoiding the house, driveway and lawn wasn't the most difficult part. It was climbing over fences and fallen logs in the woods that proved to be awkward in long skirts and a corset. I wouldn't have been able to maintain my dignity without Harry's assistance, but I still tore my hem and muddied my boots.

Although he'd let me go the moment my feet touched the earth, I could still feel his hands on my waist. I fussed with my skirts to give my nerves a few moments to settle. "Next time, I'm wearing men's trousers."

He was silent. I expected he was also trying to regain a semblance of balance after being close to me, but when I looked up, I realized his attention was on the gate's heavy lock.

"I think this is the bridleway Lord Kershaw recently blocked." He looked around and spotted something through the trees. "Is that the gamekeeper's cottage?"

We headed toward it, but it wasn't until we drew closer that I realized it was in fact the gamekeeper's cottage, only we'd approached it from the rear instead of the front. "It is very close to the bridleway. No wonder the poachers abandoned it when the cottage was built here all those years ago."

Dappled light filtered through the trees. Although it

hadn't rained for a few days, the ground was damp. Soon, the leaves would fall, laying a carpet of autumnal colors. I breathed deeply, drawing in the scent of earth, trees and fresh air.

"You like the outdoors," Harry said. It was a statement rather than a question. "I noticed in Brighton that you enjoyed the sand and the sea, and I know you enjoy walks in London's parks, too."

"I suppose I do, but I've been a city girl my entire life."

He tried opening the cottage door only to find it locked. "Do you miss Cambridge?"

"Sometimes. I miss my friends. We correspond regularly, but it's not the same. But I like my life in London, too. Living in a luxury hotel does make the chaos of the city more bearable."

He flashed me one of his dimpled grins. "I'm sure it does."

He set to work opening the lock, then entered the cottage first. Once he was satisfied it was empty, he signaled for me to enter, only to find I was already inside.

Something was amiss. Indeed, several things weren't right. The rug was rumpled, the cushions were piled up together, and the pictures had been removed from their frames and not replaced. "Someone has been here since Harmony and I came." I picked up the photograph of Mr. Shepherd with his parents. "Either they were in too much of a hurry to put everything back exactly the way it was, or they didn't care."

Harry inspected the bookshelves. "The place is hardly ransacked. They were respectful. These books have been removed from the shelves then replaced, going by the patterns in the dust."

I joined him and immediately noticed the difference to last time. "They were dustier. The intruder has definitely looked through them then put them back. I wonder what they were looking for."

"And whether they found it."

Harry entered the kitchen while I went to inspect the bedrooms. There were signs of further disturbance in each of them. After a thorough inspection, I joined Harry in the kitchen.

"They searched in here, too," I said. "What have you found?"

He handed me a card with Marylebone GuestHouse printed in bold lettering above a London address.

"Esmond Shepherd must have stayed there at some point," I said. "It might be relevant, but he could have stayed there some time ago. There's no indication of how old this is."

As I said it, I remembered another piece of evidence I'd found last time. I'd picked it up off the floor where it must have fallen, and placed it in a drawer before leaving, not thinking it was relevant. I opened the drawer and rummaged through the contents until I found it.

"He visited London quite recently." I showed Harry the return train ticket. "That's dated three days before he died. He could have stayed at the guesthouse while he was there." I slipped both the ticket and the card inside my bag. "I'll visit tomorrow."

He studied me for a moment and I suspected he was about to ask if he could join me. My case was probably more interesting than any he currently had on his plate, after all. But he did not. He simply suggested it was time to leave. "It's getting late."

"There's plenty of time before the last train," I assured him.

"That doesn't leave until four-forty-five." He checked his watch. "We can make the train before that if we hurry."

"I'm not finished yet. I have one more stop to make."

"No, Cleo. We are *not* going to the house. Sir Ronald won't want you questioning the family."

"We're not going to question the family. We're going to sneak in."

"That's even worse. It'll be crawling with servants."

"We're just going into the fernery. I want to inspect the plants for one of a similar shade to the stain I saw on Lord Kershaw's finger."

Harry's gaze narrowed. "How can we be sure no one will be in there?"

"We can't. That's why we have to be quiet."

He shook his head. "It's a bad idea."

"This isn't like you. You're not usually this hesitant. Don't worry. We won't be breaking and entering. The door from the outside will be unlocked during the day. And if we're careful, we won't be seen."

Still he refused.

I remained silent and arched my brows, defiant.

He finally gave in with a heavy sigh and indicated I should walk ahead of him out of the cottage. "Just when I'm almost back in Sir Ronald's good books, you're going to reverse the progress I've made."

"You shouldn't care so much about what my uncle thinks. I don't." I gasped and rounded on him. "You're not actually considering taking him up on his offer to return to work at the hotel, are you?"

"You're forgetting he has made no such offer. I'm still skeptical that he will, but that's beside the point. The point is…" His jaw firmed and he sighed again. "I don't want things between he and I to be permanently cold. That's all. I have my reasons."

I didn't dare ask what those reasons might be. Some things once said cannot be unsaid, and I suspected he would say something I wasn't ready to hear.

* * *

THE FERNERY COULD BE ACCESSED from the garden as well as the house, allowing us to hide behind trees and bushes to check the coast was clear before advancing. We crept up to the door like thieves and opened it just a crack to listen. All was silent, so we entered, closing the door softly behind us.

It felt tropical inside, the air thicker and hotter than in the woods. Harry and I followed the path, inspecting the plants as we went. Despite being sure we were alone, we didn't speak. Harry tapped me on the shoulder if he thought he'd found a plant of the right color, but after the sixth attempt, he gave up. He only tapped my shoulder again to show me his watch. It was time to leave.

Satisfied I'd inspected most of the plants, I nodded. We

exited the fernery into the garden, only to stop dead upon the sound of someone snorting.

We'd been caught.

I steeled myself for the confrontation, and tried to think of an excuse for my presence at the house, uninvited and with a man in tow.

But the snorter merely snorted again. I turned to the noise and released a breath. Renton the butler sat slumped on a wicker chair, his eyes closed, his head tilted back and mouth open. He emitted another noise. This time I realized it was a snore, not a snort.

Harry touched my hand to get my attention. With a finger to his lips, he nodded in the direction of the trees. Together, we crept away from Renton to the safety of the thick trunks, then continued until we'd left the house well behind.

"That was the butler," I told Harry as we headed back to the station. "According to Harmony, he likes a tipple in the afternoons then nods off. He was the only member of staff whose whereabouts she couldn't verify at the time of the gunshot. Apparently, he was in his room taking a nap, but I'm not convinced."

"Why not?"

"He got to the body very quickly for an older man whose bedroom is located on the top floor."

"Perhaps he was napping on that chair, not in his room."

"Perhaps." I still wasn't convinced, however. Renton was more exposed in the garden, especially with guests going between the house and the tennis court. He could have been asleep elsewhere, though. From the look of it, he did like his afternoon naps, so that part of his alibi was believable.

But if his naps were the result of stealing his lordship's brandy, and Esmond Shepherd had proof and threatened to take that proof to Lord Kershaw, Renton would have a motive to murder Shepherd.

* * *

FRANK WARNED me as he opened the hotel's front door upon my return that Mrs. Short was taking one of the maids to task in her office. The housekeeper had caught the girl reading a note that morning while she was pushing her cleaning cart along the corridor on the fourth floor.

"Surely she can't be in too much trouble for taking a moment to read her note," I said.

"The note was from her beau, setting up a rendezvous for Saturday," Frank said.

I groaned. The maid had fallen foul of Mrs. Short's new rule. "I assume the beau is another staff member?"

"A footman. Mrs. Short was furious, so I heard. She told the girl to come to her office at the end of the day and they'd discuss her future here at the hotel. She's been in tears all day, so Harmony told me. We think she'll be dismissed on the spot, her beau, too, if she gives up his name."

"He didn't sign the note?"

"No. Rather wise not to, as it turns out."

I was pleased to see Mr. Hobart strolling through the foyer holding the leather satchel he used to carry work home to read on the train. He hadn't left yet. If anyone could convince Mrs. Short she had overreacted with her new rule, it was him. As he walked, he glanced frequently over his shoulder, back to the senior staff corridor.

"Is the maid still with Mrs. Short?" I asked him.

"You heard about that." His lips formed a grim line. "I'm afraid so."

"Can you do something?"

He steered me away from two guests who'd stopped nearby for a chat. "Sir Ronald has forbidden me from stepping in. He says it's a good idea, in theory."

"While in practice, it's going to be a disaster." I shook my head sadly. "The staff aren't children. They won't like it if the maid and her beau are dismissed over this."

"Then hopefully the maid is able to keep his name to herself. Otherwise, they'll both be without a job and a home, and we could find most of the staff go on strike to support them."

It could be a disaster of monumental proportions.

"Miss Fox, I almost forgot. My brother telephoned earlier. He wants you to telephone him back. You can use the one in my office for privacy. Ask Peter to unlock the door for you. I must dash if I want to catch the train that will get me home in time for dinner."

I thanked him and approached Peter. As I waited for him to unlock Mr. Hobart's office door, I heard muffled voices coming from Mrs. Short's office. "I'll be a moment."

"Miss Fox!" Peter hissed. "Is that wise?"

"We'll soon find out."

I knocked on Mrs. Short's door and received a brusque response to enter. Inside, the housekeeper sat behind her desk with the maid standing on the other side, not allowed to sit. I was struck by how similar Mrs. Short looked to my uncle when he was at his most bullish. Both short and jowly, they exuded an air of barely constrained frustration that threatened to explode at any moment.

"Yes, Miss Fox?" she snapped. "Is something the matter?"

"I've just returned to the hotel and heard that my note may be the cause of some confusion." I cast a look at the maid, blinking back at me with eyes red and swollen from crying.

Mrs. Short's gaze fell on a torn piece of paper on her desk. It appeared as though it had been folded many times to make it as small as possible.

"Ah, there it is." I reached for it, but Mrs. Short snatched it away.

"*Your* note?" she said, incredulous. "This was found in Mary's possession."

"She must have picked it up, thinking it was rubbish. Was it in the corridor on the fourth floor, Mary?"

Mary nodded so quickly and vigorously a strand of her hair fell out of the pins holding it back.

"So foolish of me," I said lightly. "I thought I'd put it in my bag, but it seems I dropped it. I've been wondering where it got to. May I?"

Mrs. Short hesitated, clearly torn as to whether she could believe me. I already knew she didn't like me, but I also knew she didn't like anyone, so I wasn't overly concerned about lying to her. If I could save Mary from dismissal, my lie would be worth it.

I held out my hand. "May I have my note back, please."

Mrs. Short seemed to be in a trance as she handed it over.

I scanned it quickly. Neither the recipient's name nor the sender's was on it. I'd counted on them being extra careful, and was right. Thank goodness. I folded the note. "As I thought. It is mine. I am sorry to be the cause of such a fuss, and for you to have wasted your time, Mrs. Short. Do forgive me."

Mrs. Short rallied; her trance-like stare replaced with her usual fierce one. "Am I to believe *you* are meeting a gentleman at the Paragon Theatre to see the latest penny gaff?"

"I don't think that's anyone's business but my own." I waved the folded piece of paper at her. "Besides, there is nothing in here to suggest it's from a man. Is there?"

"The handwriting is masculine."

"I'll tell my friend that. I suspect we'll have a good laugh about it." I tucked the note into my bag. "I presume Mary will be cleaning rooms again in the morning. She does an excellent job. Just as good as Harmony Cotton. I particularly like the way she folds towels." I waited, smiling, forcing Mrs. Short to respond one way or another while I was still there.

"You may go, Mary," she bit off.

Mary went to leave but stopped. "Tomorrow?"

"Don't be late for work."

I followed Mary out of the office, not giving Mrs. Short any opportunity to so much as glare at me. The maid and I left in such a hurry that we caught Mr. Chapman the steward hovering near the door. He'd clearly been listening in. He quickly scurried off to his own office, closing the door firmly behind him.

Mary slowed her pace. "Thank you, Miss Fox."

"Don't mention it. But please be more careful in future."

She nodded and hurried in the direction of the service corridor while I entered Mr. Hobart's office to use the telephone.

D.I. Hobart had some intriguing news for me. According to a former colleague of his, a Morcombe man had been arrested on suspicion of selling stolen goods two years ago. They had to let him go after they couldn't find enough evidence, and he seemed to have stayed out of trouble since, but D.I. Hobart suggested I look for a connection between the man and Esmond Shepherd.

"Don't approach him," he warned me. "He might be dangerous if he feels cornered. I don't want you getting into trouble, or getting Harry into trouble either."

When he put it that way, I agreed with him. If we were caught searching his premises, the man was within his rights to call the police and have us arrested. "I'll be careful. What's his name?"

"Faine. Martin Faine. He lists his address as the Red Lion Inn."

So Mr. Faine wasn't just a good source of information, and an agitator who wanted the bridleway reopened. He was a fence of stolen goods, too. Everything he'd told us now had to be re-examined through a new lens.

After hanging up from D.I. Hobart, I returned to the foyer. It was growing late, but I had no dinner plans that evening, so I spent some time chatting to guests. I enjoyed finding out where they were from, and why they were visiting London. Many of them lived in the countryside and had business interests in the city. Some had come for the theater, or had been shopping. Some came to London for all three reasons.

It was while I was mingling with the guests that Uncle Ronald emerged from the lift. He greeted me amiably and joined in with the conversation I'd been having with a couple from Cardiff, but I got the impression he had something to say to me.

Once the couple left, he turned to me. "I have good news for your investigation, Cleopatra. Lord Kershaw and his family have brought their visit to London forward. They're coming tomorrow to shop for Janet Browning's wedding and are staying here." He leaned in, a look of excitement on his face. "You can speak to them."

"I don't quite understand, Uncle. If you believe the poacher did murder Esmond Shepherd, why do you want me to interrogate Lord Kershaw's family?"

He held up a finger. "Not interrogate. *Speak* to them. Don't raise their suspicions. The reason being, you may need to exonerate them if you can't locate the poacher. Call it insurance, in case you fail with your primary goal."

Nice to know he didn't have a lot of faith in me. "Very well."

I made to leave, but he called me back. "Question them gently, Cleopatra. I cannot overstate that enough. Is that clear?"

"Don't worry, Uncle. I can be subtle."

His frown deepened, telling me what he thought of that statement.

* * *

THE FOLLOWING MORNING, Harmony joined me for breakfast, even though it was her day off. She knew all about my intervention between Mary and Mrs. Short. Apparently, it was the main gossip in the residence hall.

"Mary is ever so grateful," she said, holding a coffee cup in both hands to warm them. "So is her footman beau."

"Just as long as they're more careful in future. I can't do that again. Mrs. Short is already suspicious, and won't fall for it a second time." I cracked open the shell of my boiled egg with the back of a teaspoon. "How do you and Victor communicate without getting caught?"

"We use notes, too, but we're more careful about how we pass them and when we read them." She placed a boiled egg in an eggcup and sliced the top off with a bold strike of the knife. "I can't believe we have to stoop to passing notes. It's childish and ridiculous. Just because Mrs. Short is miserable, she wants everyone else to be miserable, too. It's not fair."

"*Is* she miserable?"

Harmony merely shrugged as she scooped out the contents of her egg with a spoon.

"Do you think if a man was interested in her, she'd be less strict on the housemaids?" I asked.

"The fellow who would put up with her doesn't exist, so the point is moot." She picked up her coffee cup and, finding it empty, refilled it. She then topped up mine. "What are you doing today?"

"This morning I'm calling at a guesthouse. Harry and I found evidence in the gamekeeper's cottage suggesting that he'd stayed there. I want to find out why Shepherd was in

London. It may or may not be relevant, but it's something I can do here without returning to Morcombe."

"Is Harry going with you?"

"No."

"Why not?"

"He's busy with his own investigations, and I don't need him there. You're most welcome to join me, though, since it's your day off."

"Thank you, but no. Victor has the day off, too, so we're spending it together."

"Somewhere away from Mrs. Short, I hope."

"If this nice weather holds, we thought we'd go for a picnic in the countryside. Like Berkshire, perhaps. Morcombe had some nice parks."

I chuckled. "I forbid you to go anywhere near Morcombe. You two so rarely have a full day off together. No investigating."

"Very well, but if you think of anything, let me know. We're leaving at ten."

* * *

THE SIGN on the gate of the Marylebone Guesthouse boasted warm beds, home-cooked meals, and good service. No price was stipulated. That alone was a clue that a room would be on the expensive side. Given it was also a handsome building in a central part of London, I was quite sure it would cost more than a gamekeeper could afford. Perhaps Esmond Shepherd hadn't stayed there, after all.

That theory was proved incorrect. When I explained I was investigating the death of Esmond Shepherd, the landlady gasped in shock. "But he stayed here not long ago!" She showed me the registration book and pointed to his name. "One night, last week. I can't believe he's dead now. And you say he was murdered? Well, that is a surprise. Who would want to kill such a charming, handsome man?" She patted her hair where it was graying at the temples.

"Do you know why he was here?" I asked.

She gasped again. "Surely his death has nothing to do

with his stay in my guesthouse. I run a respectable establishment, Miss."

"I can tell." I made a point of admiring the clean floor tiles, the ornate ceiling rose and electric lighting. "You have a very fine home. I'm not yet sure if Mr. Shepherd's demise has anything to do with his visit to London, but I'm quite sure this guesthouse was simply the place he stayed at while he was here. Don't worry. The name will not appear in any newspaper articles about his death."

She relaxed a little. "Thank you. As to your question, I don't know. He didn't say why he was here, just that he was visiting."

"Did he make a reservation ahead of his stay?"

"No. He simply showed up on the doorstep and inquired as to availability for one night."

"Did he go out while he was here?"

"Twice. Once in the evening, and again in the morning before he left." She waved in an easterly direction. "I happened to notice that both times, he turned left out of the front gate."

I thanked her. Outside, I also turned left. The street was rather long, with a mixture of houses, shops, dining establishments, a church and even a home for orphans. I stopped at several, but no one could remember a man named Esmond Shepherd who fit the description I gave.

I returned to the Mayfair Hotel where Frank greeted me warmly. It was a pleasant change to his usual grunts and scowls. The reception from Goliath and the other front-of-house staff was equally warm. Word had spread about my intervention between Mary and Mrs. Short.

I thought Peter was approaching me to speak about that incident, but another matter was on his mind. "The Kershaw party arrived early, and their rooms aren't ready. They aren't supposed to check in until two."

"Have they all arrived? Even the Brownings?"

He nodded. "The ladies are waiting in the small sitting room and the men have gone out. Mr. Hobart is overseeing the preparations of the rooms himself. He didn't want the maids doing a poor job in their haste to finish. You know how he likes everything to be perfect."

I did indeed. The manager kept a file on each guest that listed their preferences, dislikes, and other information about them, including personal details. Not only did he want their room to be perfect, but he wanted them to have an enjoyable experience. That was why he went out of his way to greet them by name, inquire about family members, home renovations, recent holidays and even their pets. His notes were thorough, particularly for a family like Lord Kershaw's who had not only stayed often at the Mayfair but were personal friends of my aunt and uncle.

"Mrs. Short will be put out," Peter went on. "She won't want Mr. Hobart looking over her shoulder."

"Indeed not." I was a little surprised the manager found it necessary to intervene in the housekeeper's domain. She was just as much a perfectionist as he was.

"You may want to join the guests, Miss Fox," Peter said. "Lady Bainbridge and Miss Bainbridge are with them."

I could tell from his face that he was concerned. He was right to be. I doubted my aunt was feeling up to playing hostess, unless she'd taken a dose of her tonic. "Where is Floyd?"

"According to the footman who is currently acting as Mr. Bainbridge's valet, he is still asleep after a late night out."

I asked Peter to send in sandwiches, then headed to the small sitting room. Despite its name, it was rather large, although not on the same scale as the main sitting room where the hotel served its famous afternoon teas every day. Used only by the family, the small sitting room was more personal. Family photographs were assembled on tables and Bainbridge heirlooms inherited by Uncle Ronald were housed there. My aunt and uncle's suite had more items she'd inherited from her parents—my grandparents—but this sitting room was very much a Bainbridge room. It oozed old world nobility from the elaborately carved mahogany pedestal table to the Whistler painting hanging above the marble fireplace.

As I expected, Aunt Lilian appeared to be struggling to entertain her guests. She looked as frail as Lady Elizabeth, seated beside her on the sofa and attempting to make conversation. Aunt Lilian's shaking hands and pained expression were a clear sign she hadn't taken her tonic. That, at least, was a blessing. It meant she was at least *trying* to limit her consumption.

On my aunt's other side sat Lady Kershaw. Flossy was engaged in conversation with Janet Browning, as far from the older women as they could get. They spoke quietly between themselves, occasionally giggling. Both looked up on my arrival and beckoned me to join them to discuss Janet's wedding plans.

I declined and sat with Mrs. Browning instead, seated alone on the other sofa. Aunt Lilian gave me a small nod of gratitude. It was accompanied with a thin, tight smile that quickly vanished in a wince of pain. Her head must be pounding, poor thing.

As much as I wanted to claim I'd made my choice of companion because I wanted to be a dutiful niece and good hostess, it was purely because I wanted to ask Mrs. Browning some questions. It wasn't that she was my preferred choice of all the ladies. It was simply that it would be easier to have a difficult conversation with the one on her own, far enough from the others that we wouldn't be overheard.

And I had to ask some very difficult questions indeed.

CHAPTER 9

*A*ccording to Mrs. Browning, her husband and brother would join them at the hotel later. They had business in the city first. My suspicious mind immediately wondered about the nature of their business and whether it had anything to do with Esmond Shepherd's demise. If it did, Mrs. Browning gave no indication.

Indeed, she gave little indication about anything except that she was politely tolerating my presence. She'd been reading a letter when I sat down, and I suspected she wished to continue to read it in peace. I wasn't moving, however. Not while her solitude gave me the perfect opportunity to question her, subtly, of course.

Janet suddenly giggled at something Flossy said, reminding me of how immature she was. Too immature to marry, in my opinion. Her own mother had married young, too, after the man who was now her husband pursued her from the age of fourteen. It was difficult to imagine Mrs. Browning as a girl. She was aloof and serious. It wouldn't be easy to extract answers from her.

"The gardens at Hambledon Hall will be lovely for the wedding," I began.

"Autumn is too cold for an outdoor reception. It will be held in the ballroom." Mrs. Browning returned to her letter.

I wasn't going to be put off so easily. "Lady Kershaw must

be as excited to host the wedding in her home as you are to see your daughter married."

"I was born and raised there," she said without looking up from the letter. "It's only right that my daughter is married at Hambledon."

This wasn't going at all well. I continued with my breezy tone, despite my frustration. "If you require any assistance with the arrangements, you should speak to Miss Cotton while you're here. She assisted Floyd with the planning of an elaborate wedding recently. I'm sure she'd be—"

"Isn't that your maid? The dark girl?"

I clasped my hands tightly on my lap in an effort to continue to keep my tone light. "Miss Cotton is my maid when she isn't organizing major events for the hotel."

Mrs. Browning looked down at her letter again. "We don't need anyone's help, particularly that of a maid."

"I'm sure the staff at Hambledon are used to hosting grand events. Even though the wedding will be held inside, it must be a worry that the outdoors might not be up to its usual perfection, without a gamekeeper."

Her jaw stiffened. "A gamekeeper doesn't garden, Miss Fox. Gardeners do. You may not be a country girl, but I'm surprised you don't know the difference. You do *seem* intelligent."

I had to admit it was a terrible way to broach the topic of Esmond Shepherd's murder, but broach it I had. I wouldn't let the effort go to waste. "Speaking of Mr. Shepherd, his family and yours seemed to have a close relationship."

"The Shepherds worked for us. That is—was—the extent of the relationship."

"That's my point." When she didn't respond, I continued. "I'll let you in on a little secret. One of the hotel maids was recently caught in the men's area at the residence hall. She was dismissed instantly. Now, you could argue that the male staff member should have been dismissed, too, but while management don't know his identity, he is safe. By all accounts, Esmond Shepherd visited the rooms of the Hambledon Hall female members of staff quite a bit over the years and everyone knew, yet he wasn't dismissed."

Mrs. Browning folded the letter in half and pinched the

fold between her thumb and fingernail. "I should have known you liked to wallow in gossip, Miss Fox."

Despite the temptation to ask why she should have known, I stayed silent. I probably wouldn't like the answer, and besides, silence often forced the other person to fill it.

Mrs. Browning didn't disappoint. "You shouldn't believe every rumor you hear. Mr. Shepherd wasn't as bad as they make him out to be. While he could be charming, and the maids did like him, it never went beyond a little flirtation here and there."

"The maids and nannies left your family's employ because of him."

"Again, just gossip. It's true the previous nanny did leave after their relationship ended, but not because of Mr. Shepherd. Her brother needed her to keep house for him. I think his wife just died."

"If they were in a relationship, it didn't need to end because of her move. Unless she moved far away?" I posed it as a question, to prompt her to offer an answer.

It worked. "She returned to London. Somewhere near Marylebone, I believe."

Marylebone! Well, well.

"Let me assure you, Miss Fox, that Miss Crippen was the only Hambledon employee of interest to Mr. Shepherd, and there was nothing sordid about their relationship. I believe they were in love, at some point. They must have been." A defensive note crept into the aloofness. There was a hint of something else in her tone, too: jealousy.

"Why do you say that?" I asked.

"He *must* have been in love." She whipped her thumb and fingernail along the letter's fold again, repeating the move twice more before realizing she was doing it. She set the letter down on her lap. "So, there you have it. The gossipers were right about the former nanny, but wrong about the housemaids. Mr. Shepherd would never stoop *that* low."

"Because he didn't need to," I added.

Her lack of a response was telling. It meant she agreed with the statement. If I were to guess, I'd say Mrs. Browning had held some affection for Esmond Shepherd. Yet, while her tone was both defensive and jealous, there was no sorrow in it. She hadn't been upset by his death.

Had her affection been reciprocated? If so, how far had they taken it?

As if she sensed she'd given away too much, she suddenly stiffened. "The reason I'm telling you this is because gossip isn't always correct."

"I most certainly agree, Mrs. Browning. Thank you for putting that particular rumor to bed. I feel so much better now." I cleared my throat. "There is another, however. Indeed, I'm a little hesitant to even bring it up."

"Then don't."

"It might help explain the close connection between the Shepherds and Wentworths."

She sighed. "You're talking about the rumor that my grandfather was Susannah Shepherd's father."

Out of the corner of my eye, I saw Lady Elizabeth's head turn sharply toward us. There was nothing wrong with the elderly woman's hearing.

"Sorry for my impertinence, but *is* that rumor true?" I asked.

"How should I know? My grandfather didn't confide in me. I was a little girl when he died. Susannah Shepherd died before I was even born. Whether the rumor is true or not, it no longer matters. It happened so long ago. Susannah Shepherd is nothing more than a name on a headstone now."

She was also a face in a photograph in Esmond Shepherd's cottage. A photograph that someone had picked up to study.

"Now it's my turn," Mrs. Browning said.

I blinked at her. "Your turn for what?"

"Clarifying gossip I've heard." She nodded at Aunt Lilian, staring blankly at the platter of sandwiches that a footman had brought in a few moments earlier. As hostess, she ought to invite us to enjoy them, but she'd not said a word. "She's dying, isn't she?"

"No! She's ill, but she'll be better soon."

Mrs. Browning didn't look like she believed me. "She and your mother were estranged for a number of years, were they not?"

I saw no reason to lie to her. My aunt and uncle had probably confided in Lord and Lady Kershaw already anyway. "They were, at the insistence of their parents. They didn't like my mother's choice of husband."

"That's not the entire reason, though. Is it?"

I stared at her. "Pardon?"

"Your uncle was in love with your mother first."

"What?"

"Sir Ronald loved your mother, but she spurned him for a professor of mathematics. He settled instead for the less interesting sister, since she became the sole heiress to her father's fortune."

I clenched my back teeth to stop myself from snapping at her. I was offended and outraged, but I wouldn't give her the satisfaction of showing it. For one thing, I didn't want her knowing it could be the truth. For another, I'd asked similarly offensive questions of her. It would be hypocritical of me to be cross.

Flossy and Janet giggled again. The cheery sound was at odds with my dark mood.

I leveled my gaze with Mrs. Browning's, doing my utmost to keep my features schooled. "I never knew Aunt Lilian in her youth, but I've heard she was vivacious and a beauty."

"I didn't say she wasn't. I merely said she was the less interesting sister, so I've been told." She picked up her gloves and the letter and stood. "I'm a little hungry." She joined the other ladies and selected a sandwich from the platter. She didn't rejoin me, but instead sat with Janet and Flossy.

She hadn't been wanting or even expecting confirmation of the rumor. She simply wanted to cause offence. That was the difference between us. I was aware my questions would be hurtful, but I needed to know the answers for the sake of finding a murderer. She had asked hers for the sole purpose of offending.

I picked up the platter of sandwich fingers to offer them around. Realizing what I was doing, and that she should be the one offering, Aunt Lilian snatched the platter from me. Unfortunately, she tilted it and the sandwiches fell onto the floor.

"Cleopatra!" she snapped. "Look what you've done."

I went to pick them up.

"Leave it. Fetch someone to clean it up."

I exchanged glances with Flossy as I left. Hers was full of sympathy, her girlish good humor nowhere in sight.

I met Mr. Hobart as he was heading in my direction. Three room keys dangled from his fingers. "The sandwiches fell on the floor," I said. "Can you send in someone to clean up, please."

He signaled to a passing footman and gave him instructions. Once he was out of earshot, Mr. Hobart frowned at me. "Are you all right, Miss Fox? You seem upset."

I drew in a deep breath and let it out slowly. "My aunt is unwell and would like to retire but she doesn't want to abandon her friends."

"Then I have good news. Their rooms are ready. I was just on my way to offer to escort them personally."

"That is a relief. Do you mind if I escort them?" I wanted to return to the sitting room to show my aunt's scolding hadn't affected me. To disappear now would be cowardice.

He handed me three room keys. "They're not all together, unfortunately. The Brownings are in one of the two-bedroom suites, while Lady Elizabeth is on her own with Lord and Lady Kershaw's room beside hers. All are ready."

"I was surprised to hear that you saw to the preparations yourself, to ensure nothing was missed in the rush. Was Mrs. Short not available, or do you not trust her to be as much of a perfectionist as you?"

Mr. Hobart's eyes crinkled at the corners with his smile. "I felt it was necessary to remind her that I am the manager, and that she answers to me."

It took me a moment to realize that Mr. Hobart's pointed reminder was a result of not being consulted before Mrs. Short made her new rule about staff relationships. Always polite and professional, he'd tried to make the point as subtly as possible. I hoped it hadn't been too subtle for the blunt housekeeper to comprehend.

The footman emerged from the small sitting room, carrying the tray of sandwiches. "Shall I ask the kitchen to send in more, Miss Fox? I asked Lady Bainbridge, but her answer was…unclear."

"Have them sent to these rooms." I showed the footman

the keys, each attached to a brass fob embossed with the room number. He memorized the numbers then walked off.

Before I re-entered the small sitting room, Mr. Hobart again asked me if everything was all right. "Does Lady Bainbridge require medical assistance? Shall I telephone her doctor?"

"I think she just needs rest." And not to take more of her tonic, I wanted to add but didn't.

* * *

THE MARYLEBONE GUESTHOUSE was located on Wimpole Street, conveniently near Hyde Park, Regent's Park, the zoo, and the shopping district. I doubted Esmond Shepherd stayed there for its proximity to London's sights, however. I suspected he chose it because it was close to Miss Crippen, the former nanny.

It took two hours, but I eventually spoke to someone who knew the name Crippen. A waitress cleaning tables after the lunch-time rush at a chophouse told me that a Mr. Crippen often dined there, either alone or with colleagues from work. Hopefully he was the nanny's brother, the one who'd lost his wife and asked his sister to keep house for him.

"He always orders pork chops with mashed potatoes and beer. He'll probably be here tonight at around five, since it's Friday."

"Where does he work?"

"He's a clerk in one of the solicitors' offices near here, but I don't know which one."

I thanked her and continued my search for Mr. Crippen, only to stop after an hour. There were two solicitors' offices in the vicinity of the chophouse. I decided not to inquire at either of them. I preferred not to speak to him at his place of work. I'd return to the chophouse at five.

I told Harry as much when I spoke to him at his office. I'd found myself stopping in Soho after leaving Marylebone. Visiting Harry was a far more palatable option than returning to the hotel.

I found him writing a report. "Have you finished an investigation?" I asked.

"I have. The missing money was located where the shop-keeper left it. He'd simply forgotten it was there. Poor fellow's getting on a bit, and his mind's going, so his wife says."

I took a seat opposite him. "I'm glad it wasn't theft." I waited while he finished his report, pretending to read a newspaper but actually admiring him. He drew his brows together as he concentrated and tapped a finger on the page when he couldn't think of a word.

When he finished, he set the paper aside for the ink to dry. "Is this a social call or do you need my assistance for the investigation?"

"Both."

The answer took him by surprise. He looked pleased. His face soon fell, however. "Are you all right, Cleo?"

"I'm a little out of sorts. Investigating friends of my family isn't as easy as I thought it would be. In fact, it's troubling me that I may discover the killer is one of them."

"Have you made a breakthrough?"

I told him about my conversation with Mrs. Browning, including her hints of jealousy. "I think she was a little in love with Shepherd. Whether or not she acted on that, I don't know. I can't imagine she did. She seems too much of a snob to stoop to swooning over the gamekeeper."

Harry smiled crookedly. "His lower position could have been part of the attraction."

"She also told me that the former nanny left the Kershaws' employ to move back to London to keep house for her brother after his wife died. She let slip that he lives in Marylebone. I've spent the last few hours asking after him and finally found out that he often dines at a chophouse after work."

"I thought you said his sister is keeping house for him. Why is he dining out often?"

"Perhaps she's not a very good cook. The waitress said Mr. Crippen will probably be there tonight after work. I plan to ask him where I can find his sister. According to Mrs. Browning, Miss Crippen *was* in a relationship with Shepherd, but its end wasn't the reason she left Hambledon Hall. I'd like to know if that's true, and if Miss Crippen has any thoughts on who may have wanted to kill him."

"You mean beside herself?"

"Indeed."

"What if Crippen declines to tell you anything about his sister?"

"I'll use my persuasive charms on him."

Harry grinned. "Poor chap doesn't stand a chance."

"Will you come with me? If you don't have any plans already, that is. I don't want you to change anything for me. I can manage a suspect in a chophouse alone."

He leaned forward. "Cleo, I don't have any plans tonight. I will happily dine with you."

My spirits momentarily lifted before flattening again. "I'm afraid I can't stay to eat. I have to dine with my suspects at the hotel restaurant at eight. My interrogation of Mr. Crippen will be brief. I simply need to find out where his sister lives."

He sat back. It could have been my imagination, but he seemed a little flat now, too.

"I'm sorry, Harry. I wish I could stay, but this is important to the investigation, as well as my family."

He smiled again. "It's important to keep your uncle happy. Anyway, it sounds like a jolly evening ahead for you with a few of your suspects in one place."

"I do enjoy a good meal with my interrogation," I joked. "Although I'm not sure if I'll be able to ask too many questions at dinner. It will depend on who I'm seated next to." I pulled a face. "I hope it's neither Mr. nor Mrs. Browning."

He clasped his hands on the desk and twiddled his thumbs. "So…that's the business side. Now for the personal."

"Pardon?"

"You said this was also a social call."

"Did I?" I murmured.

Harry got up and rounded the desk then sat on the edge near me. "Something's the matter. What is it?"

"Nothing."

He tilted his head to the side and regarded me with an earnest, unwavering gaze that disarmed me altogether. He didn't need to speak another word.

"I can't explain it," I said. "I feel…odd."

"Are you ill?"

"Nothing like that. Aunt Lilian was a little terse with me

earlier, but I was feeling this way before that, so I can't blame her. I suppose the best way to describe it is that I feel unbalanced."

"I see. Is there something I can do to help balance you?"

"I doubt it. It must just be this case. That's the only explanation for it."

He nodded thoughtfully. "Well then. We should solve it as quickly as possible so you can return to normal." He pushed off from the desk and indicated the door. "Shall we make our way to the chophouse?"

I watched as he plucked his hat and jacket off the stand then opened the door. He indicated I should go first. I frowned as I passed him. There was something about him, something…curious. He didn't smile or frown. He didn't even watch me. Yet, like my emotional state, I couldn't put my finger on what had changed.

But something *had* changed.

* * *

THE CHOPHOUSE WAS PACKED with men dressed in business suits who must work in the nearby offices or perhaps even at Whitehall, enjoying beers and meals at the end of the working week. The only women there were waiting on tables, so I felt a little out of place. The waitress I'd spoken to earlier recognized me and pointed out Mr. Crippen, sitting alone in a booth by the window, enjoying an ale and reading a newspaper while he waited for his meal to arrive.

I slipped onto the seat opposite. "Mr. Crippen?"

He lowered the newspaper. "Yes?" He was a young man, no older than late twenties, with a thick crop of brown wavy hair and a clean-shaven jaw. His hazel eyes were wide, but that could have been because he was surprised to be addressed by a stranger, and a woman at that.

"Forgive the intrusion. My name is Cleopatra Fox, and this is my associate, Mr. Armitage. We're private detectives investigating the murder of Esmond Shepherd, the game-keeper at—"

"It wasn't me! I didn't do it!" His panicked gaze flicked between Harry and me.

For a moment, I thought he'd try to run off. Harry must have thought so, too, because I felt him tense beside me, ready to take up the chase if necessary.

"Nobody is accusing you of anything," I assured Mr. Crippen. "We just want to talk." I shelved my question about his sister and followed my instincts instead. His response piqued my curiosity in a slightly different direction. "Why do you think we're here to accuse you of murder?"

Mr. Crippen swallowed heavily. "No reason."

"You were arguing with him in the woods before his death, weren't you?" When he didn't respond, I lied. "I saw you."

My gamble paid off. He gave in. "We did argue. But that's all. I said my piece and left him alive and well."

"Did you stay at the Red Lion in Morcombe?"

He nodded. "I decided not to stay the extra night. It was pointless. So I caught the next train back to London."

This was the man the Morcombe police were accusing of murdering Esmond Shepherd. Except he wasn't a poacher. He was a solicitor's clerk. As I suspected, the poacher never existed.

Sergeant Honeyman may have been wrong about many things, but Mr. Crippen *was* a suspect. Not only was he in the vicinity at the time of the murder, but his sister had been in a relationship with the victim. He'd also been angry enough to argue with Shepherd.

Angry enough to kill?

CHAPTER 10

*M*r. Crippen was keen to talk. I didn't have to prompt him to tell me about his confrontation with Shepherd. He seemed to think talking about it would exonerate him.

"My sister is a good woman," he began. "She has never been in trouble before, never put a foot wrong, until *that* man came along." Hearing his voice rise, he quickly glanced around to make sure he hadn't been overheard, then leaned forward. "Shepherd convinced her he was in love with her. He took advantage of her gentle nature, her goodness, and made her fall in love with him. It was easy with his handsome face and honeyed words." He sat back. "I didn't know any of this at the time. It wasn't until it all ended that she told me, when she paid me a visit on her day off. She was upset. Shepherd had lost interest in her and moved on to a new girl, a maid at the house, or some such." He shrugged, the detail not important to him. "My sister was heartbroken, but Shepherd didn't care. He was cruel to her, calling her a desperate and sad pest he couldn't get rid of. He demanded she leave him alone. He even told her she should leave the employ of the Kershaws. The nerve of him!"

I could imagine how it had been. Shepherd had simply lost interest in her, but she thought she'd done something wrong and wanted to know what. Her questions were persistent, and he loathed being held accountable for his feckless nature. Mrs. Browning had led me to believe the couple were in love. Perhaps Miss Crippen had been, but Esmond Shepherd never had. It was clear he had been a predator who knew how to manipulate women.

"My sister complained to Lady Kershaw about his behavior, but her ladyship wanted nothing to do with it. She told her to 'buck up' and 'get on with it.'"

"Did she dismiss your sister?" I asked.

The arrival of his meal distracted him for a moment. He waited until the waitress left before continuing. "Not in so many words, but her ladyship made it clear that she ought to resign."

"It's fortunate she could return to London to keep house for you." Realizing how that sounded under the circumstances, I apologized profusely. "That was terribly unfeeling of me."

He gave me a blank look.

"You need help at home after the passing of your wife," I clarified.

He frowned. "I've never been married."

That was another point Mrs. Browning had got wrong.

"Where can we find your sister? We'd like to—"

"You're not talking to her about that man. She's upset enough." He picked up his knife and fork but didn't give his chops any attention. "The murder was nothing to do with either of us. In fact, I wasn't the only one arguing with Shepherd that day. When I approached his cottage, I saw him with two other men. I saw one of them clearly, but the other had his back to me and was partly obscured by a tree."

"Can you describe the one you saw?" I asked.

"Full black beard, dressed like a laborer. He wore a gray cap. I noticed it because I wore a similar one."

The description matched Mr. Faine, the agitator we'd met in the Red Lion who was up in arms about the blocking of the bridleway.

Harry indicated the food. "Please eat. There's nothing worse than cold mashed potato." He watched as Mr. Crippen cut into his chop. "Did you hear what the argument was about?"

"A pathway, or something of that nature. Shepherd told

the black-bearded man he was going too far. His tone was scolding, annoyed." Mr. Crippen forked the meat into his mouth.

They must have been discussing the bridleway, with Shepherd telling Faine to cease his demands for it to be reopened.

"Did the third man say anything?" Harry asked.

"The gentleman? Yes, he did. Now what was it…?"

"You said you never saw him so why do you presume he was a gentleman?"

"His accent. He said something along the lines of 'We're not pleased with your vehemence.' He may not have used the word vehemence, but that's the gist. He sounded annoyed, too. The black-bearded man didn't like being scolded and told them in no uncertain terms that he was only doing what they'd discussed. He got quite heated."

"Did either he, Shepherd or the gentleman become violent?" I asked.

"No. The conversation ended, they left, and I went to speak to Shepherd." He scooped up a forkful of mashed potato. "May I eat in peace now?"

"Thank you for your time, Mr. Crippen," I said.

We left him to his meal and exited the chophouse. The sky had darkened while we were inside, but it wasn't yet night and the streetlights hadn't come on. I didn't ask Harry to walk with me back to the hotel, and he didn't offer. He simply did it.

"Faine wasn't telling us the entire truth." I realized how unrealistic the notion of a thief being truthful was and gave a wry huff. "It sounds like Shepherd and the unknown gentleman wanted Faine to agitate for the reopening of the bridleway. The question is, why did they want it reopened? Indeed, why did Lord Kershaw want it closed in the first place? Whatever the reason, the gamekeeper didn't agree with it."

"I don't think that's true," Harry said.

"Why do you say that?"

"Shepherd and the gentleman scolded Faine for being too vehement in his campaign. They wanted him to agitate, but not with such vigor. I suspect they just wanted it to *appear* as though Faine wanted the bridleway reopened. They didn't actually want the campaign to succeed."

That made more sense. "If they didn't want him to succeed, that means they wanted the bridleway to remain closed. The question is, why?"

Harry had already thought of an answer. "We know Faine is a thief. We know valuable items went missing from the Hall."

"You think Faine, Shepherd, and the third man stole from the Kershaws? That they're using the bridleway to move the goods unseen across the estate and the neighboring estate, avoiding Morcombe and the police altogether? If that is the case, Faine pretending to want the bridleway reopened, means no one will suspect him of the thefts. Considering he's known to police, that's rather clever. If they look into the thefts, it'll throw them off his scent."

Harry nodded. "I agree, but…"

"What is it?"

"You won't like my theory."

I urged him to continue with an arch look.

"The third man in the confrontation could have been Kershaw himself," Harry went on.

"To claim the insurance money?" I asked.

"It's a possibility. We can't ignore it."

He was right, we couldn't. But I didn't think it was viable. I'd not seen any evidence that the Kershaws were in financial difficulty. I conceded that Lady Kershaw's jewelry and the paintings could have been fakes, made to look like the original to fool guests, but the meals had been bountiful and there was more than enough staff in attendance.

On the other hand, Lady Kershaw hadn't seemed upset when she noticed the silver candlesticks missing. Perhaps she was in on it, too.

Whether Kershaw was involved or not, Harry and I both agreed that the argument and the bridleway had something to do with the thefts. What I couldn't see was the connection to the murder. I said as much to Harry as we passed Nelson's Column in Trafalgar Square.

"Thieves having a falling out?" he suggested.

"The argument didn't sound heated enough for it to escalate to murder. Anyway, Crippen said they left."

"They could have met up again afterward, at which point it did become heated. Perhaps the man Crippen couldn't see properly had the rifle from the armory with him. If those two men argued, Faine might have attempted to wrestle it off him, at which point it accidentally went off, killing Shepherd."

It did fit although it seemed unlikely. The shot seemed to have been fired from a distance, otherwise Shepherd's wound would have been much uglier.

"If that theory is correct," I said, thinking it through, "the unidentified gentleman is neither of the two on my suspect list—Lord Kershaw and Mr. Browning. They both came from the direction of the house following the shooting." It was still a good theory, however. It just meant our list of suspects wasn't definitive.

"Are you busy tomorrow?" I asked Harry as we walked.

"I can always spare time for you, Cleo. Do you want to return to the village?"

"I do. Some of my suspects will be here in London, so there won't be any risk of bumping into them in Morcombe."

We continued to discuss the suspects until we reached the hotel. Often, at that point, Harry wouldn't walk me all the way to the door. He would watch from across the road or further along the street. This time, he greeted Frank then entered the foyer behind me.

"Thank you, Harry," I said.

"My pleasure." He removed his hat and stroked the brim with his fingers. "Enjoy your evening, Cleo. Don't let the investigation spoil your dinner."

"Spoil it? It'll make it more enjoyable."

His smile faded when he spotted someone approaching behind me.

I turned to see Floyd and groaned.

Floyd lifted his chin. "Evening, Armitage."

"Good evening," Harry said, his cheery greeting in contrast to Floyd's cool one. "I was just walking Cleo back after interrogating a suspect together."

"She's safe in here and she's late for dinner, so…" Floyd glanced pointedly at the door.

"I'm not late." I checked the time on my pocket watch to make sure. "I have an hour and a half to get ready."

"Lady Elizabeth wants to retire early, so dinner will be at seven instead of eight. Harmony's been waiting for you for an age. She won't have enough time to do your hair now."

"You know far too much about a ladies' toilette routine, Floyd." I turned to Harry. "Thank you again for your help this afternoon."

"I didn't do much. You did all the work."

"Even so." I smiled at him, picked up my skirts, and hurried toward the stairs. I didn't have time to wait for the lift.

Floyd came up alongside me, puffing a little from the exertion. "If you don't need Armitage's help, stop going to him. It looks bad."

"I don't care how it looks to other people. We're just friends."

"I mean it looks bad to *him*. You're giving him the message you can't do it without him. I know you, and I know you most certainly don't need his help. Or anyone's, for that matter."

I took his hand and squeezed. "That is sweet of you to say. Thank you, Floyd."

"So you'll stop letting him think he has a chance?"

I released his hand. "Sometimes you do go on too long."

"I'm serious, Cleo. Don't encourage him when you know nothing can come of it. It'll only hurt more in the long run when it has to end."

There were a thousand things I could have said to Floyd in response, but I kept them all to myself, except one. "There is nothing going on between Harry and me. Nothing at all."

"Is that how you want things to remain?"

I quickened my pace.

"I'm simply trying to protect you, Cleo. My reaction is nothing compared to what my father's will be."

I stopped and rounded on him. "Unlike you, I'm not afraid of your father. Anyway, the point is moot. Harry and I are colleagues, and I'm growing very tired of—"

"Reminding me that you don't want to marry anyone. Yes, yes, I know. All right, I'll stop." He took the stairs two at a time to keep pace with me as I hurried. "Thank God for your self-imposed ban on marriage," he muttered.

I'd been about to tell him I was tired of him reminding me that Harry had once been a hotel employee, which made him an unsuitable suitor in Uncle Ronald's eyes. Instead of telling him, I changed the topic.

"Did your father mention that he asked me to find the gamekeeper's murderer?"

"That's not what he wants you to do," he said tartly. "He asked you to look for definitive evidence to convince everyone the poacher did it and the Wentworths are innocent."

"That's almost the same thing," I said dismissively.

"It's not."

"Can I ask you to do something for me at dinner, Floyd?"

He sighed. "As long as I don't have to flirt with Mrs. Browning."

"Why?"

"I don't mind flirting with her when her husband's not around. But when he sees us enjoying one another's company, he glares daggers at me. He seems like the sort of fellow who'd challenge me to a duel, then cheat so he could win. Believe me, the ice queen isn't worth the trouble."

"Then I hope for your sake you're not seated next to her. But if you do happen to speak to Lord Kershaw, can you ask him if the missing rifle has been returned to the display on the armory wall."

We reached the fourth floor, both a little out of breath from the quick pace. "I'll try to be subtle about it so as not to raise his suspicions," he assured me.

"Oh, dear," I teased. "Perhaps I should ask someone else."

He shot me a withering glare before heading to his suite and I headed to mine.

* * *

I WAS SUPPOSED to sit next to Mr. Browning, but Lady Elizabeth asked if he could swap places with her. He obliged, looking rather pleased about the rearrangement. I wasn't sure if that was because he didn't want to be forced to make conversation with me, or because it meant Floyd couldn't flirt with his wife.

Once she was settled into her chair and the waiter had moved on, Lady Elizabeth leaned closer to me. "I hope Lady Bainbridge will forgive me for ruining her seating arrangements, but I did so want to talk to you, Miss Fox."

I glanced at my aunt. She hadn't seemed to notice the change of seats. She was too busy having a conversation with Richard, the head waiter, while simultaneously contributing to the conversation Lady Kershaw and Janet were having with Flossy. She'd obviously taken a dose of her tonic again to get her through the evening, or as much of it as possible. In another hour or too, a crushing headache would ruin the rest of her night.

"Is there a particular reason why you wanted to talk to me, Lady Elizabeth?" I asked.

"As a matter of fact, there is." She paused while the sommelier filled our wineglasses, then continued when he moved on. "This afternoon in the sitting room, I overheard you and Cicely discussing Susannah Shepherd."

I'd hoped she wanted to bring it up after noticing her interest in my conversation with Mrs. Browning. I hadn't expected her to mention it already, however. It seemed Lady Elizabeth had no desire for small talk. "I'd only just learned the gamekeeper had a sister," I told her.

Lady Elizabeth picked up the wineglass. She regarded me over the top of it. "You were asking Cicely about the rumor that my father also fathered Susannah."

It would seem she had no interest in politely skirting the issue. I liked her directness, but it threw me off for a moment. As I was trying to decide how to respond, she spoke again.

"I don't know if it's true. My parents certainly never mentioned it to me." She peered into the glass at the small ripples in the wine caused by her shaking hand. "I've often wondered what it would have been like to have Susannah as my half-sister. I think it would have been awkward, if I'm honest. I don't blame my father for taking the secret to his grave. He probably thought it best for everyone."

"So, you *do* believe it?"

"It explains the relative privilege the Shepherds have

always received. Their cottage is always well maintained, and the gamekeeper's position has always been paid a very good salary."

"And no Shepherds were ever dismissed, in your father's, brother's and now nephew's tenure as earl."

"Indeed." She put down the glass. "The gossip about my father being Susannah's father has swirled for years, so I don't see the relevance to Esmond Shepherd's murder. It simply has no bearing on anything. Even if Mr. Shepherd learned it was true and went public with the knowledge, my father and Susannah are both long dead, so it's of no consequence."

I attempted an innocent look, but she didn't believe it.

"I know you're trying to solve the murder, Miss Fox, hence all these questions. You may be able to fool the others, but you can't fool me."

I released a breath. "It's true. I'm trying to prove your family innocent, so there are no lingering doubts."

She sighed as she shot an exasperated glance at Lord Kershaw. "My nephew is a dear man, but he doesn't always think things through. He should never have influenced Sergeant Honeyman's investigation. It makes us all look guilty." She turned to me again. "Thank you, Miss Fox. If there's anything I can do to help, please ask. I may be old, but I know a thing or two about Esmond Shepherd."

"Such as?"

"He was a womanizer. Several nannies and maids have left because of him, and my silly niece-in-law just lets them go. Mr. Shepherd was charming with her and the other young women, but not with me. That's the thing about being old. Nobody bothers to flirt or try to charm me." Her eyes twinkled merrily as she lifted her wineglass. "On the other hand, it means I see people as they truly are, warts and all, because they're not trying to be something they're not in my presence." She continued to watch me as she sipped.

Did she see me? Did she know I had members of her family on my list of suspects?

"What else can you tell me about Susannah Shepherd?" I asked.

"Other than she may have been my half-sister?" Lady

Elizabeth shook her head. "I hardly knew her. She was quite a bit younger than me, and she was the gamekeeper's daughter while I was the earl's. I do remember when she died. So young, she was."

"Twenty-one," I said.

"Everyone was so distraught, particularly her mother, poor thing. It's fortunate she and her husband had Esmond, so Mabel Shepherd could funnel her love into another child. She had so much love to give, did Mabel." Lady Elizabeth smiled sadly. "She spoiled Esmond, though, which may explain why he ended up the way he did."

"You mean his womanizing?"

"I do."

"Do you recall the last nanny who left?" I asked.

"Miss Crippen? She was a pleasant woman; quiet, well-mannered. Pretty enough, but no beauty. I believe she was one of Mr. Shepherd's conquests. She left when he moved on to a new girl." She *tsked* in irritation.

Her openness compelled me to be open with her in return. I suspected she would appreciate my directness as much as I appreciated hers. "I met Miss Crippen's brother this morning. He told me *he* was the one I saw arguing with Esmond Shepherd on the morning of the murder. It was he who stayed at the village inn then left suddenly. Mr. Crippen isn't a poacher. He works in a solicitor's office here in London."

"I'm not surprised. I never believed there was a poacher. How clever you are to have found him, Miss Fox."

"I wasn't looking for him. I was looking for Miss Crippen."

"He *is* a suspect, I presume?"

"Of course."

"And did you speak to Miss Crippen?"

"No."

"Send her my regards if you do."

We paused our conversation while the soup course was served. Once the waiters had dispersed again, I asked her about the candlesticks. "Did you notice they went missing during our stay?"

She lowered her spoon to the bowl and frowned at me.

"Missing!" She frowned harder. "Which candlesticks are you referring to?"

"The large silver ones that sat on the dining room mantelpiece. They were there one day and gone the next."

She scooped up a spoonful of oxtail soup only to watch a few drops spill back into the bowl. "Marion must have removed them. She never liked them. She called them ugly once, but never again after she saw my reaction. I was horrified. They're family heirlooms."

Valuable ones, no doubt.

Lady Elizabeth seemed upset to know they were missing, so to distract her, I asked her about the legend of Henry the Eighth's visit to Hambledon Hall. "I heard he had his eye on one of the maids, but her beau rescued her from under the king's nose."

Despite the salacious nature of the tale, Lady Elizabeth seemed to enjoy retelling it. If it had been a recent occurrence, she wouldn't have wanted anyone to know about the lascivious royal's failed attempt at seduction. That's the thing about scandals. They grow less hurtful and more amusing with the passing of time.

"Do you know the path the lovers used still exists?" she asked.

I couldn't believe my good fortune that she'd been the one to introduce the topic of the bridleway. "I heard Lord Kershaw recently blocked it."

She gazed down the table at her nephew, listening to something Uncle Ronald was saying. "He has, the silly fool. I can't think why he would bother."

"The villagers are upset. A man named Faine is leading them in the fight to reopen it."

"I don't blame them for being upset. To have something taken away from you after so long... Most upsetting indeed."

She'd shown no recognition at the mention of Mr. Faine. If she knew him, he was of no consequence to her. "You have a great understanding of village life and its challenges, Lady Elizabeth. Having lived in Cambridge and then London all my life, I can't begin to comprehend what it was like to grow up in the countryside."

"Oh, it was a wonderful childhood," she said dreamily. "I

had a lot of freedom to do as I pleased. I was always scraping my knees or getting leaves tangled in my hair." She chuckled. "I loved going into the village with my mother, too. I remember how colorful everything was. The ribbons and buttons in the haberdashery, the boiled sweets in the confectionery shop. There wasn't much need for silks and satins, but the draper would order them from London especially for my mother once a year."

"She didn't have her clothes made in London?"

"She preferred to purchase everything locally, to help the Morcombe traders. My parents were conscious of doing their duty in any way they could, big or small. I do think they both *liked* supporting the village. It wasn't a hardship."

"They sound like good people."

"They were. My father was strict but fair, and my mother was gentle-natured. It was my privilege to take care of them as they aged."

"They instilled that sense of duty in you, Lady Elizabeth. I heard the villagers praise you for all the good things you've done over the years."

"I like to call many of the village women my friends, so it's a relief to know the feeling is mutual." She chuckled again. "Otherwise it would be awkward the next time I go."

I laughed.

"Not that I get into Morcombe very often these days." She glanced at her niece, Mrs. Browning, sitting in silence between Lord Kershaw and Floyd. "It would have been nice for Janet's wedding dress to be made by the local seamstress, but Cicely insisted the London seamstresses are better. I suppose she doesn't have the connection to the village that she once had."

"She married young and moved away."

Lady Elizabeth gave no indication of her thoughts on Mrs. Browning's age at the time of her marriage, or indeed what she thought of her niece's choice of husband. She smiled at the waiter who took away her empty soup bowl and bestowed another smile on the next one who deposited a poached salmon dish in front of her.

After a few mouthfuls, she said, "I must commend your cook, Miss Fox."

"I'll pass on your compliments to Mrs. Poole."

"Please do. Now. All this talk of weddings has me wondering." She picked up her wineglass and regarded me with a mischievous smile. "What about you? I overheard Miss Bainbridge tell Janet that you have no intention of marrying anyone. I imagine you can't be short of suitors, so I assume you're avoiding matrimony through choice. Will you indulge a curious old spinster and tell me why?"

"I like my freedom." A lively, clever and kind woman such as Lady Elizabeth, coming from a wealthy and titled family, would have had her fair share of gentlemen suitors, yet she'd remained unwed. It must have been her choice, so I felt comfortable adding, "I'm sure you understand that."

Her next words had me doubting myself, however. "Forgive me, Miss Fox, but I feel compelled to ask. Are you *quite* sure you wish to remain a spinster forever? It can be very lonely, even when you're surrounded by people." Her gaze wandered to the members of her family. All of them had a partner in their husband or wife, and soon Janet would, too. Did she feel like the odd one out?

Before I could answer, she continued. "Perhaps you haven't met the right man yet, the one who makes it worthwhile to give up some of your freedoms." She put down her knife and rested her hand on my forearm. "Will you accept some advice from an old woman who has observed a thing or two? Don't wait for the perfect man to simply show up. You may wait a long time and then find it's too late."

"Is that what happened to you, Lady Elizabeth?" I asked gently.

She didn't seem to hear me. Her voice turned dreamy again. "That's the thing about time. When you're young, there seems to be an endless amount of it. There's no reason to hurry, so you put off doing things because there are a thousand other demands on your time. Then one day you wake up and realize you're no longer young. You're not even sure *when* you became old. By then, it's too late. Your dreams for the future are out of reach. All the men who showed any interest moved on years ago, your body is too frail to go exploring new places, and your mind can't quite grasp how to do new tasks."

Lady Elizabeth gave her attention to her food, and seemed disinclined to talk further, but I couldn't end the conversation on such a melancholy note. "No one is too old to form new friends or adopt a pet for company. And as long as one has an imagination, there are new adventures to dream up."

Whether she heard me or not, she gave no sign. I fell into silence, too, my own thoughts occupying my mind to the exclusion of all else.

CHAPTER 11

*A*fter dinner the gentlemen went to the billiard and smoking rooms, while the ladies retreated to the hotel's private sitting room. It felt like an age before the men joined us. Although I'd hoped it would be the perfect opportunity to learn more from my female suspects, I found it difficult to weave my questions into conversation. The only thing I managed to discover was that Lady Kershaw didn't know why her husband had closed the bridleway path to the public. When I mentioned admiring the pair of silver candlesticks on her dining room mantelpiece, she pretended Lady Elizabeth had summoned her and went to join her.

I sat with Flossy and Janet. We discussed the wedding, the house where Janet would live with her new husband, and eligible gentlemen for Flossy, before there was a suitable lull in which I could ask Janet a question relevant to my investigation.

"And how are you and your family holding up after the dreadful event at Hambledon Hall last week?" At her blank look, I clarified. "The death of the gamekeeper."

"Oh. That." Janet sighed. "It did put a dampener on the end of our visit to Hambledon, but then I quite forgot about it. I simply have so much on my mind of late." She frowned. "Although, now that I think about it, it may have affected my mother somewhat. It's understandable, really. She'd known the gamekeeper since she was a girl."

Mrs. Browning had seemed untouched by Shepherd's death when she spoke to me, but I'd wondered at the time if that had been an act. "How has it affected her?" I asked Janet.

"She seems sad. More than usual, I mean. She's taking laudanum to help her sleep, which she only started to do after we left Hambledon." She suddenly clutched my hand. "I probably shouldn't have said all that. She wouldn't want others to know."

Mrs. Browning was attempting to converse with Aunt Lilian, but my aunt appeared to be sinking into a low mood after the effects of her tonic wore off. She would be suffering through a raging headache by now, and perhaps feeling ill. Flossy and I exchanged glances, both of us knowing she needed rescuing, yet neither of us wanting to be the one to suggest she retire. She was so unpredictable that she could very well snap at us in full view of our guests.

The arrival of the gentlemen was a blessing. Uncle Ronald went to my aunt's side and asked if she required anything. She took the opportunity to say she was tired, and Lady Elizabeth followed suit. Both bade us goodnight and allowed Uncle Ronald to escort them from the sitting room.

"Tea?" I asked our guests.

Floyd made a scoffing sound. "Or something stronger?"

My offer was declined, but Lord Kershaw and Mr. Browning wanted port, and Mrs. Browning agreed to a sherry. Mr. Browning plucked his watch out of his waistcoat pocket, but instead of opening the case, he simply raised his brows in question at Floyd.

"It's too early," Floyd told him.

I joined Floyd at the drinks trolley one of the footmen had wheeled in when the men arrived so we could serve ourselves. I assembled five glasses. "What was that about?" I whispered.

"I mentioned I was going out later to my club, and now Browning wants to come with me."

"You don't sound pleased about it."

"He's in his fifties!"

"Are you implying he's too old to keep up with you young bucks?" I teased.

He removed the stopper from a crystal decanter. "I just

think it's pathetic when someone his age wants to go out carousing with fellows my age." He poured port into one of the glasses. "Also, he's a boorish prig."

"And your friends are refined and cultured?"

"At least we treat women respectfully, even the courtesans. Browning was just telling me in the billiard room that he's looking for a replacement, since his last one became too fat. If I had a wife, at least I wouldn't dishonor her by taking a mistress."

"That's very mature of you, Floyd. I have a newfound respect for you."

He finished filling three glasses with port and replaced the stopper in the decanter. "I'll have my amusement now, while I'm young and unfettered. Once I get a wife, I'll settle down and be dull like the rest of the married men."

"There goes my respect again."

"What did I say?"

"Just pour the sherry. I'll have one, too." I moved two empty glasses closer to him. "Did you manage to find out anything useful for my investigation?"

"No, sorry. I tried, but Kershaw always steered the conversation in another direction without answering. Most of the time he simply avoided me."

"Deliberately?"

"I suspect so." He glanced toward our guests. "He's watching us now. He suspects we're investigating him."

"*I'm* investigating. *You're* assisting me. Although I think I've gleaned as much as I can, for now. Hopefully, you'll have some luck later with Browning." I indicated the port glasses. "Fill his up a little more."

Floyd obliged.

I patted his arm. "Enjoy the rest of your night."

"I'll try." He turned his back to the room, downed one of the glasses of port then refilled it. "That ought to help."

* * *

THE HANDWRITING on the piece of paper slipped under my door was difficult to decipher. With Harmony's help, I managed to work out that it was from Floyd and that Mr. Browning had told him the antique rifle was still missing from its position on the armory wall. Over a simple breakfast of poached eggs, toast and coffee, Harmony and I discussed its possible whereabouts in light of what we'd learned from our suspects, but we didn't come up with any new ideas.

I met Harry at the train station as arranged. On the journey to Morcombe, we discussed what to do once we arrived, but couldn't come to an agreement. I wanted to confront Faine about his criminal history, but Harry didn't think that would get results. Faine, he thought, would lie.

Harry suggested we look through his belongings for stolen goods instead.

D.I. Hobart had given Faine's address as the Red Lion Inn, but we doubted he actually lived there. We were wrong. The innkeeper informed us that Faine had use of a room in the old coach house in exchange for performing work at the inn from time to time. Part of the coach house had been converted into accommodation years ago, when the railway came to Morcombe and the number of coaches passing through diminished significantly. There were four rooms, but Faine's was the only one in use. The innkeeper also informed us that we wouldn't find Faine there. He was currently working at a building site at the edge of the village.

Perfect.

We told the innkeeper that we merely had more questions for Mr. Faine about the bridleway, then we pretended to leave the vicinity of the inn altogether, only to return via a side gate attached to the courtyard. It was quiet. If any horses were in the stables, they made no noise. The courtyard and outbuildings would have once bustled with grooms, and coachmen stopping on their journey to or from London, but the railway had ended the inn's glory days. Now, locals enjoyed a drink after work, and ramblers stopped for a pie before returning to the city on the train, but it was nothing like it must have been in its heyday.

We skirted the central well and an old trough with a puddle of water pooled at the slimy bottom and approached the large coach house with three enormous arched entrances.

Through one, I could see an old cart and some rusting equipment. The second led through to an empty space, and the third marked the entry to the four flats; two on the ground floor and two above. Harry picked the lock on the only door that was locked.

Faine may live in a converted coach house, but his flat resembled a pigsty. The smell struck me first. It was a mix of unwashed man and rotting food. There were dirty clothes strewn about the floor, and dirty dishes piled on the table. I didn't dare look into the bucket placed beside the unmade bed. I used a broken tennis racket to move the clothes and test for loose floorboards, while Harry looked inside and above the narrow wardrobe.

The squeak of a floorboard as I pressed on it with my foot drew his attention as he closed the wardrobe door. Our gazes connected. He dropped to his knees and pried the floorboard up. He reached into the cavity to his elbow and felt around. When he withdrew his hand, I thought at first he'd found nothing, but he opened his palm to reveal a silver teaspoon.

I picked it up. It was solid silver, going by its weight. The bowl was shaped like an acorn and the letter K was engraved into the stem. I'd used teaspoons identical to it at Hambledon Hall.

I tucked the spoon into my bag. "Is this the only thing in there?"

Harry nodded. "The space is a good size. A number of items could be hidden in it. How large were the candlesticks?"

"About the length of my arm. They were very impressive."

"They wouldn't have fit in there. Wherever he stored them, I suspect they've already been sold or melted down, along with the rest of the spoons. That one got left behind."

It was unlikely we'd find anything further, but I was keen to continue looking. The sound of voices in the courtyard changed my mind. We were too exposed. We'd found the evidence we needed, so there was no point continuing to look for stolen goods when they would have been moved on.

We waited for the men to disappear into the stables then

we slipped out of Faine's flat. We didn't speak until we'd left the Red Lion well behind us.

"I should probably give this spoon to Lord Kershaw when I see him at the hotel," I said. "He can decide whether to press charges or not."

"Hold on to it, for now. It proves our theory about thieving from the Hall, and we don't want the thieves to know we're aware of their operation. Until we discover if the thefts are related to the murder, we won't say a word. Besides, we're not sure if Kershaw himself is the third thief."

"I don't believe he orchestrated the burglary to collect the insurance money," I said. "But I agree that we shouldn't tell anyone. I want to see if the thefts continue now that Shepherd is dead, and I want to find out for certain who the third man is, the gentleman, as Crippen called him."

"In a village the size of Morcombe, there wouldn't be many who sound cultured. The mayor, perhaps, or a doctor."

"Or the vicar." I nodded toward the church and its neighboring vicarage.

We passed the window of the teashop where we'd listened to the gossip about the Wentworth family from the four women. It was busier today, and the proprietress was occupied behind the counter and didn't see us. Two of the other women sat at a table in the window, though, and recognized us. They smiled and waved. We went inside and greeted them.

"You must have enjoyed your previous visit to Morcombe to be returning here so soon," said Mrs. Smith, the elder of the two. "The weather isn't as nice today, but at least it isn't raining."

"Won't you join us?" asked her companion, Mrs. Clayborn.

"Not today," I said. "We were curious about the bridleway, and Mr. Faine's attempts at encouraging Lord Kershaw to reopen it. Was anyone else equally vehement in their desire to have it reopened? Someone with influence in the village, perhaps?" Without specifying 'a gentleman', I wasn't sure how to describe the man we were searching for.

The two women looked at one another. "Not that I can think of," Mrs. Smith said. "Mr. Faine was the driving force behind the campaign. Most who agreed with him were local traders and shopkeepers. I suppose you could say they have influence."

It wasn't the sort of influence I meant. *Drat*.

"The campaign may fall apart now, anyway," Mrs. Clayborn added.

"Why is that?" Harry asked.

"Some of the zeal seems to have gone out of Mr. Faine's efforts. There was supposed to be a village meeting last night, but he didn't even bother to go. He was drunk at the Red Lion." The women exchanged looks again, this time full of disdain for the inebriated Faine.

We thanked them and left the teashop.

"Why would Faine no longer be interested in campaigning against the closure of the bridleway?" I asked, trying to think it through. "It was a fake campaign, as far as he was concerned. He didn't want it reopened. He wanted it closed so they could move their stolen goods through the woods with ease. Could it be it no longer matters, now that Shepherd is gone? Has the thieving enterprise fallen apart without him?"

"Faine and the third man could try to continue it."

While Faine's sudden disinterest in his campaign was a mystery, I was growing more convinced of Reverend Pritchard's involvement as the third man, the one Mr. Crippen had overheard arguing with Shepherd. He sounded like a cultured gentleman, and he'd been in the vicinity of the woods at the time. He also had a murky past that he was trying to keep obscured. A thieving past, perhaps?

If I had to make a wager on the third man, I'd put all my money on him. The problem was, how to find out for certain?

Harry suggested we speak to him again. As a seasoned criminal with no reputation to lose, Faine would be a difficult nut to crack, but Reverend Pritchard might be more easily manipulated into admitting guilt.

His housekeeper refused to let him know we wanted to speak to him, however. "Unless it's an emergency, he doesn't want to be disturbed. He needs peace and quiet to write tomorrow's sermon. He pours his heart and soul into it, he does. Very devout is our Reverend Pritchard."

Out of curiosity, I asked, "What qualifies as an emergency for a vicar?"

She looked uncertain for a moment before declaring, "A crisis of faith."

"We'll come back later," Harry said.

"He'll be preparing for the service *all* day."

"Then he's very devout indeed."

As we walked away from the vicarage, I muttered words of frustration under my breath. I felt sure we could make him talk.

Harry wasn't as disappointed as me. Indeed, he had another suspect in mind, someone with far greater access to the house than the vicar. "Butlers put on cultured accents. Some sound more upper class than their employers."

I gazed along the road that led to Hambledon Hall. "That's true. The Kershaws' butler is one such fellow, and he also has easy access to the silverware." I set off in the direction of the house. "We'll question him now. It shouldn't be too difficult without the family at home."

"Unless he's napping," Harry said, matching my strides. "Or drunk."

* * *

THE BUTLER WAS neither drunk nor napping. He was in his office in the service area, going through paperwork. The footman who escorted us closed the door as he left, giving us privacy.

Renton gave me a quizzical look. "Miss Fox, this is a surprise. The family are in London, staying at your hotel, as I'm sure you are aware."

"We're here to speak to you. This is my friend, Mr. Armitage. He's a private detective."

Renton's bushy eyebrows shot up his forehead. "Is this regarding the death of Mr. Shepherd?"

"It is. We've been tasked with proving the murderer is the missing poacher."

"The poacher! Yes, of course." The eyebrows settled as Renton relaxed. "Lord Kershaw hasn't said anything to me about hiring a detective."

"He isn't the one who hired us."

Renton frowned. "Who did?"

"I'm not at liberty to say."

"Why are *you* involved, Miss Fox? I don't understand why *you* are here when *he* is the private detective."

"Miss Fox is assisting me," Harry said before I could answer. "Considering her unique situation as a witness, I thought she'd be helpful."

Renton turned back to me. "Do Sir Ronald and Lady Bainbridge know you are here?"

I smiled through my clenched jaw. "I'm a grown woman and can do as I please." I softened my snippy response by adding, "In any case, my uncle approves."

"Very well, I'll answer your questions."

I could well imagine this imperious fellow being the third man that Crippen overheard in the woods arguing with Esmond Shepherd. He sounded cultured and gentlemanly and was far bossier than I remembered him being while I stayed at Hambledon Hall last weekend.

"You mentioned that a *thief* murdered Mr. Shepherd," Renton went on. He addressed Harry, even though I'd been the one to mention the thief.

"It's a possibility," Harry said. "What do you know about the thefts from the house?"

Renton's gaze flicked between us, perhaps wondering how much we knew. "Some candlesticks went missing, as well as some cutlery and a few other valuable items."

"Who do you think took them?"

Renton shook his head. "I don't know. The house is usually locked up at night, so I doubt anyone broke in. It's easier to enter the house during the day when the servants are busy and the doors unlocked."

"Even so, wouldn't a stranger be noticed?"

"One would assume so."

Harry waited, but Renton didn't expand on the theory. "Then wouldn't it be logical to assume the thief was someone known to the household?" Harry prompted. "Someone who could freely walk in and out without raising suspicions?"

Renton's jaw stiffened. "It's possible one of the staff may

be involved, but I cannot confront anyone without proof. Lady Kershaw has asked me to wait until we have it."

"Isn't the silverware under lock and key?" I asked. "In my experience, the butler is the only member of staff who has access to it."

His jaw stiffened even more. "Are you accusing *me* of theft, Miss Fox?"

"It would be remiss of us not to consider you. Indeed, given what we know, you should be at the top of our list."

The jaw slackened with his gasp. "Not all of the items stolen were locked away in the silverware cupboard! And any number of people could have come in here and taken the key!"

"That isn't what I meant," I said.

"Then what *do* you mean? What do you know? Or think you do?"

I ignored his questions and asked my own. "Where were you when you heard the gunshot that killed Esmond Shepherd?"

He shifted uncomfortably in the chair. "I was napping."

"Your room is on the top floor, yet you arrived very quickly at the scene."

"I wasn't in my room. I was here, in this chair. Sometimes I nod off. It's old age."

"It's his lordship's brandy, but let's not quibble about it."

For a moment, I thought Renton would explode with rage as his face flushed scarlet. But the color soon vanished, and his cheeks turned quite pale. I suspected he'd remembered I was related to a friend of his employer and was therefore not someone he could scold like a maid.

"I won't tell Lord Kershaw about the brandy, if you tell me who you think stole the silverware."

Renton's gaze searched the office, perhaps searching for a way out of the dilemma he found himself in. Finding none, he finally looked at me. "I don't know, but I can assure you, it wasn't me. I have worked here for more than thirty years. I'm loyal to Lord Kershaw and he has promised to be loyal to me. I'll be given a cottage in the village and a good pension when I can no longer perform my duties here. Why would I jeopardize that by stealing from him when I've had ample opportunity over three decades?"

I had to admit it seemed unlikely. That didn't mean he wasn't a murderer, just probably not a thief. "What are your thoughts on Esmond Shepherd?"

He blew out a measured breath and sat back. "I didn't like him. He was too sure of himself and was a seducer of young women. He behaved appallingly toward them at times."

"Then why didn't Lord Kershaw dismiss him?"

"You would have to ask his lordship."

"There are rumors that he was treated well because Shepherd's sister, Susannah, was the daughter of the fourth earl, and the family connection added a measure of permanency to Esmond Shepherd's tenure as gamekeeper, and that of his father before him. Were you working here then?"

"I am not *that* old, Miss Fox. I've been here thirty-three years. Miss Susannah Shepherd was deceased by that point, and the fourth earl was in his dotage. As to the truth of the gossip, I cannot comment. It's undignified."

I didn't press him. He was too loyal to Lord Kershaw to spread rumors about the family. "Did you have any run-ins with Esmond Shepherd?"

"No. We had little to do with one another. He belonged outside, I worked inside. Our paths crossed most days, but we didn't stop for idle chatter. We were both busy."

I rose to leave, but Harry had one more question. "You mentioned the house is locked up at night. Did Esmond Shepherd have a key?"

"No." Renton stood and indicated we should walk ahead of him to the door. "Would you like a carriage to take you into Morcombe, Miss Fox?"

"No, thank you, we'll walk. Renton," I added, "I've promised not to mention the brandy to Lord Kershaw, and I will keep that promise. But you have to promise something to me in return."

"If it is within my power to do so then I will."

"Don't tell any of the Wentworth family that I was asking about the stolen property."

"And why not?"

"You don't need to know why, just like I don't need to know why you take a nip of brandy during the day."

Renton acknowledged my blackmail with a stiff nod. He bade us a curt goodbye then made sure we were escorted out of the house by a footman.

"What do you think?" I asked Harry as we walked along the gravel drive.

"I don't think he's involved in the thefts."

"Agreed. My money is firmly on Reverend Pritchard now. It's a shame we can't speak to him."

"Perhaps we don't have to. There may be another way to get answers. Those candlesticks wouldn't have fit in the cavity below Faine's floor. So where were they hidden?"

I smiled as I followed his train of thought. "Perhaps they're still in their hiding place."

While the vicarage was off-limits with both the house-keeper and Reverend Pritchard inside, the church was most likely empty.

It wasn't, but the parishioner there left soon after our arrival when she'd finished praying. Once she was out of sight, Harry closed the door. We would hear it opening again if someone arrived.

We then set about looking for hiding spots for items the size of the candlesticks. There weren't many places in the nave or altar. Harry headed into the sacristy, but I had another thought. Finding the candlesticks would be a very important piece of evidence, but we both suspected they'd already been sold on or melted down, along with the rest of the silver spoons. But there was another piece of evidence that could prove Reverend Pritchard was a thief, and we were in the right place to find it.

I entered the parish office while Harry checked the sacristy and vestry. Low bookshelves weighed down by thick volumes of registers didn't interest me as much as the filing cabinet crammed with correspondence and other paperwork.

It took a few minutes, but I eventually found a letter in a slim folder dedicated entirely to Reverend Pritchard. It was addressed to Pritchard from the bishop of the London diocese, stating that he was being moved to a different one. A second letter from the bishop of the Diocese of Oxford welcomed Pritchard. While neither letter stated the specific reason he was moved to Morcombe, the second one did express the need for urgency due to what the bishop called Pritchard's 'problem' at his former parish.

The parish church where he was located before Morcombe was mentioned as St. Michael's in Marylebone. I knew of it. Indeed, I'd walked past it more than once the day before. It was located near the guesthouse where Esmond Shepherd had stayed a few days before his death.

CHAPTER 12

I showed the letters to Harry before we left the church. He'd not had any luck finding the stolen candlesticks, but my discovery meant we hadn't wasted our time. The letters provided a possible connection between Shepherd and the vicar that we'd not previously known.

I said as much as we walked through the churchyard. "I think we're wrong about the reason Shepherd went to Marylebone. He didn't go to speak to Miss Crippen, the former nanny. I think he went to St. Michael's to find out more about Reverend Pritchard, his partner in crime. Perhaps he wanted something to use against the vicar if he tried to extricate himself from their thieving enterprise."

It made sense that the vicar was a necessary third member of the scheme. If Shepherd was the brains behind it, and Faine was the fence, they needed a third man whose presence in the dining and drawing rooms wouldn't raise suspicions, someone who could slip in and out with silverware hidden inside his coat. Someone trusted in the community, who could be blackmailed because of his problematic past.

"What did Pritchard say when you originally questioned him about Shepherd?" Harry asked.

I thought back to my earlier conversation with the vicar, shortly after we'd met over the dead body. "He said Shepherd wasn't a churchgoer, and that he'd only met him once."

Harry lifted a hand to wave. I turned to see Reverend

Pritchard watching us through the vicarage window. I waved, too. The vicar didn't wave back.

"There's one more question the letters from the two bishops raise," I said as we continued toward the railway station. "Reverend Pritchard came from St. Michael's church in Marylebone. Miss Crippen, the former nanny, is from the same area. It's possible she knew the vicar. What if she knew the reason he left?"

"And informed her lover, Esmond Shepherd?" Harry finished. "Shepherd blackmails Pritchard, so Pritchard kills him to avoid paying." Harry's bright eyes told me what he thought of the theory. He liked it a great deal.

As did I. We needed to confirm our theory with Miss Crippen.

"It's Saturday," I pointed out. "Mr. Crippen won't be at work today, and he only goes to the chophouse after work. We'll have to wait until Monday afternoon to follow him home."

"You're forgetting something," Harry said.

"What am I forgetting?"

"That you have an assistant who plans ahead. I thought knowing where Crippen lived might prove useful, so after I escorted you home yesterday, I returned to the chophouse. When Crippen left, I followed. He lives in a flat above a book-shop on Marylebone High Street."

"Excellent! But I do have one quibble."

"Oh?"

"You're not my assistant. We're equal partners."

Harry's gaze softened. "I like the sound of that."

"Just as long as you don't expect a raise with the promotion. I'm afraid you get nothing out of it this time."

"On the contrary. I get a lot of pleasure out of this arrangement." He took my hand, stopping me. "Cleo—"

The distant whistle of a locomotive interrupted him. I let go of his hand and picked up my skirts. "Come on, Harry! If we miss this train we'll have to wait an hour for the next one."

* * *

The walk to Mr. Crippens' flat took us past the very church where Reverend Pritchard had worked up until six months ago. We decided to enter and see what we could glean from the new vicar. Unlike Pritchard, he was not out of sight in the vicarage writing his sermon for the following day.

He greeted us amiably. "I haven't seen you here before, but that is of no consequence. I consider it an honor to marry a young couple of my parish, even those who are not regular churchgoers."

"We're not getting married," I said. "We're private detectives. This is Mr. Armitage and my name is Cleopatra Fox. We're trying to determine the final movements of a man by the name of Esmond Shepherd. Did he come in here and ask you some questions?" At the vicar's befuddled look, I added, "Middle-aged, quite handsome. He would have come in about ten days ago."

"I'm afraid we get a lot of people looking through registers. Their faces blend together."

"Mr. Shepherd wasn't looking at parish records. He would have been asking after the former vicar, Reverend Pritchard."

The vicar's friendly demeanor vanished. "What is the meaning of this?"

"We simply want to know if you recall a man asking about Reverend Pritchard."

He shook a finger at me. "I will not answer you, young lady. Take yourself off these premises immediately!" He pointed at the door. "Go!"

"I thought everyone was welcome here," Harry said, a thread of steel in his tone.

"Only those with good in their hearts, not troublemakers and muckrakers."

"We're trying to solve a man's murder. It may be linked to the reason why Reverend Pritchard left this parish."

The vicar's face turned thunderous. "Get out of my church!"

"Harry," I said sharply, before he could respond. "We won't learn anything here."

I led the way outside and down the steps to the pavement. Harry's long strides meant he soon streaked ahead. He was seething. Fortunately, it didn't take long before he'd worked the anger out of his system and his strides returned to normal. I was going to run out of breath if he let it consume him much longer.

"Sorry, Cleo, but I can't abide hypocrites. He talks of people with good in their hearts and yet he protects Reverend Pritchard, a man who did something the bishop called a 'problem' in his letter."

I glanced over my shoulder to the church, expecting to see the vicar still spouting his fire and brimstone rhetoric at us from the steps. He was not. "At least we can be sure Pritchard did something terrible, otherwise his replacement wouldn't be so insistent on keeping it private."

Harry followed my gaze, frowning. "Yet he didn't seem to recall Esmond Shepherd. If Shepherd had asked the same question as us, the vicar would certainly remember, given his reaction to our inquiry."

"Unless he lied, and he did remember him."

* * *

THERE WAS no answer to our knock on Mr. Crippen's door, so Harry and I decided to begin our inquiries at the bookshop below their flat. Still bruised from our encounter at St. Michael's, I prepared myself for a nasty tirade telling us to mind our own business. I was pleasantly surprised when the bookshop owner was keen to talk about Miss Crippen when I mentioned her.

"I'm worried about her," he said, leaning over the counter, his voice low. "She used to come in every day after she moved back in with her brother, but about six weeks ago, she stopped. I haven't seen her since."

"Perhaps she moved out," I said.

He shook his head emphatically, causing his spectacles to slide down his long, straight nose. "Her brother comes in and buys books from time to time. They're the sort of books a young woman would enjoy, so I'm quite sure she's still up there. Sometimes I hear *two* sets of footsteps, a heavier one and lighter one." He looked at the ceiling. "I think he's keeping her prisoner in the flat."

"Why would he do that?"

He leaned forward even further. "I can't be certain, but usually when a female is kept prisoner by her family, it's because she fell in love with a wrong 'un, and the family are stopping her from running away with him."

Esmond Shepherd certainly fit the description of a wrong 'un.

"Has anyone come here looking for her?" Harry asked.

"Just you two, as far as I am aware. Someone could have come when the shop is closed, and I wouldn't know."

"In your opinion, is Crippen a violent man?"

"No. He seems quite ordinary. But you never can tell, can you?"

His answer eased my mind somewhat, but a kernel of concern remained. "May we wait in here for Mr. Crippen's return?"

"Of course. There's an excellent display of poetry books in the front window. You can pretend to browse while you watch the street."

Harry and I waited at the window, each of us holding a book of poems. Mine was rather good and I became distracted by a poem about fairies. Fortunately, Harry was more alert.

"There he is," he said, keeping his head bowed as if reading. "He's entering the building now."

We set down the books and raced out of the shop. I waved my thanks to the bookshop owner and followed Harry through the door that led to the flat above the shop. Taking the stairs three at a time, he reached Mr. Crippen well before me.

"Where's your sister?" Harry demanded.

Mr. Crippen paled. He swallowed heavily. "Y-you again. Wh-what is the meaning of this?"

"It's a simple question. Is your sister inside? Are you holding her against her will?"

"No!" Mr. Crippen eyed Harry carefully. "I presume you've been talking to the bookshop owner below. You shouldn't listen to a word he says. He reads too many horror novels."

Before Harry could grab Mr. Crippen by the lapels and shake the answer loose, I stepped between them. I had an inkling about the reason for Miss Crippen's confinement. In fact, confinement was the best word for it.

"She's pregnant, isn't she?" I asked.

Harry's release of breath came out as an audible sigh of realization. "She's not your prisoner?"

With Harry no longer looking so threatening, Mr. Crippen took on an air of indignation. "She is staying indoors of her own volition now that she's showing. We don't want anyone to know about the baby. Phyllida isn't married."

"Is Esmond Shepherd the father?" I asked.

The muscles in Mr. Crippen's jaw bunched and his lips pinched.

"We won't tell anyone," I assured him.

He gave in with a grunt. "Yes, he is."

"May we speak to her about him?"

Mr. Crippen agreed, on the condition that we treat her gently. "She's been very upset since learning of his death."

We found Phyllida Crippen preparing tea in the small kitchen. She was unprepared for visitors, going by the unwashed hair hanging past her shoulders and loose-fitting housecoat over her dress. She quickly drew the housecoat closed over her swollen belly.

I introduced us. "We're private detectives, looking into the death of Esmond Shepherd."

Tears welled in her eyes and she touched her lips as she composed herself.

"We believe you can give us some answers we've been seeking," I went on.

She placed two more cups and saucers on the tea tray. "Come into the parlor where it's more comfortable." She spoke softly, but her voice was steady and her gaze met mine.

She handed the tray to her brother, then led the way into the parlor. She removed a pile of romantic novels from the sofa and placed them on a side table. I studied her as she served the tea. She was quite young, probably no more than twenty, with the milky complexion of a girl not used to the outdoors. There was a gentleness about the way she moved and a great deal of shyness, particularly in regard to Harry. She hardly looked at him.

It would probably be best if I asked the questions. "You left Hambledon Hall three months ago, is that right?"

"Yes. When I became sure that I was…" She settled her hand over her belly.

"Did you tell Mr. Shepherd about the baby?"

She glanced at her brother. He encouraged her with a nod. "I did, as soon as I realized. I presumed we would marry, but…" She swallowed heavily. "That's when he told me there was someone else. He wanted nothing more to do with me. He urged me to leave Hambledon while I still had my good reputation intact and could get a reference from Lady Kershaw."

Mr. Crippen's face twisted with his sneer. "Shepherd was a cad."

Miss Crippen looked as though she would like to protest, but thought better of it. She sipped her tea.

"We want to establish Shepherd's movements in the days leading up to his death," I went on. "Three days before he died, he came to London. He stayed at the Marylebone Guesthouse, not far from here. Did he come to London to see you?"

"No. I don't know why he was here. It was a shock to see him on our regular evening walk."

"It was the surprise on Phyllida's face that made me realize he meant something to her," Mr. Crippen added. "She'd refused to tell me the name of the father, but after seeing her reaction that day, I assumed it was him."

"You must have suspected it was someone from Hambledon Hall," Harry said.

"I presumed it was Lord Kershaw. It's often the way, with a young female servant taken advantage of by the lord of the manor." He shrugged, as if it was so common as to be ordinary, accepted even.

"Did either of you approach Shepherd when you saw him here?" I asked.

"No," Miss Crippen said. "I wouldn't let my brother go after him. I'd made up my mind about the baby's future, you see, and it didn't involve Esmond." She rubbed her belly again. "He'd already showed his lack of interest. A confrontation wouldn't change his mind."

According to the landlady at the guesthouse, Shepherd

had left the building twice during his stay, once in the evening after his arrival and again the following morning before his departure. "Did you see where he was heading?"

"He walked along Wimpole Street, then turned into Queen Anne Street."

Queen Anne Street connected to the street where St. Michael's was located. "Do you go to church?"

My question took them both by surprise.

"I used to, before I was showing," she said.

"Which church?"

"All Saints on Margaret Street. Why?"

Instead of answering, I asked another question. "How well did you know Reverend Pritchard?"

She blinked in surprise. "Not very well. I went to his services on Sundays, as did most of the staff. He seemed like a good man, very pious, but he'd only been there a short while before I left." She gasped. "Do you think *he* killed Esmond?"

"It's a line of inquiry we're following. So, you didn't know that Reverend Pritchard was based at St. Michael's here in Marylebone before he went to Morcombe?"

"You're mistaken, Miss Fox. He was from Cornwall."

"He lied about being from Cornwall, because he didn't want anyone investigating his past. He left his previous post under a cloud."

"Oh! I wonder what happened."

Mr. Crippen lowered his teacup. "Do you know, I think I've heard something about this. Our neighbor attends St. Michael's, and happened to tell me several months ago about the vicar being caught out in some scandal or other. No names were mentioned, and he didn't know the particulars of the scandal, only that it necessitated the vicar's swift move out of the parish. Our neighbor wondered where he'd gone. It was all very hush-hush, he said."

"Are you saying Morcombe's Reverend Pritchard is that same vicar?" Miss Crippen asked me. "Oh, dear. Poor Lady Kershaw. She'd be mortified if she knew. She dislikes scandal."

"Don't we all," Mr. Crippen muttered into his teacup.

Miss Crippen lowered her gaze.

"Did Lady Kershaw know about your condition?" I asked.

"No. She knew about my liaison with Esmond, but not the outcome."

"Her ladyship *must* have guessed," Mr. Crippen said with a sneer. "She just didn't want to know for certain, because then she'd have to acknowledge they employed a snake."

"She knew what he was like, by all accounts," I said. "As did Lord Kershaw. Why do you think they put up with a gamekeeper who seduced their female staff? Why not dismiss him?"

Miss Crippen shrugged. "He was a good gamekeeper, I suppose. He'd been employed for a very long time, and his father before him, I believe. Tradition counts for much."

"It's everything for some," her brother added in another mutter.

Miss Crippen cradled her belly with one arm. "Now that I think about it, it is strange that they kept Esmond on. They didn't seem to like him very much."

"Why do you say that?" I asked.

"They both went out of their way to avoid him. If they saw him approaching, they changed direction and disappeared. Lord Kershaw must have had meetings with him, of course, to arrange shoots and so forth. Even so, he always looked as though it was a chore. I thought it was odd. Esmond was *so* charming."

Her brother grunted. "Until he got what he wanted. Then he changed his tune and the man's real character was revealed."

Miss Crippen pressed her lips together in an effort to stop them trembling. She failed.

Harry handed her his handkerchief. "What about other members of the family? For example, Lady Elizabeth. Did she dislike Shepherd, too?"

Miss Crippen accepted the handkerchief with a light blush infusing her cheeks. "Thank you, Mr. Armitage." She dabbed the corner of her eye. "I'm not sure what Lady Elizabeth thought of him." She suddenly lowered the handkerchief to her lap. "But Mrs. Browning loathed him."

"Why do you say that?"

"I overheard them arguing once, her and Esmond, in his

cottage. I was meeting him there, but didn't enter when I heard their voices. I could hear them clear as a bell. They probably thought they couldn't be overheard there."

"What were they arguing about?"

She frowned in thought. "At the time, I assumed it was me. But now, in light of his…wandering eye, it makes more sense that they were arguing about Miss Browning."

"Janet!" I had a terrible feeling about this.

Miss Crippen nodded. "I heard Esmond say something like, 'You're jealous of her?' Since I believed I was the only one in his affections, I thought he meant me. I presumed Mrs. Browning was infatuated with him and became upset to discover his feelings were engaged elsewhere. I think they were lovers, once, a long time ago."

It seemed logical to me. To have confronted him so boldly meant Mrs. Browning had more than feelings for him. It meant her feelings had been returned at some point, otherwise she would have suffered in silence, too embarrassed to admit she liked him.

"Esmond called her pathetic," Miss Crippen went on. "She retaliated by telling him he was awful, that she was too young."

"Too young?" Harry echoed.

"Again, I thought she was referring to me. To someone of Mrs. Browning's age, I am young, but I'm twenty. Old enough. Janet Browning is just nineteen. She's also old enough, but a mother must worry about her daughter's heart being lost to a man much older than her."

"Her heart *and* her reputation," Mr. Crippen added. "The Brownings would want a good marriage for their daughter, and no man of good breeding will—" He cut himself off with a cough.

Miss Crippen lowered her head again and sniffed.

I agreed with her that it made more sense for Mrs. Browning to be worried about Janet, not the nanny who'd been there less than a year, nor any other servant. It made even more sense for her to worry if she knew Esmond Shepherd was the sort of man who would take advantage of Janet then set her aside when he tired of her.

"What did Shepherd say in response to Mrs. Browning?" Harry asked.

"He said she revolted him now."

"Now? Are you sure that's the word he used?"

"Quite sure. That's why I presumed they were lovers once, when they were both younger. Also, he called her Cicely."

For a gamekeeper to call the sister of his employer by her first name implied they were very close indeed. I was inclined to agree with Miss Crippen. Mrs. Browning and Shepherd *had* been lovers. She discovered he was pursuing Janet and confronted him. Instead of agreeing to stop his pursuit, he accused her of jealousy. That must have been galling for Mrs. Browning, a mother worried about her daughter.

It meant she had a strong motive to murder him.

I was still considering the implications, but Harry had moved on. "Did you notice anything in the house go missing?" he asked.

Miss Crippen looked taken aback. "No."

We rose to leave, but Harry hadn't quite finished. He directed his question to Mr. Crippen, however, not Phyllida. "You discovered Shepherd was the father of the baby three days before you traveled to Morcombe to confront him. Why the delay?"

"Phyllida didn't want me to talk to him. She begged me not to, and I agreed to let sleeping dogs lie. But I couldn't. After three days of stewing in my anger, I decided to go. That was Monday. I made a reservation for two nights at the inn, as I wanted to stay long enough to make plans with him for the baby's future, but then I heard about his death."

"Why not stay and see if your sister could make a claim for an inheritance?"

Mr. Crippen bristled. "Because I wasn't thinking about money at that point. I wanted the man to *marry* her, not pay her. I admit that I panicked when I heard he was murdered. I thought it best not to get involved, so I left. I didn't kill him, Mr. Armitage, and I resent the implication that I did." He jerked open the door and lifted his chin. "Good day to you both."

"Thank you for your time," I said.

"And apologies for the difficult questions," Harry added.

"At this juncture, they are necessary." He placed his hat on his head and offered a shallow bow to Phyllida Crippen.

She blushed profusely and lowered her head. Realizing she still clutched Harry's handkerchief, she held it out for him to take.

"Keep it," he said with a smile.

Mr. Crippen snatched it off her and pressed it into Harry's hand. "I'd like to remind you about your promise to be discreet."

"Her secret is safe with us," Harry assured him.

I fully intended to keep our promise. However, it may not be possible if Mr. Crippen or his sister turned out to be a murderer. I said as much to Harry as we walked back to the hotel. It was growing late, and prematurely dark, thanks to the clouds blanketing the city. It had been a long day, and it wasn't over yet. I was due to dine with my family and the extended Wentworth clan again. Hopefully I'd have an opportunity to ask them some more questions.

Despite the prospect of getting answers, I wasn't looking forward to it. How was I supposed to ask Mrs. Browning about her former lover's interest in her daughter without offending her?

CHAPTER 13

Once again, Harry insisted on escorting me into the hotel, not just to the door. Frank narrowed his gaze at Harry as we approached. Harry doffed his hat, smiled, and thanked him. Frank scowled further. Loyal to my uncle, he assumed Harry had deserved his dismissal from his position as assistant manager.

Goliath, standing in the foyer just inside the door, swept down upon us like a giant bird when he saw us. "You shouldn't be here, Mr. Armitage."

"Call me Harry."

"Sir Ronald is—"

"Cleopatra! Armitage!" My uncle's booming voice had a number of guests turning toward him.

Goliath winced. "Sorry."

Harry clapped him on the shoulder. "No need to worry. It's perfectly fine."

Uncle Ronald barreled up to us. As he was much shorter and a great deal wider than Harry, they looked almost comical facing off in the vast foyer, but there was nothing amusing about my uncle's expression. He looked worried.

"What is it, Uncle?" I asked.

"Dinner has been canceled. Your aunt and Lady Elizabeth are both feeling a little low this evening, so we decided not to go ahead." At the mention of Aunt Lilian, the reason for his worry became clear.

"Is Aunt Lilian all right?"

"She's having one of her episodes. It's best not to disturb her." He heaved a sigh. "I'll take Kershaw to my club." He turned to Harry. "What are you doing here?"

Before Harry could respond, Mr. Hobart emerged from the senior staff corridor, carrying his leather satchel. He must be heading home.

"Good evening, Sir Ronald, Miss Fox. I wasn't expecting you, Harry."

Despite Mr. Hobart's statement, Uncle Ronald seemed to think he was the reason for Harry's presence at the hotel. "You two talk about hotel business on your way out. Cleopatra, I want a word before you go up."

"Hotel business?" Mr. Hobart asked, glancing between Harry and my uncle.

"Mrs. Short's new rule and the problems it's causing," Uncle Ronald clarified. "Armitage always had valuable insights where the staff were concerned. Perhaps he can advise on how to stop the situation boiling over."

Mr. Hobart adjusted his grip on the case's handle. "Perhaps he does. We'll talk it through as we walk."

"I doubt you need my input," Harry said. "I'm rusty when it comes to managing a hotel."

"Nonsense," Uncle Ronald declared. "That sort of knowledge isn't lost in a matter of months." He shooed them toward the door. "You don't want to miss your train, Hobart."

I watched Harry and Mr. Hobart cross the foyer, briefly stopping to chat to some guests who recognized Harry, before leaving altogether. Why had Harry come into the foyer this time? I got the distinct impression it was so that he was seen, but who did he want to be seen by?

I narrowed my gaze at my uncle. "You were very polite to Harry just now. Thank you."

He grunted. I didn't expect anything more. He was hardly going to admit he'd made a mistake in dismissing Harry. He would never admit fault. I was simply grateful he'd not berated Harry, as he'd done in the first months after dismissing him. More recently, my uncle had allowed Harry to remain in the foyer while he was investigating a case. That had been the first sign that Uncle Ronald was softening toward Harry. Today's cordial encounter was another.

I nodded at Goliath who looked as relieved as I felt.

"Take the lift up with me, Cleopatra," Uncle Ronald said as he walked off.

I fell into step alongside him. "Has something happened with the staff?"

"According to Hobart, Mrs. Short's rule is causing a great deal of discontent among the staff. He would like me to intervene. I'm reluctant, however. The rule has its merits. I only want respectable staff working here, naturally."

"I know he spoke to you about it a few days ago. What I meant was, has something happened since then?"

"Your maid, Miss Cotton, expressed her concerns, too, to Floyd. Floyd asked her to repeat them to me, which she did. Very articulate and persuasive, she was."

Good for Harmony! "So you're going to overturn Mrs. Short's rule after all?"

The lift door opened, and a trio of guests stepped out. John, the operator, waited for Uncle Ronald and me, but Uncle Ronald slowed his pace.

"While I do see Miss Cotton's point," he said, "I think we need to see how it plays out." He lengthened his strides again. "Anyway, Hobart informed me earlier that he has it in hand."

I smiled at John and stepped into the lift. "So, he doesn't really need to talk it through with Harry? Were you just trying to get rid of him?"

"Fourth floor, John. No, Cleopatra, not at all. Armitage is welcome here. It's good for the regular guests to see him again."

I wanted to ask why, but not in front of John, or anyone else. I suspected I knew the answer, anyway. Uncle Ronald wanted Harry to return as assistant manager.

"I presumed Armitage wanted to talk to his uncle about the hotel," he said. "That is why he came here, after all."

I didn't dare tell him Harry was helping me. I didn't think he'd want me involving Harry in this investigation. To Uncle Ronald, Harry was an outsider, nothing more than a former employee. While it was all well and good for him to assist me in an investigation that benefited a hotel guest, Uncle Ronald would draw the line at a matter involving his close friends.

* * *

THE FORMAL DINNER may have been canceled, but I still had to eat. I went in search of Floyd and Flossy and found them together in her suite. Flossy was in her bedroom choosing outfits, while Floyd lay on the sofa, idly flipping the pages of one of his sister's fashion magazines.

"Cleo!" he said without getting up. "Just the person. What do you think about sporting pantaloons being worn by women all the time, not just when bicycling and what not?"

I peered over his shoulder at the article he'd been reading. It suggested bloomers worn by female bicyclists would be ideal as all-day wear, not just for riding or playing sport. "I think it sounds liberating."

He wrinkled his nose. "I'm not so sure women should wear men's clothes. It's a recipe for confusion."

I patted his shoulder. "Only for people who are easily confused."

"I know you're being mean, but I'm too tired to care." He yawned as he lowered the magazine to his lap.

"Late night with Mr. Browning?"

"Late and as horrid as I thought it would be. Give him a few drinks and he turns into even more of a swine. I have a newfound pity for Mrs. Browning."

I thought about her affair with Esmond Shepherd. Not for the first time, I wondered when it had happened. "Did you learn anything from him that might be pertinent to my investigation?"

"Not unless it's important to know that he likes to gamble."

That may very well be important. "See what else you can find out."

"I'll do what I can. We're dining with him and Kershaw at Father's club, since the family dinner has been canceled. Mother's not up to it, apparently." He sat up and regarded me seriously. A serious Floyd was worrying. "Cleo, will you check on her later?"

"Your father's with her now."

He glanced at the door that led to the bedroom where the shush of rustling silk was accompanied by Flossy's humming. "The thing is, I don't think Father is the best person to be taking care of Mother. He doesn't restrict her use of the tonic. He lets her have her way."

Flossy appeared in the doorway, holding up her favorite pink dress. "Cleo, just the person. Do you think I've worn this too much lately? I know I look good in it, which is why I often choose it, but has everyone seen it too many times, do you think?"

I squeezed Floyd's shoulder again. "I'll try to look in on her later."

He patted my hand. "Thank you, Cuz. You are the best."

One cousin satisfied, I turned to the other. "I thought we weren't dining out tonight."

Flossy grew quite animated as she bounced on her toes and tried to contain her smile. "Mother and Mrs. Browning suggested Janet and I are old enough to dine on our own in the hotel restaurant. Janet is about to get married, after all, and I'm nineteen, too."

"What about Mrs. Browning and Lady Kershaw? Where will they dine?"

"In their rooms, I presume." She placed the dress against her body. "What do you think?"

"I think you should wear whatever you feel comfortable in."

She pouted. "That's no help. I want to look pretty."

"Then wear this one. It does look lovely on you."

"It suits your eyes," Floyd said from the sofa.

"My eyes aren't pink, idiot."

"They will be after a few glasses of wine. I'd better warn Chapman that he might have to send for strong footmen to escort two drunk girls up to their rooms later."

Flossy pulled a face at her brother before grabbing my hand and dragging me into the bedroom. "Help me choose an outfit, Cleo. Will you join us tonight? You're more than welcome. We'll have such a laugh together."

Joining two of the giggliest girls of my acquaintance sounded a little painful. Although it could be a good way to get Janet to talk about Esmond Shepherd, I declined. For one thing, she wouldn't reveal too much in Flossy's presence. For another, the person I really wanted to speak to was her mother, and Mrs. Browning was apparently dining alone in her room.

"Thank you, but I'm tired," I said. "You two enjoy your night out."

I left my cousins and made my way to my suite, only to change course when I spotted Lord Kershaw waiting at the lift. I pretended I also needed the lift and joined him. "Good afternoon, my lord."

My voice startled him. "Miss Fox, I didn't see you there. Are you heading out?"

"Actually, I wanted to speak to you. Do you have a moment?"

"I, uh, I'm afraid not. I'm running late. Indeed, I'd better take the stairs. The lift is taking too long." He touched the brim of his hat and hurried off to the staircase.

I knew that my uncle had informed Lord Kershaw I was investigating the murder, so I wasn't offended by his snub. If I had something to hide, I'd avoid speaking to the person investigating the murder of my gamekeeper, too.

Instead of being annoyed at not getting anywhere with Lord Kershaw, I decided to take the opportunity of his absence and speak to his wife instead. Hopefully she wouldn't be as rude as her husband, although she could still turn me away at the door. What I needed was a guaranteed method of getting inside, and I knew just the thing. No English lady of good breeding could turn away another holding a tea tray.

It was well past the hour for afternoon tea, but I worked with the theory that cups of tea were always welcome. Instead of taking the guest lift down, I took one of the service lifts, situated at the end of the corridor. They were used by maids to move their cleaning carts between floors, and for waiters transporting food to rooms directly from the kitchen. Unlike the guest lift, it went all the way down to the basement service rooms.

The kitchen was one of my least favorite places in the hotel. It was always busy, hot, and noisy. I worried about getting in the way and being shouted at. Although the *chef de cuisine,* Mrs. Poole, wasn't as intimidating as her predecessor, I didn't like to intrude on her domain, particularly in the hectic lead-up to dinnertime.

I spotted Victor at one of the counters in the heart of the kitchen, chopping something with impressive speed. The tea station was near the entrance, not far from where a junior cook sat on a stool, writing down orders given via the speaking tubes located in each room. I waited until he finished writing and passed on the order to another junior cook.

As he turned back to the speaking tube, he caught sight of me. "It's Miss Fox, ain't it? Blimey! What are you doing down here?"

"I'm after a pot of tea. Can you prepare one, please? I'll take a tray up to my room, with two cups."

Victor spotted me and came over, wiping his hands on a cloth. "Afternoon, Miss Fox. What brings you down to the pit?"

"Tea. I'm going to take it up to Lady Kershaw so she'll be forced to invite me in, at which point I'll question her."

"Sounds like a dastardly plan. Harmony tells me you've made considerable progress."

"It doesn't feel like it, sometimes, but I suppose we have."

"'We', eh?" He smirked. "Armitage muscled his way in again, has he?"

"I asked him to help."

"Why? You can do it without him."

I tried to think of a way to answer without admitting the reason was because I simply enjoyed Harry's company.

Victor was too perceptive, however. "Your secret is safe with me."

"There's no secret regarding Harry." The kiss we'd shared in St. James's Park several months ago flashed in my mind. I shook my head in an attempt to dislodge it, then changed the topic. "Speaking of Harmony." I kept my voice low and glanced around. While I didn't think Mrs. Poole would forbid relationships between staff, I didn't want to put my theory to the test, either. "You two are being careful, aren't you?"

"I know how to avoid getting caught. It would be easier if

we didn't have to avoid anyone, though. Harmony's worried."

"I'm sure she is." Out of the two of them, she had more to lose. If she had to leave the hotel, she'd only get another job as a maid, whereas at the Mayfair she was promised further administrative roles if they came up. Victor could walk into any kitchen and start work immediately. "I know she tried speaking to my uncle about it, as have I, but he thinks the rule has merit. I doubt he'll change his mind unless he's forced to."

The junior cook brought over the tea tray and handed it to me with a smile. He'd added a small vase of daisies for decoration and seemed keen for my approval. I asked him his name then thanked him. By the time I turned around, Victor had gone.

I caught the service lift up to the fourth floor and carried the tray to Lady Kershaw's room. She opened the door upon my knock and blinked at me in surprise. "Miss Fox!"

"Good afternoon. I hope you don't mind the intrusion. May I come in? The tray is growing heavy."

As if she were an automaton and I'd flipped her switch, she stepped aside. I placed the tray on a low table in the sitting room.

"This is an unexpected delight," she said, not looking at all delighted.

"I'm glad to hear it. I was worried I'd be intruding."

Her lips thinned in a humorless smile. "Not at all. Please, sit. You've gone to so much effort." As hostess in her own room, she poured the tea, proving once and for all that manners were ingrained as deeply within a lady as a sense of honor was in a gentleman.

I accepted the cup and waited until she'd taken her first sip before I began my interrogation. "You are aware I'm investigating the death of Esmond Shepherd."

"Your uncle informed my husband that you're attempting to prove the poacher did it."

I didn't correct her. For the sake of my aunt and uncle's friendship with the Kershaws, I'd let her continue to believe I was following that particular thread. "Did you know that Reverend Pritchard isn't from Cornwall?"

Her eyes momentarily flared with surprise. "He has been open about his former post with me."

"But not with Lord Kershaw?"

She chose her next words carefully. "Reverend Pritchard asked me not to discuss it. He was worried my husband wouldn't understand, although I assured him Lord Kershaw wouldn't want the good reverend persecuted for love any more than I do."

Love? So, he wasn't a thief. He hadn't been moved on from his former parish because he stole from the church. Or so Lady Kershaw believed. It was possible the vicar had lied to her because the truth was less palatable.

I kept my features schooled so as not to reveal my surprise at her revelation. If Lady Kershaw suspected I didn't already know, she might close up. "I quite agree. I'm glad you see it that way, too. Love, in all its facets, should be encouraged. It's a shame the bishop doesn't think so and forced Reverend Pritchard to move to another diocese altogether, away from his love."

"At least Morcombe isn't far from London, and they can be together sometimes. Although, naturally he's reluctant to continue now that they've been discovered."

"That's a shame. Have you tried encouraging Reverend Pritchard not to give up? Perhaps he'd listen to you."

"Oh, no, it's not Pritchard who is reluctant. It's his lover." She lowered her gaze to her lap and all but whispered the next sentence. "His *male* lover."

A man! I thought it would be either a man or a married woman. Either would be scandalous, but the former was also illegal.

"I couldn't possibly talk to Pritchard about it," Lady Kershaw went on. "The conversation would be much too awkward."

Pritchard being moved on from his former church for loving a man was just as strong a motive as him being moved on because he stole from the parish, perhaps even stronger given the salacious nature of it. If Shepherd found out about the vicar's proclivities, Pritchard might do anything to stop him telling anyone.

The theory didn't quite fit, however. The new vicar at St.

Michael's hadn't remembered Esmond Shepherd asking about the reverend a mere ten days earlier, yet he'd become extremely angry when we did. It was the sort of anger that would remain with him well beyond a week or two. I was now even more inclined to believe that Shepherd hadn't gone there to ask after Pritchard.

What had the new vicar said? He received numerous requests to look through parish records. Could Shepherd have gone to St. Michael's with the intention of finding out something from the church's registers?

Lady Kershaw cleared her throat to get my attention. "May I ask what our vicar has to do with the poacher?"

"Possibly nothing, but his lie made him look suspicious."

"Please don't drive our reverend out, Miss Fox," she said grimly. "I know it seems…unnatural to some, but his particular kind of love makes him very devout. It drives him to go above and beyond for the sake of his soul, you see."

"I see," I said, hardly listening as I considered what else I needed from Lady Kershaw. "Speaking of scandal and subterfuge, I've been made aware of Esmond Shepherd's… wandering eye, as someone put it. There are numerous rumors that he seduced the young maids at Hambledon."

"Rumors are not fact. If you have any questions about Mr. Shepherd's employment, you must speak to my husband. The gamekeeper reports directly to him."

Speaking to her husband was an impossibility while Lord Kershaw avoided me. Even if he hadn't run off at the lift, I doubted he would have told me why he never dismissed Esmond Shepherd, and why his father and grandfather before him didn't either. If Susannah Shepherd's parentage was the reason, then the secret would most likely be taken to his grave. Unless someone else knew.

There *was* something I could put to bed here and now, however. Something that would tell me once and for all whether Lord Kershaw was the third man whom Mr. Crippen had overheard arguing in the woods before Shepherd's death, the one with the cultured accent.

"Let's not discuss the unfortunate incident anymore," I declared. "Let's enjoy our tea."

Lady Kershaw visibly relaxed as she picked up her teacup again.

I pointed my teacup at her wedding ring, a wide band of platinum set with a diamond surrounded by intricate filigree. "I wanted to tell you how much I admire your taste in jewelry. The ruby necklace you wore last night to dinner is a particular favorite of mine."

Lady Kershaw's entire face lifted. This was a topic she liked. "It's a favorite of mine, too. Would you like to see it?"

"Yes, please."

She disappeared into the adjoining bedroom and returned moments later with the necklace. A fat ruby pendant dangled from the center, with four smaller rubies on each side. Between the rubies were small diamonds, sparkling in the room's electric lighting.

"I didn't get around to putting it back in the hotel safe," she said, handing it to me.

I made a great show of admiring it by holding it closer to the lamp. I wasn't a gem expert, but it looked real to me. I checked the back, having learned that was how a fake piece could be spotted. Jewelers creating fakes often didn't bother to replicate the parts that wouldn't be seen while worn. There was a jeweler's mark on the clasp of the ruby necklace, and the clasp itself wasn't a modern design.

"Where did you have it made?" I asked.

"I didn't. That belonged to the past three Kershaw countesses. It's quite old. These are the matching earrings."

I admired the earrings and checked them over, too, but I was already sure the set was original. They hadn't been sold off and replaced with cheaper fakes to make it appear as though the family were financially well off. That confirmed my earlier thought that Lord Kershaw was still as wealthy as everyone presumed. It was very unlikely he was the third thief in Shepherd and Faine's operation, selling off silverware and other items from his own house while also claiming the insurance money.

I'd already discounted the butler, the vicar, and now Lord Kershaw. That left just one man who fit the description Crippen gave, and who had access to the house and its contents and was also a suspect in the murder.

Mr. Browning.

I had even more reason to speak to his wife now.

CHAPTER 14

*H*armony heard that my family's dinner plans were scuttled. At a loose end herself, she decided to join me for a light meal in my suite. I ordered via the speaking tube and our food arrived shortly afterward, accompanied by a strawberry tartlet.

"They only sent up one," I said. "I didn't order it, but I would have thought whoever assembled our tray would realize I was dining with a second person based on the other dishes and provide two."

Harmony plucked the tart out of my hand. "That's for me."

"How do you know? It's my room."

"Victor brings me leftover strawberry tarts because he knows they're my favorite. He must have guessed I was here." Smiling to herself, she set it aside for later.

I sighed. She was fortunate to have someone who provided her with strawberry tarts. I realized it was my own fault that I didn't have a special man to bring me little tokens of affection, but that didn't improve my mood. It only dampened it further.

"You two are so happy lately," I said.

"Things are good between us. Better than good. I don't want anything to change."

"I hope for your sake it doesn't." I tucked into my salmon, not waiting for Harmony. "Apologies for my haste," I said after swallowing my first mouthful. "I want to catch Mrs. Browning before she retires. I don't want her to have a reason to turn me away when she sees me on her doorstep."

"Eat as quickly as you like without giving yourself a stomachache. But if you have the time, can you tell me what you're going to ask her. I'm wildly curious about this case, since I was there at the time of the murder. I'm also quite bored."

I gave her a sympathetic look. "I'll not only tell you what Harry and I have learned so far, but I have a task for you to do tomorrow after you finish your cleaning round."

She listened as I told her we'd found a silver spoon hidden in Faine's room, which confirmed he was stealing from Hambledon Hall. I mentioned the letters we'd found in the church office, and how that led us to a confrontation with the new vicar at St. Michael's in Marylebone.

"That's where I'd like you to go tomorrow," I said. "The vicar who took over from Pritchard will recognize me, but you're a stranger to him. I want you to ask to see the parish registers."

"Christenings or marriages?"

"Both. I don't know what to look for, but I'm hoping it will be obvious when you see it."

"How will that tell you what Pritchard did to earn himself a hasty removal to Morcombe?"

"It's nothing to do with him. According to Lady Kershaw, he was quickly moved on because he likes men. I want you to look through the parish records because I think that's why Shepherd was there. I don't yet know what he was looking for, or if it's relevant to his murder. It's possible it isn't, and he was killed by Pritchard after all when he attempted to blackmail the vicar."

"Blackmail sounds like something Shepherd would do. Horrid man."

"Your opinion will continue to decline after you hear what we learned from the former nanny, Miss Crippen. Keep this to yourself, though. I promised not to spread her secret." I told her about Esmond Shepherd's abandonment of Phyllida Crippen in her time of greatest need.

Harmony was furious, but not shocked. "Men like him don't take responsibility for their actions. Unfortunately, it happens all too often. Those are the sort of men who should be stopped visiting the rooms of maids with rules like Mrs. Short's. Not genuinely good men with honest intentions."

"I agree. But there's more. Miss Crippen told us that she overheard Mrs. Browning arguing with Shepherd. It sounded like they'd once had a relationship but it had soured, and she was warning him not to go near her daughter, Janet."

"That's why you want to speak to Mrs. Browning tonight? I don't envy you. Good luck, Cleo. You're going to need it."

Indeed I would. Mrs. Browning was prickly at the best of times. Confronting her about such a sensitive topic would be difficult.

* * *

I TRIED the same tactic on Mrs. Browning that had been a success with Lady Kershaw. I arrived at her door with a tea tray. She didn't move aside and let me in, however.

She crossed her arms over her chest. "I didn't order tea."

"I thought you might appreciate it, nevertheless."

"I have a headache, and I don't want tea. Goodnight, Miss Fox."

"I thought you might try to avoid me, so let me tell you why you should let me in. Either you can give me your version of events, or you can talk to Scotland Yard."

"The murder isn't a London matter."

"It will be when they learn Sergeant Honeyman is over-looking evidence because your brother told him to."

Her nostrils flared.

"Believe me, I am the kinder option of the two, and the one that will draw less publicity. I don't want to upset your family, because that will upset my family. I offer you discretion and understanding."

She considered my proposal with another flare of her nostrils then grabbed the tray out of my hands and led the way through to the sitting room. She set the tray down on the table so heavily that the cups rattled in their saucers.

"Let's get this over with," she snapped as she poured the tea.

I cleared my throat to give myself a moment to compose

myself. I didn't want her to see that I was as rattled as the cups. What I had to say first could see me unceremoniously banished. "You had an affair with Esmond Shepherd."

The stream of tea missed the second cup and spilled onto the saucer. She lowered the teapot to the tray. "So that's how it is."

I waited silently.

"Who told you?"

"I can't tell you that. The affair, Mrs. Browning…when did it begin?"

"It wasn't an affair. That implies one of us broke marriage vows. It happened before I married Mr. Browning."

Mrs. Smith from the Morcombe teashop claimed Lady Cicely Wentworth, as Mrs. Browning was called then, married at seventeen. "You were very young," I said.

"But not naïve. I knew what men were like, that they coveted young women. I just didn't realize Esmond was like that. Not then. He was only four years older than me, so it seemed perfectly all right. To me, at least."

"You thought he loved you."

"Yes, and I loved him, at the time."

"You say you knew what men were like, despite your tender age. Is that because Mr. Browning pursued you from the age of fourteen?"

I'd managed to surprise her again, but she quickly schooled her features. She finished pouring the tea and handed me a cup. "It wasn't as debauched as you make it sound. It's true that Gordon was keen on me from the moment he saw me, and that I was only fourteen, but he didn't act on his desire. Others must have noticed, however, so when my relationship with Esmond was discovered, I was married off to Gordon before anyone else found out. I had to be urgently removed from Hambledon."

That explained why she'd married a commoner, and not waited for a titled nobleman.

"Is Janet the daughter of Esmond Shepherd?" I asked.

"No. She was born in my third year of marriage to Gordon. Esmond and I didn't continue our secret liaisons after my wedding day. I simply meant the urgency was because no one wanted me to run off with Esmond. Could you imagine the scandal if I had? My family would have been humiliated."

"You continued to love him, though."

She nodded. "I loved him for years. I looked forward to visiting Hambledon, just so I could catch a glimpse of him. We never renewed our relationship, despite a few attempts on my part. I would wait for him in my room, or his cottage, hoping he would stumble upon me and…" Her cheeks flamed and she took a large gulp of tea. "Call me a fool, but I thought he never married because he was heartsick over losing me. I didn't realize he'd lost interest a long time ago. Looking back, it was probably around the time I got pregnant."

It seemed like another good opening to mention Janet, but I hesitated. Asking a woman if her daughter was having a relationship with her former lover seemed like a step too far.

Mrs. Browning noticed my hesitation. "Get it over with quickly, Miss Fox. It will hurt, but only for a moment."

I drew in a deep breath. "Did Esmond Shepherd and Janet…?"

"No! Lord, no. I told him I'd shoot him if he went anywhere near her." She huffed out a humorless laugh. "That's not an admission of guilt. I merely threatened him, I didn't kill him."

"When did you threaten him?"

"It was around three months ago, just before the last nanny left."

That matched Miss Crippen's account of overhearing them in the gamekeeper's cottage.

"Is that all, Miss Fox? Or do you have more muck to rake?"

"Something has bothered me ever since learning that Esmond Shepherd is a cad who seduces the young female staff. Why has he never been dismissed when everyone seems to know what he's like, including your brother?"

"Not just my brother. Our father, too. He was furious when he caught us. Apoplectic. Yet he didn't dismiss Esmond. As far as I'm aware, he didn't even scold him. I took the full force of his anger." She watched me over the rim of her teacup as she sipped. "I presume it's because there's truth to the rumor that my grandfather was Susannah Shepherd's father, and that connection meant each successive earl was reluctant to dismiss her little brother, since old William Shepherd had been dreadfully wronged." She pulled a face. "It's all so murky. It happened so many years ago, that I doubt anyone knows the particulars, even Aunt Elizabeth."

"What year was Susannah born?"

She lifted her gaze to the ceiling as she calculated. "She was a lot older than me and died aged twenty-one in fifty-five, so that means she was born in 1834, two years after my father was born."

I frowned. "Your father was born in '32? Then he would only have been sixty-eight if he were alive today."

"Yes. He died five years ago. So?"

"His sister, your aunt the Lady Elizabeth, is eighty."

"There was a large age gap between the siblings, and she has a healthy constitution. What of it?"

"Nothing," I said quite honestly. I couldn't think how it might be relevant, if at all.

"Is that all, Miss Fox? Or have you come to ask me more questions about your aunt's jealousy of your mother?"

I'd been prepared for her waspishness, but her directness still took me by surprise. I allowed myself a moment in which to settle my jangling nerves. Once my tension eased, I wondered if she went on the attack because she was hiding something. It was a good way to throw me off balance.

It wouldn't work, however. There was one more thing I needed to discuss with her. "Your husband went out with my cousin last night. Floyd told me all about it."

"You have spies everywhere."

"He doesn't spy for me. He simply gave me his impression of Mr. Browning."

Mrs. Browning huffed into her teacup before sipping.

"He likened him to Shepherd, actually, in their mutual fondness for young women." I watched her carefully, but she looked neither surprised nor upset. Even so, I didn't like myself for telling her. "I'm sorry. That was cruel."

She lowered the teacup to the saucer and held my gaze with her own. "You can hardly be shocked, after learning Gordon took an interest in me when I was fourteen. But I do want to make one thing clear. Neither he nor Esmond succumbed to their urges with any underage girls."

"You were seventeen when you married," I pointed out.

"Old enough for marriage, Miss Fox."

The conversation had veered from the direction I wanted to take it, so I steered it back. "Did your husband know about your relationship with Shepherd?"

"Yes, but he wasn't jealous of Esmond if that's what you're asking."

"There was no issue between them? No awkwardness when you visited Hambledon Hall?"

"Why would there be? My husband has no need to be jealous of a gamekeeper."

"Did they become friends?"

She scoffed. "Don't be absurd."

"Did you ever see them talking?"

"They had to talk when we went shooting."

"Are those the only occasions you saw them talking?"

She frowned. "What are you getting at, Miss Fox?"

I sipped my tea to allow the silence to unsettle her into responding. It didn't work. She sipped her tea, too, and waited. I tried approaching my theory from a different angle. "Did you know some valuable items went missing from Hambledon Hall?"

"No. What does that have to do with anything?"

"It appears that Shepherd may have been involved in the thefts, but he must have had help from someone from within the household."

"Staff can't be trusted these days."

"Floyd told me your husband likes to gamble."

Her eyes flashed. "You think Gordon is in financial difficulty so has been stealing from my brother, along with Esmond. They had a falling out, so Gordon shot him." She laughed, a brittle sound that raked across my nerves. "I was told you were smart, Miss Fox. What a disappointment to find that you're simply fanciful."

"You aren't in financial difficulty?" I pressed. "Or does your husband not share that information with you?"

Any pretense of civility vanished. "Get out. You give me a headache."

I left, feeling like I'd just been in the ring with a champion pugilist. Even so, I'd managed a solid blow or two of my own. If I had to guess, I'd say she had no idea what the family's financial situation was, and she loathed being in the dark.

Mrs. Browning's mention of my aunt reminded me that I'd promised Floyd I'd check on her. I knocked on the door to her suite. When there was no answer, I tried the handle. It was unlocked.

I opened the door a fraction. "Aunt Lilian? It's me, Cleo. May I come in?"

Silence.

I entered and closed the door behind me. I felt my way along the dark corridor to the sitting room. Finding the light switch by feel, I turned it on.

"Turn it off!" cried Aunt Lilian from the sofa as she flung her arm over her eyes.

I quickly turned the light off again. "Sorry, I didn't see you. I called out, but there was no answer."

"What do you want, Cleopatra?"

"I'm just checking to see if you're all right."

"Why wouldn't I be?" she snapped.

"I know you feel unwell if you haven't taken your tonic for a while."

She didn't respond.

I turned to go, but stopped. Sometimes the right thing to do was the most difficult thing. I steeled myself and plunged in. "It will be hard weaning yourself off the tonic at first, but you *will* feel better in the long run. If you want to try, I will be here to help you."

"How can you help, Cleopatra? You don't know anything about what I'm going through."

"I'm sorry," I said again. "I'll leave you be."

"You're just like your mother," she said, her tone icy. "She poked her nose into my business and treated me like a child, too."

I blinked back tears as I left her suite and returned to my own. I didn't blame her for lashing out. It was the addiction talking, not my sweet aunt. Knowing that didn't make me feel any better, however. Indeed, it only made me feel worse. I wanted my loving Aunt Lilian back, but unless she wanted that, too, I couldn't help her.

* * *

SLEEP WAS ELUSIVE. My theories chased around the evidence in my head, only to be diverted by my concern for Aunt Lilian, and ways I could have handled the situation better. Despite snatching only a few hours, I got up at five and sat at the desk. Writing down my thoughts often cleared my head, allowing space for sleep to take over.

Not this time. I heard a soft shush of sound. Wrapping my dressing gown tightly around me, I stooped to pick up the piece of paper someone had slipped under the door. It was from Floyd, who once again had written me a note after returning home from a late night out with Mr. Browning.

I quickly opened the door, only to have to catch Floyd as he toppled against me.

"Sorry, Cleo," he slurred. "I was leaning on your door for…I don't really know why."

I wrinkled my nose. "You stink of alcohol and cheap women."

"One woman, and certainly not cheap." His lips curved with a sleepy smile. "She was worth it."

"*Ugh*. You're disgusting."

"And you're…" He rubbed his chin as he tried to think of a suitable insult. "Annoying."

"So everyone is telling me lately." I waved the paper in his face. "What did you want to tell me? I can't read your drunk writing."

"I'm not drunk."

I straightened his crooked tie. "I don't need to be a detective to see the evidence to the contrary."

"This isn't my drunken state. This is my tired state." He took the note from me. He squinted at the writing then turned the paper around, then around again. "The gist of it is that Browning is a turd. He tried to borrow money from me after he lost at cards. When I refused, he picked my pocket. Someone saw and alerted me. Can you believe it, Cleo!" He pointed his finger at me, stopping a mere inch from my nose.

179

"No need to remind me I used to be just as bad, but I assure you, I never stole from anyone to fund my gambling habit. Also, unlike Browning, I admitted I had a problem, and I made attempts to stop."

"You only admitted it *after* you found yourself in hot water, and you didn't get out of it yourself. Harry got you out of it."

"I said I made *attempts*." He tapped the end of my nose with his finger. "He's downstairs in the smoking room."

"Harry?"

"Brown turd." He laughed. "Did you hear that, Cleo? Brown turd. I combined his name with what he is and the result is so witty. I'm smart *and* amusing when I'm drunk."

"I thought you were simply tired."

The lift door opened further along the corridor, and Mr. Browning emerged. He spotted me speaking to Floyd. Instead of heading to his own room, he approached.

"Evening, Miss Fox," he said, a little loudly considering the late hour and everyone was asleep.

Instead of telling him to keep his voice down, or point out it was no longer evening, I smiled. He didn't sound as drunk as Floyd, but he was certainly suffering the effects of alcohol, going by the way he swayed. The perfect opportunity had just presented itself.

Floyd leaned against the doorframe and crossed his arms over his chest. "Go to bed, Browning."

"I want to speak to your pretty cousin."

"She doesn't want to talk to you."

"Actually, I do," I said.

Mr. Browning licked his smirking lips and tried to enter my suite. Floyd blocked him with an arm across the doorway.

"We can talk here," I said, realizing I'd given the wrong impression.

Mr. Browning's top lip curled with his sneer. He directed the sneer at me then Floyd. "She's not worth it anyway."

Floyd drew himself up to his full height.

Mr. Browning chuckled and began to walk off.

"Were you jealous of your wife's relationship with Esmond Shepherd?" I asked.

He spun around and marched back to me, proving he

wasn't as drunk as he seemed. His fists opened and closed at his sides. "What did you say?"

I'd said it purely to make him stop. It had worked, but I changed my mind about pressing him on the thefts. My questions could wait until broad daylight when he was sober. Perhaps then he'd remember his gentlemanly manners.

He leaned so close I could see the fury burning in his eyes, despite the poor light. My heart pounded, drumming out a warning not to antagonize this man further.

Floyd's drunkenness meant his warning system wasn't working as well as mine. "She said, were you jealous of your wife?"

Mr. Browning flinched as if he'd been struck, but he didn't take his hard gaze off me. He raised a fist and for a heart-stopping moment, I thought was going to hit me. Instead, he unfurled the fist and poked me in the shoulder. "You are one of *those* women, aren't you? You may look pretty and feminine, but you act and think like a man. You're not natural. You're a *freak*. Bainbridge, you should lock her in a cage and charge admission so normal people can come and see her. You could earn a—"

Floyd slammed his fist into Mr. Browning's stomach.

Mr. Browning doubled over, wheezing.

Floyd rolled his shoulder and stood a little taller. "Disparage my cousin again and I'll smash your nose. Try explaining *that* to your wife."

Mr. Browning's wheezing subsided enough that he was able to straighten. "I'll tell Sir Ronald about this. Wait until he hears that his friend was assaulted by his own son."

That knocked the wind out of Floyd's sails and rendered him quite speechless.

"Thank you, Floyd. I'll take over from here." I gave Mr. Browning a pitying smile. "Your brother-in-law is Uncle Ronald's friend, not you. I wouldn't be surprised to find that both men think you deserved that punch after what you said. But if you do find you want to tell Sir Ronald, then I must warn you that I will tell everyone that you stole from Hambledon Hall."

Floyd stared at me, open-mouthed.

Mr. Browning's nostrils flared, rather like his wife's did

when I said something to offend her. "That's an absurd accusation."

"Only if it isn't true. I know that you, Shepherd and a man named Faine stole valuable items from Lord and Lady Kershaw."

Mr. Browning's lips twisted with his smile. "If that were so, why weren't the police notified?"

"Because Lord and Lady Kershaw knew *you* were the one stealing from them, and they overlooked it because you're family. This way, they're able to help you pay off your debts without embarrassing you. As you were stealing items that have no sentimental value, they don't feel compelled to stop you. You knew Lady Kershaw despised those candlesticks, and teaspoons can be easily replaced."

Mr. Browning took a step toward me, but Floyd intercepted him.

"Did Shepherd take more than his share?" Floyd asked. "Is that why you killed him?"

"I didn't kill him." Mr. Browning kept his voice low and glanced around. "Don't spread that lie, Bainbridge." He tugged on the hem of his jacket to straighten it after Floyd's punch wrinkled it. "It's true that we were partners in a little… scheme. It was only a few things that were easy to melt down or sell off. Except for that blasted rifle."

"What rifle?" I asked.

"The one made by James Purdey & Sons that was displayed on the armory wall. It was originally made for royalty and is now a collector's piece, worth a fortune to the right buyer. The problem is, those sorts of buyers aren't easy to find and Faine couldn't get rid of it using his usual network."

"Is the rifle still in Faine's possession?"

"I suppose so." He rubbed his hand across his mouth again. "Listen. I didn't kill Shepherd. There was no falling out, or anything like that."

"What was Shepherd's role in the scheme?"

"He knew of a way to get Kershaw to close the bridleway, so the goods could be moved without anyone from the public stumbling on us."

"What way?"

"I don't know. He wouldn't tell us."

"Kershaw wasn't suspicious as to the reason for wanting the bridleway closed?"

He shrugged. "I assume whatever Shepherd had on Kershaw shut down any questions. Anyway, you're probably right and he knows I'm in it up to my neck." He huffed a humorless laugh. "He's the one you should be looking at for the murder, not me. Kershaw could have killed Shepherd because he was tired of being blackmailed." He seemed to take great delight in realizing that his brother-in-law had a strong motive for murdering the gamekeeper.

I wasn't sure if ending the blackmail was a good reason for murder, however. Why end it now? And why end it with murder when telling the police about the thefts would have sufficed? He could have got Sergeant Honeyman to overlook Mr. Browning's involvement, if necessary.

It would be interesting to see if Lord Kershaw reopened the bridleway now that Shepherd could no longer blackmail him. It would certainly add weight to the argument that he was the murderer.

Floyd and I watched Mr. Browning make his way back to his room. Once he was inside, I kissed Floyd's cheek. "Thank you for defending me. You really are a sweetheart."

"I know, but don't tell anyone. It'll ruin my reputation." He winked and sauntered off toward his own suite.

I smiled, my mood dramatically improved now that I knew what step to take next.

CHAPTER 15

*H*arry was keen to return to Morcombe with me. I'd not wanted to search Faine's property alone and he agreed it was necessary to go immediately. But first, he suggested he telephone his father and find out what he could about the bullet that shot Esmond Shepherd.

I had an even better idea, however. "I'll contact D.S. Forrester at Scotland Yard. I think it's time to involve an active member of the police force, not a retired one."

"Or a corrupt one," Harry added. "The local man, Honeyman, is entirely under Kershaw's thumb."

Harry listened with a frown as I told Monty Forrester about the investigation over the telephone, and what information I needed from him. The frown only appeared when I called the detective sergeant by his first name.

An hour and a half later, we once again ventured into the courtyard of the Red Lion Inn, being careful not to be seen. It was Sunday morning, and the inn was quiet. Indeed, the village seemed quiet. Shops were closed, and an overcast day kept the ramblers away. We hid behind some beer barrels in the courtyard, watching the converted coach house for any sign of Faine. After twenty minutes, however, no one emerged from his room and I grew impatient.

"I'll draw him out if he's in there," I said. "I'll suggest we have a drink together. Then you go in and search."

"That's a terrible idea. He'll know you're up to something."

"I'll be convincing."

Harry shook his head. "We should look in the stables or the other coach house, somewhere we haven't already searched."

It was a point we'd discussed on the train journey. Harry was convinced the rifle wasn't in Faine's room or we would have found it last time. I thought a second, more thorough, inspection was required before reaching that conclusion.

Five minutes later, when Faine still hadn't emerged, I decided to go ahead with my plan to draw him out so Harry could search. I got up, only to be jerked back down by the hand.

Harry put a finger to his lips then pointed at the stables. Faine appeared in the doorway, scratching at his scraggly beard as he strode across the courtyard. He passed us without looking our way and left the courtyard altogether.

Harry signaled to go, and together we cautiously approached the stables. He entered first, setting down the small case he'd brought with him near the entrance, and looked inside. Moments later, he signaled for me to follow. "It's empty except for one horse."

The horse was contentedly munching oats in its stall and paid us no attention as we set about our search. I expected to find the rifle in a cavity under the floor, just as we'd found the teaspoon under the floor in Faine's room. I pushed aside straw and stamped my feet on the cobblestones in search of a loose section that could indicate there was a hiding space underneath.

I hadn't got very far when Harry joined me, carrying a long bundle wrapped in a blanket. "Found it hidden in the rafters." He unwrapped the bundle to show me a rifle bearing an elaborate engraving on the silver escutcheon. "It's an antique Purdey."

"Just as Mr. Browning claimed."

If the bullet that killed Esmond Shepherd matched one fired from the rifle, then this was the murder weapon. It was time to telephone Monty to see what he'd learned.

Harry tucked the bundled-up rifle inside his coat and

picked up the case. We went in search of a telephone, only to find that the village's public silence cabinet was located in the post office and it was closed. We had no choice but to got to the police station.

I was surprised to find Sergeant Honeyman there, considering it was Sunday. He was chatting to the constable manning the front desk. It seemed to be just the two of them on duty. I suspected very little happened in Morcombe most days, let alone on a Sunday. The murder of Esmond Shepherd would have been a unique incident.

"I remember you from Hambledon Hall," Sergeant Honeyman said to me. "You're Lady Kershaw's friend."

"I'm Cleopatra Fox." I was surprised he remembered me, since he hardly spoke to me on the day of the murder, despite me being one of the first at the scene. I didn't tell him that, however. We needed his help and I didn't want to offend him. "Mr. Armitage and I are private detectives. We've been investigating the murder of Esmond Shepherd and have something for you. We discovered this in the stables of the Red Lion Inn where Mr. Faine lives."

Harry unveiled the weapon and set it down on the desk in front of the sergeant.

The constable whistled and bent to inspect the rifle closely.

Honeyman, however, narrowed his gaze at me. "I had a telephone call from Scotland Yard earlier. I was ordered to give you my full cooperation. Why are you chasing my tail?"

"Because there was no poacher."

"There was."

"No, there wasn't, as you are well aware."

Honeyman opened his mouth to argue, but Harry cut him off. "Sergeant, remind me what the consequences would be if you disregard Scotland Yard's orders?"

The constable melted into the background, eager to distance himself from his superior's corruption.

The sergeant glared at Harry for a moment before giving in with a grunt. He picked up the rifle. "It's a fine piece. Faine had it, you say? He's a bad apple that one. It wouldn't surprise me if he stole this and shot Shepherd with it when Shepherd saw him." He seemed satisfied with his theory, perhaps because it meant Faine got the blame, not a member of Lord Kershaw's family.

"We're not sure if it's the murder weapon," I said. "We need to undertake a scientific experiment to compare a bullet shot from this gun with the one recovered from Shepherd's body."

"It won't work."

"Bullets shot from old rifles like this will have unique markings visible under a microscope, unlike modern machine-made weapons that appear to be all the same. If there's a match to the recovered bullet, then we'll know this is the murder weapon."

"I know about the science, Miss Fox," Honeyman bit off. "The problem is, we don't have a microscope here to inspect the bullets."

Harry set his case on the desk. "I brought mine." He looked pleased that he was going to put one of his favorite instruments to good use.

Honeyman snatched up the rifle. "Constable, fetch the evidence box for the Shepherd case. You two, come out the back."

He retrieved a bullet from a locked cabinet and led the way through the station to a courtyard. We watched as he fired a bullet from the rifle into a sack packed with fabric scraps that had clearly been used as target practice before, going by the dozens of holes. Sergeant Honeyman retrieved the bullet and handed it to Harry.

Back inside, Harry set up his microscope and inspected the bullet. He then invited Honeyman and me to look, while the constable handed him the bullet retrieved from the victim. He swapped the bullets and inspected the second one under the microscope.

"They're different," he said, straightening. "That rifle isn't the murder weapon."

I peered through the microscope's eyepiece. "Are you sure?" Even as I said it, I could see the difference to the first bullet. The pattern of grooves on the Purdey were clear, but were barely visible on the bullet retrieved from the body. I stepped aside to allow the sergeant to look.

"I missed church because of this," Honeyman said with a

shake of his head. "You be sure to tell your friends at the Yard that I don't appreciate being ordered to go on wild goose chases based on the imaginings of a private detective who should be sipping tea instead of interfering with police investigations."

"I wouldn't have to interfere if you did your job properly in the first place," I said.

"Are you suggesting we're inept here at Morcombe?"

"No, Sergeant. That's not what I'm suggesting at all."

If he realized I was calling him corrupt, he showed no sign. He took the rifle and both bullets. "Amateurs."

I marched out of the station, forgetting that Harry had to pack up his microscope. He joined me moments later.

"I can't believe it's not the murder weapon," I said as we walked off.

"It could have been another from the armory, a more modern rifle."

"None were missing when Harmony and I checked after the murder, and there was no time for one to be returned before Harmony arrived. The murder weapon must still be in the woods or elsewhere in the house, depending on where the killer was standing at the time."

"If that rifle was stolen by Browning and passed on to Faine to sell, and it's not the murder weapon, then it's likely that neither Browning nor Faine are the murderer."

"I'm not ruling either out yet. Both have motive and opportunity."

We continued to walk through the village and found ourselves near the church as parishioners spilled out after the service. Reverend Pritchard stood at the door to see them off. He didn't smile. He was a serious, pious man, as many had pointed out to us. Now that I knew why he'd left London under a cloud, I saw him in a different light. He didn't seem quite so sinister or scheming. He seemed like an ordinary man whose life had fallen apart and he was struggling to pick up the pieces.

My sympathy for him could be a mistake. I mustn't forget that his secret meant he had a motive for murder.

Yet Shepherd hadn't gone to St. Michael's in Marylebone to investigate *Pritchard*. I was quite sure of that. Harmony would look through the parish records after her shift finished today, to see if she could find a connection to Morcombe, but as I watched the vicar, I was reminded of something he'd told me some time ago.

Esmond Shepherd wasn't a churchgoer. Indeed, he'd only gone once, and that wasn't to hear a service. It made sense that it was to look through the parish records. Had he searched here first and not found what he wanted, so went to London instead? And why St. Michael's in Marylebone? Why that particular church?

I discussed it with Harry while we waited for the parishioners to disperse and the vicar to return inside. We followed him and found him gathering his sermon notes at the pulpit.

He sighed heavily upon seeing us. "I'm afraid I don't have time for your questions. Sundays are my busiest days."

"Our questions are brief," I said. "You once told me that you met Mr. Shepherd here in the church. I presume he wanted to look through the parish records. Can you tell us which ones?"

He seemed relieved that my question wasn't about him and his past. "He looked at several, but I don't know whether it was the baptisms or marriages."

"What about the year?" Harry asked.

"I wasn't peering over his shoulder." The vicar tucked the notes under his arm and strode off in the direction of the sacristy and office, his gown billowing behind him.

I followed. "May we take a look at them?"

"Just for a few minutes. I have to pay calls to parishioners too ill or infirm to attend the service today, and I'll be locking the office. One can't be too careful these days."

"We only need a few minutes." With a specific year in mind, it wouldn't take long.

I found the register for 1834, the year Susannah Shepherd was born. Morcombe was a small village so there were few baptisms each year, and we found hers quickly. That was both a surprise and a disappointment. I'd expected to find no record at all. Its absence would explain why Esmond Shepherd went to London to look through the records of a different parish. But its presence in Morcombe meant

Susannah was baptized here. There was no need to look elsewhere.

Harry pointed to each of Susannah's parents. Mabel Shepherd was recorded as her mother and William Shepherd as the father. His occupation was noted as gamekeeper. The fourth Lord Kershaw was either not Susannah's father, or Mabel lied to protect herself and her family from scandal.

Drat. If the record of Susannah's baptism was in *this* parish register, why did Esmond Shepherd go to London at all? Was he looking for something else?

As Harry slotted the register back into the bookshelf, I approached the vicar, seated at the desk where he was writing notes about the service in a leather-bound notebook. "You were the vicar at St. Michael's in Marylebone before coming here."

The tip of his pencil snapped off as he pressed too hard on the page. "No! No, I wasn't! I came from Cornwall."

"We know the truth. We know why you left there in a hurry."

The hand holding the pencil started to shake.

"It doesn't matter to us," Harry assured him. "We won't divulge your secret unless it's pertinent to the murder."

"It's not!" Pritchard removed his glasses and wiped the lenses with his handkerchief. The ordinary activity seemed to calm him, or perhaps it was simply a way of giving himself a moment to think. He placed the glasses back on his face and pocketed the handkerchief. "You're right. I was based there before I came here. I'll swear on a thousand bibles that I had nothing to do with Shepherd's murder. As far as I'm aware, he knew nothing about my…" He cleared his throat. "…about my past."

"We don't care about that," Harry said again. "But Miss Fox has learned that the victim went to St. Michael's a few days before he died. We want to know why."

"I don't know! I haven't corresponded with anyone from that parish since I left. Please, don't dig up my past. I can't go through that again. If Shepherd's visit to St. Michael's was to do with me, he never mentioned it, and I'm quite sure the new vicar wouldn't say anything to him." He closed his notebook and stood with such force, the chair tilted on its hind legs before settling back again. "Now, if you don't mind, I have things to do."

"Shepherd wasn't asking about *you* at St. Michael's," I said. "He was looking through the parish records."

"Oh. I see. I'm sorry, but I can't help." He took a step, only to stop again. He frowned. "It might have something to do with Lord Kershaw." He shrugged. "Or perhaps not. I don't want to stir things up for him. He and Lady Kershaw have been kind to me."

"She knows your secret, too," I said. "She promised to keep it. Is that in exchange for you keeping a secret of hers?"

"No. Nothing like that. You're right. She does know about my past, and that I came from St. Michael's. It was when I informed her that she told me about her husband's connection to the Marylebone parish. It was just an offhand comment, a curious coincidence. I'm sure it means nothing."

"What kind of family connection?"

"The earls of Kershaw kept a townhouse in the St. Michael's parish for a hundred years or more. It was sold by the previous earl when the railway came to Morcombe. The train journey to London was so much shorter than travel by horse and carriage, and they could be there and back in the same day. For the few times they wanted to stay longer, they could just take a suite at a hotel."

Many of the landed gentry kept townhouses in London, and some had sold them off in recent times as keeping them was costly, particularly when they were hardly used. It was why luxury hotels like the Mayfair had become popular with that set.

Reverend Pritchard glanced from Harry to me. "Telling you that doesn't place Lord and Lady Kershaw in trouble, does it?"

"Our investigation is ongoing," I said. "Thank you for the information."

He dogged our steps as we headed out of the office. "I doubt they're involved in their gamekeeper's demise. They're good people. They've been kind to me."

"And to me," I said. Not only did I like the Kershaws, but they were dear friends of my aunt and uncle. If they were guilty, I would have a very difficult choice.

"You only have to look at the fact his lordship overturned the decision to close the bridleway," Reverend Pritchard added.

Harry and I stopped. "When?" I asked.

"The mayor received the letter from his lordship's solicitor yesterday. The bridleway's reopening is effective immediately. Apparently he discovered some paperwork that proved the public were granted access centuries ago, and he wanted to do the right thing without delay. As I said, he's a good man."

Harry and I didn't speak until we'd left the church and Reverend Pritchard behind. I walked quickly in the direction of the railway station, outstripping Harry at first.

When he caught up to me, he touched my elbow. "Cleo, what's wrong?"

"Lord Kershaw has only reopened the bridleway because Shepherd is dead. That means he closed it because that's what Shepherd wanted. Why would he do something his game-keeper wanted if it went against his own wishes? Because Shepherd was blackmailing him, just as Mr. Browning stated," I finished, answering myself.

"It doesn't necessarily mean Kershaw killed him. We don't have proof."

"The evidence is mounting." I sighed. "I don't want Lord Kershaw to be guilty, Harry."

"Because you like him? You think he's a good man, as Pritchard said?"

"Because pointing the finger at him will upset my aunt and uncle. Uncle Ronald will rant and rage at me, and Aunt Lilian will…" A sudden rush of tears clogged my throat and filled my eyes, blurring my vision. I lowered my gaze and drew in some steadying breaths until I'd regained my composure. "Her addiction is making her say things she usually wouldn't. I'm worried what she'll say if I have Lord Kershaw arrested for murder."

He took my hand and squeezed. "I can be with you if it becomes necessary to tell them."

I was about to tell him it was a task I had to do my own, but changed my mind. The thought of having his support was very appealing. "Thank you, Harry. Let's hope it doesn't come to that."

* * *

THE HOTEL STAFF were in a grim mood. I detected it the moment I entered the foyer. Frank wasn't at his usual position at the door, and his replacement said he was taking a short break in the staff parlor. I went there directly and discovered Frank along with Goliath, Peter and Harmony. They sat in morose silence, cradling cups of tea.

"What's happened?" I asked. "Has someone died?"

"Mary and her beau, one of the footmen, were dismissed today," Peter said. "Mrs. Short caught him passing a note to Mary when she was supposed to be working."

I flopped down onto one of the chairs, suddenly exhausted. The last two days had felt inordinately long. "I warned her to be careful."

"We all did," Harmony said, sounding annoyed. "She only has herself to blame."

"It's not their fault," Frank said. "When were they supposed to meet? They can't be seen talking at the residence hall because the men can't go into the women's area, or vice versa. They can't talk here because they're supposed to be working. So tell me, when?"

"Some people manage," she shot back.

"Not everyone has Victor's skill with secrecy."

She bristled. "What does that mean?"

"Nothing," he muttered.

Peter pointed at each of them in turn. "That's enough, both of you."

"Don't tell me what to do," Frank growled.

"I am your superior."

Frank rolled his eyes.

Goliath leaned forward, elbows resting on his knees. "Is there anything you can do, Miss Fox?"

"I doubt it," I said. "But I'll try to speak to Mrs. Short."

Goliath gave me a flat smile of thanks then stood. "I have to get back to work."

Peter and Frank followed him out of the parlor, while I

remained with Harmony. I poured myself a cup of tea from the kettle and sat beside her.

"How did your visit to St. Michael's go?" I asked.

She shook her head. "It was a waste of time. There was no record of Susannah Shepherd's baptism in 1834."

"We found it in the register at Morcombe. I'm sorry, Harmony. It seems I sent you on a wild goose chase. Although something *did* send Esmond Shepherd to St. Michael's after he'd been to the Morcombe church." I sipped my tea, trying to think what it could be.

"I checked other years either side of 1834," she said. "Just in case. There were a large number of entries but I managed to cover seven years' worth."

"Did you see any references to the Wentworth family at all, or the Kershaw title? It was their local parish when they came to London, until the previous earl sold their townhouse."

"No. Nothing."

We both sighed into our cups of tea. We'd been so sure the registers would yield results. They might still, but without narrowing down a year, we were searching in the dark.

* * *

Mrs. Short's reaction upon seeing me enter her office was similar to that of every suspect I'd interrogated in the past week, except *her* groan was audible. "I know what this is about, and no, I will not change my mind, Miss Fox. Mary and her beau broke not one rule, but two. Their fraternizing broke my new rule, and they also did it when she was supposed to be working. That rule has been long-standing here at the hotel, I believe, and it has nothing to do with me."

"They only broke that rule because the new one made it so difficult for them to even talk at home." I sat down, not prepared to give up without seeing where digging in got me. "They are young and in love, Mrs. Short. Can you not over-look it this one time?"

"I overlooked it the last time, at your request." She pointed her pen at me. "In fact, if you'd let me dismiss Mary then, we wouldn't be in this predicament now where I had to dismiss both. The footman could have been saved if you didn't interfere."

Her accusation stung. Not because it was hurtful, but because it was true. I was partly to blame. It meant I had even more reason to try and help the hapless couple now. "What harm is there in passing a note?"

"What harm?" she bellowed. "What harm, Miss Fox? A great deal, that's what." She jabbed the pen in my direction again. "A note leads to a liaison, and a liaison can lead to a girl getting herself into trouble. Unwed girls need to be careful."

"That's quite a leap to make, Mrs. Short."

"Not in my experience. I've been in service many years, Miss Fox. I have seen girls give their virtue to a boy they thought loved them. More often than not, the boy disappears the moment she tells him he's going to be a father. As house-keeper, all the maids are under my care. Their well-being and reputation are *my* responsibility, and if a girl is too silly to know what's good for her, then I must make the difficult deci-sions for her."

I was so stunned by her tirade that I didn't know how to answer. While she was right in general, she was still treating the maids as though they were naïve children who were unaware of the consequences. Perhaps that was true for some, but not all.

She must have thought my silence meant I agreed with her. She softened her tone but did not end the lecture there. "If the worst happened, and the footman abandoned her, Mary would be in a terrible predicament. Either she'd have to give the baby up, or she'd plunge it and herself into a lifetime of poverty and misery." Mrs. Short had leaned forward an inch or two with each sentence in her attempt to get her point across. Now she sat back and concentrated on her paperwork. "If you don't mind, Miss Fox, I have work to do before I leave for the day."

As I closed the office door behind me, I had the vague sensation that I could have said more—that I *should* have said more. But I couldn't quite grasp why. All I could think about was unwed mothers giving birth to illegitimate children. That led me to think about Miss Crippen, which led me to think about Esmond Shepherd, the father of her unborn child. Then I couldn't stop thinking about Esmond Shepherd's life. Not just his death, but his birth, too.

Pieces of the mystery became clearer—Esmond's search through the Morcombe church records, the moved photograph in his cottage, the niggling feeling this entire case hinged on the past.

I was now sure that it did. I just had to make a telephone call to prove it.

CHAPTER 16

I telephoned the Morcombe post office first thing in the morning and asked for an urgent message to be sent to Reverend Pritchard with my brief instructions. I paced the foyer of the hotel for the next hour, worrying that he'd be offended at me giving him orders. Or perhaps the postmaster didn't heed my request for urgency. Or perhaps the vicar wasn't available.

It was a relief when the clerk at the check-in desk signaled to me. I accepted the telephone receiver from him and spoke into the mouthpiece. "This is Miss Fox."

Reverend Pritchard's voice crackled down the line. "This is most irregular. I don't have the time to come to the post office to make telephone calls to London. My flock in Morcombe need me."

"This affects your flock," I reminded him. "I do appreciate your time, Reverend, as I'm sure Lord and Lady Kershaw will when they're made aware of your help."

Mentioning the names of the most important members of his flock had the desired effect and his next words lacked the acerbity of his previous ones. "Esmond Shepherd was indeed baptized here in 1855. His parents are listed as William and Mabel Shepherd."

"And Susannah's death?"

"She was buried in the churchyard in 1855 at the age of twenty-one, just five days after Esmond's baptism. The cause

197

of death is given as fever. It must have been a tumultuous time for the Shepherd family. They experience the joy of welcoming a son after years of barrenness only to lose their daughter mere days later. I can't imagine what they went through."

Nor could I. The vicar was right about the joy and the heartbreaking loss. But he was wrong about the rest.

After I hung up, I telephoned Harry's office, but the operator informed me there was no answer. I hung the receiver on its hook and thanked the clerk. I needed to talk over my findings with someone, but all the staff were at work. If I had to work, too, then so be it.

I found Harmony cleaning a room on the third floor. I joined her at the bed where she was unfolding a set of clean sheets. We'd discussed my theory that morning over breakfast, so she knew of my plan to telephone the vicar.

"You look as though you've won a prize," she said, her eyes bright. "You were right? Susannah Shepherd was Esmond's mother, not his sister?"

I signaled for her to give me one side of the sheet to help her spread it over the bed. "The parish records list William and Mabel Shepherd as his parents."

"Oh."

"They also show that Esmond was baptized five days before Susannah was buried, when he was a mere week old. Her cause of death was given as a fever. The timing can't be a coincidence, not when women who die days after giving birth are sometimes noted as having succumbed to fever rather than a result of childbirth. I'm sure that Susannah was his mother, despite what the records say."

"All right. So, if we accept that, then who is the father? Surely it can't be the fourth earl. If the rumors suggested he was Susannah's father, not her lover, then there must have been quite an age difference."

"It's more likely her lover was the *fifth* earl, the current Lord Kershaw's father. That the rumor about the *fourth* earl and *Mabel* Shepherd being lovers was wrong."

"Perhaps they were never quashed because it was better to have everyone believe that than know the truth."

She had an excellent point and I told her so.

I assisted her to pull up the bedspread and watched as she tucked it firmly into her side of the bed. I attempted an equally firm tuck on my side, but she insisted on redoing it to her standard. Harmony picked up a cleaning cloth from her cart, so I picked up one, too. We split the room down the middle, each of us wiping over the surfaces on our half.

Cleaning proved to be a good activity to do while thinking, particularly for this case. As I lifted up objects on the bedside table to clean under them, I was reminded of the photograph in the gamekeeper's cottage, as well as all the dust. The dust had built up over the previous month, after Mabel Shepherd died. Esmond, and the world, had assumed she was his mother. But if my theory was correct, she was his grandmother.

"Mabel Shepherd died recently," I pointed out. "Again, an apparent coincidence that might be more significant than we thought."

"Do you mean she may have confessed to Esmond on her deathbed that Susannah was his mother and the previous earl his father?"

"She may have confessed to more people than Esmond. Somebody studied the photograph in the cottage, most likely to look for a resemblance between Esmond and the fifth Lord Kershaw."

"Yes, but they studied it well after Mabel Shepherd died, going by the dust disturbance." Harmony flicked her cloth over the already cleaned desk in the corner of the room. "If Mabel confessed on her deathbed, that's a delay of three or four weeks. Why wait?"

She had a point.

"And," she went on, "why would someone kill Esmond over this? The parish record of his baptism states the Shepherds are his parents. There's no proof that the fifth earl is his father. Without proof, there's no motive."

"I have a theory about that. Esmond went to St. Michael's here in London after looking through the Morcombe parish records. I wasn't sure why at first, but now I wonder if it's because his baptism was registered twice. Firstly, here in London where he was born in the family's townhouse, away from the prying eyes of the village. Then mere days later back in Morcombe. The first registration could have his legitimate parents' names, and the latter one could have the false names and was carried out purely for the sake of appearances. It's easier to obscure the truth in the busy London parish than the quiet Morcombe one where everyone knows everybody else's business."

Harmony nodded along to my theory. "So I should have checked the 1855 records yesterday, not 1834."

"You can go back this afternoon."

She moved into the en suite bathroom, only to stop in the doorway. "There's one large hole in your theory, Cleo."

"What?"

"The motive. Yes, it's a scandal, but it's the previous earl's scandal, not the current one's."

"Perhaps the current Lord Kershaw didn't want his parents' memories to be mired in scandal. He may want to maintain the facade that his parents were happily married." Even as I said it, I realized I lacked a crucial piece of information to support that theory. I didn't know if his parents were married at that time. If they were, then it was quite possible he didn't want the world to know his father had an affair with the gamekeeper's daughter. If they weren't, the scandal was rather a mild one as scandals go.

* * *

I SPENT the rest of the day in a state of restlessness while I waited for Harmony to revisit St. Michael's church after her shift finished. I'd made up my mind to call on Harry and ask if he needed assistance with any of his cases, but before I left the hotel, Flossy waylaid me.

"Cleo, will you please, please come shopping with Janet and me. Neither her aunt nor her mother wants to go. They say they've had enough of shopping and everything for the wedding is purchased."

"Then why do you want to go?"

She looked at me as though I'd said something stupid. "Why not?" She clasped my hand. "Please, Cleo. It's Janet's last day in London, and we have nothing to do until afternoon tea and our mothers won't let us out without a chaperone."

Since I needed to do something to fill my time, I agreed. With a little clap of her hands, Flossy went off to fetch Janet while I asked Peter to organize one of the hotel carriages to collect us at the front door.

Fifteen minutes later, we set off in the rain. An hour later, in the men's department at Harrods, I began to regret my decision. Shopping wasn't my favorite activity, particularly when I wasn't the one choosing things. Added to which, Flossy and Janet were like bees flitting from flower to flower. Janet wanted to buy a gift for her fiancé, but she couldn't decide between a walking stick, a monocle, or a gold cigar cutter. When she dismissed them all and moved on to the tiepins, I decided to step in for the sake of my sanity.

"Tell me about your fiancé," I said. "How old is he?"

"Seven years older than me," she said, touching a silk handkerchief display on the glass-topped counter.

"Then I don't think a monocle or walking stick are a good idea."

"But they make a man look so distinguished."

Flossy agreed with me. "They make him look *old*."

"I suppose," Janet said.

"Does he smoke a lot of cigars?" I asked.

Janet bit her lower lip as she bent to study the tiepins beneath the glass countertop again. "I don't know. He doesn't smoke around me."

At least we were narrowing down our options. "What are his hobbies?"

Janet straightened. "Politics?"

"You don't know?"

"His family are quite political, so I assume he is, too. Yes, he must be. I think he plans on becoming quite the force in one of the political parties one day."

"The Tories?"

"Is that the conservative party? Yes, them."

I exchanged a glance with Flossy and was relieved to see that even she seemed to think it unusual that Janet didn't know her fiancé very well. "Haven't you spoken about his plans for the future?" I asked Janet.

She shrugged. "I'm sure he knows what he's doing. He's determined to do well for himself. He's quite ambitious."

A gentleman with plans to enter politics could have his future derailed by a scandal in his wife's family. The fifth earl of Kershaw's affair with the gamekeeper's daughter might not be enough to affect the sixth Lord Kershaw's life, but it could alter Janet's future husband's.

I studied Janet closely as she asked the sales assistant if she could take a closer look at one of the tiepins. She clutched her beaded purse tightly in both hands and tried to look mature, but she couldn't hide her smile of satisfaction as the sales assistant set out the tiepin on a white cloth. Janet seemed like a girl allowed to spend her own money for the first time, who wanted to make her first purchase special. She was innocent in the ways of the world, I was sure of it.

Her parents were wise, cunning even, and Janet was pretty and young, a combination that attracted the roguish gamekeeper. What would they do to protect her? Marry her off to the first gentleman to take an interest in her when Esmond Shepherd's roaming eye settled on her, as her own mother's parents had done?

"What do you think?" she asked Flossy and me.

"It's very elegant," Flossy said.

Janet looked pleased. "Miss Fox?"

"It's quite flashy with the ruby. Is your fiancé the sort of man who likes colorful gemstones?"

Janet deflated. "I don't think so."

The sales assistant glared at me as she returned the tiepin to the display cabinet.

"What about the one with the diamond?" I asked. "It's not as colorful as the ruby, but it's still elegant and quite sophisticated."

"Very sophisticated," the sales assistant said as she showed it to Janet.

Janet agreed and handed over the money. As the sales assistant wrapped the box for her, I pressed her about her upcoming marriage.

"How and when did he propose? It must have been a thrill for you."

"Oh, he didn't. It was all arranged before we met. I first saw him at Hambledon Hall, a week after it was all set up."

"Why there?"

"My aunt and uncle Kershaw know his parents very well. They suggested the marriage and had their solicitor draw up the contract. That's why I was able to make such a good match, you see. The benefit of having an earl for an uncle," she said with a giggle.

Flossy must have heard the story before, and knowing my views on marriage, quickly wanted to allay my concerns over the decision forced on Janet. "She wasn't keen at first, were you, Janet? But after she met him, she changed her mind."

"I was dead against it," Janet said. "I wanted to marry a man of my choosing. Then I met him and saw how handsome he is, and so tall. I'm very fortunate."

If tall and handsome were the only ingredients for a happy marriage, she would have a wonderful life ahead. I kept my cutting opinion to myself. As unwise as it was to choose a husband based on such superficial reasoning, I didn't want to be the one to upset her. I liked Janet's vivacity, so different to her mother's jaded character. Although, if I were Janet's mother, I'd worry about her naivety. I'd have waited until she was a little older before setting her up with a conservative man.

"Why not wait a few years?" I asked.

Janet's face suddenly flushed scarlet. She accepted the package from the sales assistant before hurrying to the exit.

Flossy raced after her. "Janet? Why is your face red?"

Janet walked out of the shop, strode up to our waiting carriage and climbed in. Flossy and I exchanged glances then got in too. I waited for the footman to close the door before pressing Janet.

"Is something wrong? Please, tell us. Perhaps we can help you."

She lowered her head. "It's nothing. Everything's all right now."

Flossy took Janet's hand. "We're your friends and sharing your burden might make you feel better."

Janet chewed her lower lip.

"You shouldn't take the secret to your wedding," Flossy

went on. "Share it with us and we'll advise you whether you should tell your fiancé or not. Cleo is very discreet, and wise, too."

I was pleased that I didn't have to be the one to do the coaxing, for once. I simply tried to look suitably discreet and wise as I sat opposite Janet and waited for her to talk.

She gave in with a small nod. "All right. But I assure you, it's nothing, really. While I can't say for certain, I think my marriage was arranged quickly because of an incident that happened a few months ago at Hambledon Hall. I told my Aunt Kershaw and she must have told my uncle and shortly after that, I was engaged." She shrugged slender shoulders. "It all happened so fast, but I do think that incident was what compelled them to marry me off to someone…safe."

"What incident?" I prompted.

"I was staying at their house and caught their gamekeeper watching me."

"At a shooting party?" Flossy asked.

"In the house. I was in my room, getting ready for bed. I heard a noise behind the wall panel beside the fireplace. I thought it was a mouse and went to look. I touched one of the wall panels, and must have released a mechanism. The panel opened like a door. Behind it was a large space, and the game-keeper was in it. I screamed and he fled. I told my aunt when she came to see what had upset me. Together, we found the tiny peephole in the panel that he must have been looking through into my room. She didn't know it was there, and said if she had, she would never have given me the room. She said my uncle didn't know either."

Flossy gasped. "Had the gamekeeper seen you *naked*?"

Janet lowered her head and nodded.

Flossy circled an arm around her friend's shoulders. "So your aunt and uncle thought you should be married after that?"

Janet lifted one shoulder. "I was engaged shortly after-ward, so I presume so. It all worked out for the best, though. My fiancé is a wonderful man. He'll take good care of me. I know he will."

Would he continue to take good care of her if he knew her uncle's family were linked to a scandal that could embarrass him, at best, and ruin his career, at worst? How far would Janet's family go to stop the secret from coming out?

* * *

I WAS LISTLESS when I returned to the hotel. I felt close to a breakthrough, but wanted to wait for Harmony to return from St. Michael's before I confronted Lord Kershaw. I needed solid proof before I accused his late father of being the father of the murdered gamekeeper, and that he, or one of the Brownings, murdered Esmond Shepherd to keep the secret from ruining Janet's marriage. If Harmony found nothing, my next port of call would be the General Registry Office. I hoped I didn't have to go that route. Getting records out of the GRO was time-consuming and this was something I wanted to get over with quickly. The sooner the killer was exposed, the sooner I could begin to repair the damage my investigation would cause to my relationship with my uncle and aunt.

I took the stairs rather than the lift up to the fourth floor to expend some of my nervous energy. When I reached my suite, I wondered if I should return downstairs to telephone Harry and talk it through with him. I decided not to when an opportunity presented itself.

Lady Elizabeth emerged from the lift. She thanked John, the lift operator, and walked slowly and unsteadily to her room. She stopped at her door and leaned the walking stick against the wall so that she could fish out the key from her bag. After a moment, she paused, sighed heavily and snapped the bag closed.

I approached and asked if she was all right. "Do you need some assistance?"

"I forgot that I gave my key to my nephew in the foyer earlier, so he could return my coat to my room. I realized I didn't need it as it's not that cold outside, after all. He never gave the key back, and now he's downstairs reading the newspaper in the smoking room and I'm all the way up here and can't get inside." She tapped the door with the end of her walking stick.

"Would you like to join me for a cup of tea? I can send a

message down to the kitchen through the speaking tube in my room and have someone retrieve your key."

Her face softened with her smile. "Would you? That's so kind, Miss Fox. Thank you." She took my arm and together we walked to my suite.

I sent word down to the kitchen for tea to be sent up along with Lady Elizabeth's key. We settled in the sitting room while we waited.

"Have you enjoyed your stay at the Mayfair?" I began.

"Very much so. I always like coming to London, although I do it so rarely, these days."

"Is that because your family sold their house in Marylebone?"

She showed no flicker of surprise that I knew. It must be common knowledge. "I miss that house. It was a handsome place, and very well located. My bedroom window over-looked the garden square and, thanks to its height, I could see couples having clandestine meetings behind the bushes. They thought they couldn't be seen." Her eyes twinkled with her laughter. "I was annoyed with my brother when he sold it."

"Why did he?"

"We didn't need it anymore."

"He sold it after 1855, didn't he?"

"That very year, it was," she said wistfully. "A long time ago, now."

"After Esmond was born there." I'd decided not to wait for Harmony. I was very sure of my theory, and the opportunity of speaking to Lady Elizabeth alone might not present itself again. The family was leaving the following morning.

She regarded me for a moment, her head tilted to the side. She showed no anger or concern, nor even a great deal of surprise. She almost seemed relieved. "Yes. Apparently Esmond Shepherd was born there, although I didn't know that at the time. When it became clear Susannah wouldn't survive, my brother took her home to Morcombe to die and gave up his son to Susannah's parents to raise as their own. He never entered the townhouse again and sold it soon after."

"He loved Susannah?"

"So Mabel Shepherd told me, years later."

"On her deathbed last month?"

"Oh no. After my brother died, five years ago."

"Who else knew Esmond was his son?"

"No one."

"Are you sure your brother's wife didn't know?"

"I don't think she did. It was never discussed. Not once. If she did, she hid it well. She and my brother had a perfectly good marriage, you see, and his relationship with Susannah took place before they married."

"Would your brother have married Susannah if she hadn't died?"

She tilted her head again as she studied me. "I didn't expect you to be so sentimental, Miss Fox."

"Would he?" I prompted.

"No. If marriage was his intention, he wouldn't have bedded her. He would have waited until they were husband and wife. My brother knew his duty, Miss Fox. Our parents drilled it into us from an early age that we had certain responsibilities as members of a noble family. My brother was just the heir at that time, but he had a strong sense of honor and duty. He knew he had to marry a young woman of good breeding, not the gamekeeper's daughter, no matter how much he cared for her or how many children she gave him."

The tea arrived and I directed the waiter to leave the tray on the table in the sitting room. Lady Elizabeth placed the room key that came with it in her purse while I poured.

"Not too full for me, please, Miss Fox." She showed me her shaking hand. "Halfway is safest."

I handed her a cup and saucer then sat down with mine. "It's quite the scandal you have buried in your family tree." I tried to sound lighthearted, as if it didn't matter.

"Oh yes, isn't it? If my brother were alive today, he'd be horrified to know I was talking to you about his business."

"What about your nephew, the current earl?"

She frowned. "Why would it upset him? It's not *his* scandal. Anyway, I told you. He doesn't know."

"Doesn't he?"

"As far as I am *aware*, he doesn't."

"Do you *suspect* though?"

She sighed and lowered the teacup to her lap. "Perhaps he does know. It's the only explanation for the bridleway closure. I tried talking to him about it but he wasn't interested. He brushed me off whenever I mentioned it. But he must have closed it to the public to keep Esmond Shepherd happy, after Esmond threatened to tell people about his real parents. I suspect my nephew wanted to protect his father's secret so agreed. It was a small price to pay. Anyway, he has reopened it now that…"

"Now that Esmond is no longer blackmailing him."

Her lips thinned in disapproval at the word.

"How do you think Esmond found out?" I asked.

"Through his mother, Mabel Shepherd. His *grandmother*, I mean."

"Do you know why Esmond wanted the bridleway closed?"

"It's close to his cottage. I assume he was tired of the public traipsing past his front door, and he saw this as an opportunity to force my nephew to stop them." She picked up the teacup and sipped.

I didn't mention the thefts. I no longer thought them relevant to the murder. "Are you going to tell Lord Kershaw you know why he closed the bridleway? Or that I know who Esmond's real parents were?"

"I see no reason to." She peered at me over the rim of her teacup. "Not unless I need to warn him that you are going to run to the gossip columnists."

"You know I won't," I said.

She nodded and sipped, satisfied with my response.

"But there is the matter of Esmond's murder…"

"You think my nephew did it? You think he killed Esmond to keep his father's secret from getting out?" She scoffed. "Don't be absurd, Miss Fox. Keeping the scandal from being made public may be enough of a reason to close the bridleway, but it's not enough to kill a man. His own half-brother, no less."

When she put it like that, she had a point. It wasn't a strong enough reason for such a terrible act. The shooting was calculated, perhaps even planned. It wasn't done in the heat of an argument. Even if Lord Kershaw didn't learn Esmond was his half-brother until quite recently, it would take a particular coldness to shoot someone he'd known his entire life. I couldn't imagine Lord Kershaw murdering Esmond Shepherd because they shared the same father. If the scandal came out, what of it? It would embarrass Lord Kershaw, but that was all.

I didn't throw out the theory altogether, however. "The scandal would affect Janet. Her conservative, politically ambitious fiancé wouldn't like it. He might even end their engagement over it."

Lady Elizabeth set down the teacup. "It's true. He might. But if he's affected by old gossip that has no bearing on anything at all, then good riddance. Janet will find someone else. Perhaps even someone more suited to her character than the stuffy fellow my nephew and his wife found." She took her walking stick and used it to push herself to her feet. "Thank you for the tea, Miss Fox. It was unexpectedly invigorating."

I walked her to the door. "I hope my questions haven't offended you."

She chuckled. "It takes a lot to offend me. A few impertinent questions about my family's naughty past aren't going to do it."

I watched her walk slowly along the corridor until she reached the door to her room, then returned inside my own. I sat at my desk and wrote notes to help my thoughts form. I got nowhere, however. Despite the connections between my suspects, and good theories, I lacked a powerful motive.

I checked the time on the clock. If I hurried, I might catch Harry before he left the office for the day. He might have some insights.

I was about to leave when Harmony arrived. She sported an air of satisfaction.

"You found something in the St. Michael's records?" I asked.

"I looked at the baptisms for 1855, and I found nothing."

"Then why do you look pleased?"

"Because a page was torn out of the baptism register. I brought it to the vicar's attention, and he said he hadn't noticed before. I think Esmond tore it out and kept it as proof."

"He must have. But I no longer think it matters who his

father was. It's not a strong enough motive to kill him. After all this time, it's a modest scandal, at worst. Enough for Janet's fiancé to give up on her, but not enough to kill Esmond Shepherd to stop him revealing it. I doubt even Janet would kill him if she suspected he was going to make the information public. She's in love with the *idea* of getting married more than she's in love with the man she's marrying."

Harmony flopped onto the sofa and kicked off her shoes. "What about her father, Mr. Browning? If he has debts and the future son-in-law is wealthy, he might be planning to borrow from him. Esmond could ruin his plans by exposing the scandal."

"Mr. Browning had a better moneymaking scheme with the thefts. Esmond Shepherd was more valuable to him alive, by blackmailing Lord Kershaw into closing the bridleway and turning a blind eye to the items that went missing from his house." I sighed. "I'm sorry, Harmony. I sent you to St. Michael's for nothing."

"You can make it up to me by allowing me to nap on your sofa. I have two hours before it's time to do your hair for dinner."

I'd almost forgotten we were dining with the Kershaws again, since it was their final night at the hotel. "Take the bed. It's more comfortable. I'll read a book in here."

There was a knock at the door. I opened it to find Mr. Hobart standing there. "I hoped to find you in here, Miss Fox. I have a message for you."

"From Harry?"

"Reverend Pritchard. He telephoned and asked me to pass on the following information." Mr. Hobart cleared his throat. "He happened to be looking through an old marriage register in the church and discovered a page had been torn out. He doesn't know when it was torn out or by whom, but he thought it might be relevant to your investigation, given the date."

"The date?"

"The page included marriages conducted in early 1855. He said it was a year that meant something to you." He arched his brows in question.

"It does indeed, Mr. Hobart. Thank you for coming here personally. That is very interesting."

I closed the door and turned to see Harmony was on her feet, with no sign of tiredness. "A torn page from the St. Michael's baptism register and now one from the Morcombe marriage register, both pages from the year 1855. It can't be a coincidence."

"There's only one reason Esmond Shepherd would be interested in the marriage register," I went on. "He found a record that his parents got married. He's *legitimate*, Harmony. And since he was the eldest son of the fifth earl of Kershaw, *he* was the rightful sixth earl."

That must be it! *That* was the strong motive I'd been missing. Esmond Shepherd was killed so he couldn't tell anyone *he* should be the earl. It put the man known as the current Lord Kershaw at the top of my suspect list with several exclamation marks and a circle around his name.

CHAPTER 17

J sat at my writing desk and drew a family tree in pencil, with the fourth Lord and Lady Kershaw at the top on the left. On the right, I wrote the names of Mabel and William Shepherd. I ruled solid lines from the Kershaw side to their two children, Lady Elizabeth Wentworth and her brother, the fifth earl, the man who'd married the Shepherds' daughter before he inherited the title. Their marriage would probably have angered his parents, if they'd known. I wasn't yet sure if they had. It was possible only the local vicar and the obligatory witness knew at the time.

"The marriage must have occurred in secret," I said to Harmony. "Otherwise it would be common knowledge in Morcombe."

She peered over my shoulder and pointed to the name of Esmond Shepherd. "There should be a dotted line connecting him to his adoptive parents, Mabel and William, and a solid one connecting him to his real parents, Susannah and the fifth earl."

I ruled the lines as described. "If the fourth earl didn't know about his son's secret marriage at the time, surely he found out when Susannah died." I tapped the pencil against my chin as I realized something didn't add up. "The name recorded in the parish register for burials was Susannah *Shepherd*, her maiden name, not Wentworth."

"The fourth Lord Kershaw could have used his influence

to force the vicar to record it that way, so that nobody found out his son married her."

That would explain it. It seemed he'd known after all, but perhaps not at first. "The fourth Lord Kershaw may have been the one who tore out the marriage register page. I wonder if he also tore out the pages in the St. Michael's baptism register, or if that was Esmond's doing."

"I think it was all Esmond's," Harmony said. "He must have had *some* proof, otherwise it's just slanderous gossip nobody would believe." She watched as I extended the family tree with branches for the sixth Lord Kershaw and his sister, Mrs. Browning. It just occurred to me that Mrs. Browning had a relationship with her half-brother. I wonder if she knew.

Harmony traced her finger along the lines up the tree, stopping at Lady Elizabeth. "Do you think she knows? Do you think she knew all along? She's the only one alive now who was old enough to be aware of events back then, *and* the fifth earl was her brother."

If she did know, she'd lied to my face.

Harmony leaned her hip against the edge of the desk and crossed her arms. "Why bother hiding the marriage after Susannah died? Her husband was free to marry again, and to a woman of his family's choosing if that was so important to them. Why not admit that he'd married Susannah, thereby making Esmond legitimate? By denying the marriage, he denied his son legitimacy and all that goes with it."

"I suspect that was the intention. As the firstborn son, Esmond would inherit and become the sixth earl. Any sons of a second wife would simply be spares. The best wifely prospects from the best families would never accept that, and the Kershaws wanted only the best."

Harmony pulled a face. "I've seen blood sports that are less brutal."

"When you realize that, murdering Esmond makes sense. It didn't before, but this…" I underlined his name on the family tree. "His legitimacy is the motive. With proof, he could oust the current Lord Kershaw. Imagine the upheaval."

"Proof," Harmony echoed. "Where is it? Those torn pages must be somewhere."

"Unless whoever killed Esmond destroyed them. That's

what they were looking for in Esmond's cottage after he died. Some time after we looked through it that first day, and before Harry and I went back, someone searched high and low. They must have been looking for the pages torn out of the registers, which Esmond told his killer he possessed. The question is, did they find them? And have they been destroyed?"

* * *

DINNER in the hotel restaurant was a laborious affair. Now that I was confident I knew why Esmond had been killed, and that Lord Kershaw was most likely the killer, I couldn't concentrate on the chatter around me. I tried to surreptitiously watch him while he talked and ate, bearing the new information in mind.

I was also very aware that I hadn't talked it through with Harry yet. It wasn't that I needed to; Harmony had been an excellent sounding board. I simply *wanted* to talk to him. It would have to wait until the morning.

Despite my frustration, I think I managed rather well to keep my features schooled and pretend nothing had changed. I listened to just enough conversation to contribute a comment here and there or laugh at an appropriate moment. When dinner eventually came to an end and it was time for the ladies to retreat to the private sitting room, I pretended I didn't have a care in the world. All the while, I sifted through the evidence in my head, sorting absolute facts from the circumstantial, and deciding who I needed to speak to next.

The person who emerged as most likely to tell me something of use turned out to be Mrs. Browning. While Lady Elizabeth possessed decades' worth of knowledge, I decided not to speak to her again. I suspected she'd already given me everything she would, or could. Likewise, Lord Kershaw was unlikely to admit he killed his half-brother so he could keep the title for himself. Mrs. Browning, however, had known Esmond very well. As her lover, he may have told her things he'd not told anyone else. Even if he'd not known who his parents really were in those days, he might have told her about hiding places within his cottage. Places where he could have hidden the proof of his birth.

The problem was, I didn't want to reveal that I knew about the circumstances surrounding Esmond's birth. For one thing, it could make Mrs. Browning clam up altogether. For another, it could place me in danger if she informed the killer.

I waited until tea and coffee were brought in by the waiters. I helped serve then took a seat beside Mrs. Browning. She couldn't get up without appearing rude in front of everyone.

Realizing I'd cornered her, she sighed heavily. "What is it now, Miss Fox?"

"I simply wanted to speak to you on your last night with us. Have you enjoyed your stay in London, Mrs. Browning?"

"Well enough. Thank you for accompanying my daughter this morning to Harrods. She says the tiepin was your suggestion. I think it's a good choice for her fiancé."

"He's going into politics, I hear. How exciting for them both. What an interesting life they have ahead of them."

She narrowed her gaze at me as she sipped her coffee, perhaps trying to detect if I were being sarcastic.

"I'm looking forward to their wedding," I went on. "Janet tells me it will be a lavish affair."

Her gaze narrowed further.

I couldn't work out why. "Is something the matter, Mrs. Browning? Have I offended you?"

"I don't know why you think me a fool, Miss Fox, but clearly you do."

"Pardon?"

"You sit next to the one person in this room you don't like very much, and who doesn't particularly like you, when there are several other places available."

"I like you." It sounded lame, even to me. "You intrigue me," I added with a little more confidence.

"You pretend to engage me in conversation with the sole purpose of finding out more information about my family, in the hope of pinning Esmond's murder on one of them."

"That's not—"

"Stop it," she said with pained effort. "Why do you care so much about the death of a man you never knew?" Her breath suddenly hitched. "Did something happen between you before his death?"

"No! I only met him once, in Lord Kershaw's office. He was reading a book while he waited for his lordship, but left before he arrived. Our encounter was brief and a little odd, if I'm honest."

"Liar."

I blinked rapidly. "I assure you, that's what happened. That is *all* that happened. Not every woman found him attractive."

"It must be a lie. You can't have caught him reading. He can't read very well. He would not pick up a book while he waited. He'd hum a tune or do a jig, anything but read."

I turned to face her fully. "Are you saying he *couldn't* read? Not at all?"

"He could a little, but not well. It's not for lack of trying over the years. He went to school with the village children. My father even paid for my brother's tutor to teach him, but Esmond didn't progress. He was sensitive about it and didn't want people to know. It wasn't common knowledge. I tried helping him to read and write, too, but he just couldn't grasp it. He'd jumble up the letters and write them back to front. He'd get cross from frustration, so I gave up before we had a falling out over it."

I'd heard about word blindness. It had nothing to do with a person's level of intelligence. It was simply a phenomenon that happened to a few and meant they couldn't read as well as others.

"Esmond wasn't stupid." Mrs. Browning sounded protective. Despite everything he'd said and done, she still loved him enough to ensure falsehoods weren't spread about him. "He just needed time to concentrate on the words to make sense of them."

A slow reader would want to read an important document at their leisure. They would take it home to read in a comfortable and familiar environment without others around.

That's why Esmond had torn out the pages in the registers —to read them properly and carefully in his own time. They were proof of his legitimacy, and his right to be the earl. Understanding them was of vital importance.

I thanked Mrs. Browning. Not only had she inadvertently given me the reason why Esmond had taken the pages, she'd also given me a possible location of where he'd hidden them.

Unless, of course, they'd been found and destroyed.

I spent the next little while chatting to Lady Kershaw. After half an hour, I'd scored an invitation to accompany the family back to Hambledon Hall the following day. Under the pretense of being a keen art lover, I said I wanted to take a closer look at the masterpieces acquired by several generations of Kershaw earls. Not only would such an excuse get me back inside the house, it would also allow me a measure of freedom to wander around.

My evening was cut short when the gentlemen returned. Aunt Lilian wanted to retire and asked me to accompany her upstairs, to use my steadying arm for support. Since my arm was not as sturdy as her husband's or son's, I braced myself.

I was right to be worried.

Once we stepped out of the lift on the fourth floor, she let go of my arm. She turned to me, her once-clear eyes full of despair, the shadowed skin around them bearing evidence of her exhaustion. "Does loyalty mean nothing to you, Cleopatra?"

"I, er…yes, of course, it does."

"Your uncle and I took you in. We didn't have to. We could have let you fend for yourself in Cambridge."

"I know, and I'm grateful. Aunt, what—?"

"This is how you repay us? By accusing our friends of murder?"

"I haven't accused anyone."

"You will. I know you will. You have that air about you." The muscles in her face twitched before distorting with a myriad of emotions that were too fleeting for me to identify.

Before I could assure her that I wouldn't accuse anyone without proof, she continued, her voice as thin and frail as her figure, like a woman twice her age. "Your grandparents wouldn't let us adopt you after your parents died. They didn't want us anywhere near you. Our money was good enough, but *we* weren't."

Tears stung the backs of my eyes, but I didn't let them spill. I felt compelled to defend my paternal grandparents.

They'd just lost their only child in a terrible accident, and his daughter was all they had left. They didn't want to lose me, too. And knowing Uncle Ronald as I did now, he would have found some way to diminish their influence in my life. "They only took enough money for my upbringing and education. Nothing more. They didn't want—"

"What about what I wanted?" she snapped. "Nobody *ever* asked me. Not my parents, not your mother, my husband, or your grandparents. Why do *my* feelings not matter?"

That was the heart of her pain, the reason for her melancholy, which led to her becoming addicted to the cocaine-laced tonic. It wasn't my investigation into the death of her friends' gamekeeper that caused us to reach this point. It was a lifetime of feeling inferior. Whether others had genuinely put her down, or whether it was her innate lack of self-confidence that imagined it so, I didn't know. Indeed, it didn't really matter. She felt that way, and that had plunged her into the depths of despair.

"Your feelings matter to me, Aunt." I reached for her, but she slapped my hand away.

"You hold *them* in such high regard." Her words were a little slurred, and her train of thought difficult to follow.

"My grandparents?"

"Higher regard than you hold your uncle and me. So selfish, just like your mother. She and Ronald were supposed to marry, but she changed her mind. He could have made it difficult for her. He could have insisted the arrangement go ahead, but he let her go because he wanted her to be happy. He settled for me instead." She tapped bony fingers hard against her chest. "The stupid sister. The dull one. The ugly one."

"You are none of those, Aunt. You are beautiful, inside and out." I went to circle my arms around her, but she pushed me away with surprising strength. I lost my balance and stumbled into the wall.

She spun around and raced along the corridor to her room. She did not look back and slammed the door behind her.

I tasted the salty tear as it slid onto my lips. I wasn't sure when I'd started to cry, but I couldn't stop. My heart hurt. My throat ached and my head felt woolly. I couldn't think.

Instinct took over. It was the only explanation for what I did next.

I ran down the stairs to the foyer. Philip, the night porter, said something to me. I didn't hear his words as I opened the door myself and ran outside.

Later, I tried to remember how the air had felt on my skin. Was it cold? Damp? I had no jacket or coat, just my silk evening dress, yet I felt nothing but a driving force that propelled me along Piccadilly, past the Circus, toward Soho. I pushed open the black door between the confectionery and tobacco shops, and raced up the stairs. I knocked on another door without hesitation.

It seemed to take an age before it opened. Harry stood there in trousers and an undervest. "Cleo! What is it? What's wrong?"

I buried my face in my hands and burst into great, gulping, ugly sobs.

His arms came around me and drew me against his body. The thud of his heart against my cheek wasn't as steady as I expected it to be, but he was warm and solid and wonderful.

I didn't know how long we stood on his threshold, me sobbing into his chest. It could have been seconds or several minutes. As my crying eased, my mind began to finally clear, and I realized the full implications of where I'd gone in my moment of greatest need, and why.

Harry drew away. He took my face in his hands and tilted it up. His thumbs wiped my damp cheeks and his worried gaze searched mine. "What happened, Cleo?"

"Not out here. Let's go inside."

He hesitated. Swallowed. "I don't think that's a good idea given your state. And mine."

"I don't care, Harry. I don't care."

Still, he hesitated.

Very well. If it had to happen on the threshold in full view of his neighbors, if they cared to look, then so be it. I cupped his face as he cupped mine and drew it down to my level. I stood on my toes and kissed him.

It was neither fierce nor hungry; it was full of longing.

Releasing my emotions after suppressing them for months was cathartic. It allowed for a flood of new feelings to take their place, and they filled me more completely than anything ever had.

Harry pulled away. His breaths were ragged, his eyes shining feverishly in the dim light from the stairwell. He let me go and tucked his hands behind his back. "You're upset, Cleo. You're not thinking properly. We should talk about this when you feel more yourself."

"I am myself, Harry, and I am thinking properly."

He crossed his arms over his chest, only to lower them to his sides again, then tuck them behind his back once more. He didn't know what to do with them. "Cleo… I can't do this if you mean to go on as we were. I've tried being just a friend, being patient with you…" He shook his head. "I can't anymore. Not now. Not after that kiss. Either we move forward or…" He swallowed. "Or we don't see each other anymore."

I stepped closer and reached around behind him. I took his hands in mine and looked up at him. He blinked rapidly down at me. "Since I cannot imagine my life without you in it, Harry, it seems the decision is made. We move forward. Together."

His fingers twined with mine behind his back. A slow smile teased his lips, causing his dimples to make a sudden appearance before disappearing again. I wanted to capture that smile and bring the dimples back.

I kissed him. He released my fingers and circled his arms around me and kissed me, too.

When it ended, Harry pressed his forehead to mine. "Is this real? Or am I still dreaming?"

"It's real."

"Good," he said on a contented sigh. "Let me dress and I'll take you home."

I waited just inside the door while he disappeared into the adjoining bedroom. Harry's flat was rather plain, befitting a bachelor who never brought home female guests. Photographs of his birth mother, as well as the parents who'd adopted him, added a personal touch, as did books on architecture and science. He owned a few novels, but they weren't well-thumbed like mine. There was no dust on the furniture, in stark contrast to Esmond Shepherd's cottage where dust and grime were everywhere.

Harry emerged from the bedroom fully clothed, a jacket slung over his arm. He took a coat from the stand and placed it around my shoulders, then put on the jacket. "Ready?"

The fabric at his shoulder was crumpled. I smoothed it with the palm of my hand then stroked his jaw, rough with stubble. "Ready."

He turned his face and kissed my wrist, then he took my hand and led me outside.

We continued to hold hands as we walked. "Now, tell me why you were crying. What happened?"

"My aunt said some things…" I shook my head. "It doesn't matter what she said. I wasn't crying because I'd taken her words to heart, I was upset because I didn't recognize her. Aunt Lilian is sweet and kind. The woman she has become isn't her, and I was upset because I want her back. I don't know how to go about it, Harry. I don't even know how to begin."

"You can't do much unless she wants to get better."

"I know, and in the meantime, I'll be there for her, although it won't be easy if she continues to say nasty things."

Harry squeezed my hand. "We need to speak to a doctor who specializes in cocaine addiction. Perhaps with a little guidance, we can be more useful."

"Should we ask your uncle for a name?" As hotel manager, Mr. Hobart could get his hands on the rarest of things, from tickets to sold-out theater shows, to appointments with the Prince of Wales's tailor. But a doctor specializing in cocaine addiction might be beyond him. Indeed, I doubted such a fellow even existed. It was an affliction most medical professionals didn't even recognize as a problem.

"I'll ask Dr. Garside," Harry said.

"The scientist from St. Mary's Hospital who helped us on the poisoning case?"

"The same. He's well-connected and keeps up to date on medical breakthroughs and theories. If anyone knows of a specialist in the field, he will."

My heart swelled. Harry had offered me kind words and support before, but this time he was giving me more. He was giving me a practical solution, and that gave me hope.

I stopped between lampposts and drew him into another kiss. He lifted me onto my toes in his eagerness. Even though we were on a main street, it was late at night and the light was poor. If someone we knew happened to pass by, they wouldn't know it was us. Although we'd moved our relationship a giant leap forward tonight, we still had obstacles to overcome. The greatest obstacle of all being my family. I didn't want to be forced to face that obstacle until we were both ready.

We continued our walk but stopped holding hands as we drew closer to the hotel. Harry asked if he could see me in the morning, but I had to decline.

"I've made arrangements to go to Hambledon Hall, and I don't want to lose the opportunity to look around inside." I told him what I'd learned that day, beginning with the telephone call from Reverend Pritchard and finishing with Mrs. Browning's revelation about Esmond Shepherd's difficulty reading.

Harry didn't say anything, but I could see he was worried. "I'll come to Morcombe, too. Meet me in the teashop when it's all over."

"I'll be all right," I assured him. "There won't be any danger to me."

"I'm not worried about your safety. I want to make sure you haven't changed your mind about this."

I laughed softly before kissing him again. "I won't, but your company on the journey home will be welcome."

Someone standing behind Harry cleared his throat, making me jump. Harry stepped aside to reveal Victor, arms crossed over his chest. Despite the formidable pose, he looked amused and rather smug.

"You're lucky Philip fetched me and not Sir Ronald or Mr. Bainbridge," he said. "He suspected you'd gone to see a… friend and thought it best if another friend went to check you'd arrived safely, rather than send a family member after you. I was just finishing my shift."

If I'd been capable of clear thought at the time, I would

have realized Philip would worry. It may not be terribly late and there were still many respectable people making their way to and from theaters and private parties, but it was nighttime and I was a lone female. To think of fetching Victor, who was not only my friend but someone who was still in the building rather than in his room at the residence hall, was well done indeed.

My hasty goodbye to Harry wasn't as heartfelt as I would have liked given the momentousness of the evening, but I felt awkward in front of Victor. When we reached the door to the hotel, I turned around and waved.

Harry stood there, watching, and waved back.

CHAPTER 18

*R*enton the butler didn't express his displeasure at seeing me at Hambledon Hall with words. He was polite as he took my coat and passed it to the footman, his tone pleasant as he welcomed me back, along with Lord and Lady Kershaw, and Lady Elizabeth. It was the way he followed me about the house that was the clue to his distrust.

As I moved from one reception room to the next, studying the portraits and landscapes in their ornate gilt frames, he pretended to have something to do in that same room. He ran a gloved finger along pristine tabletops and moved decanters before returning them to their original position. He adjusted hanging pictures that were perfectly straight and checked a doorknob, commenting to himself that it was loose.

All the while, I made notes in my notebook on the paintings I'd found. I appreciated art, so the ruse was easy and enjoyable. I'd resolved to wait all day if necessary, but a short while later, as I studied a Constable landscape in the drawing room, a footman whispered something in the butler's ear. With an annoyed glance in my direction, Renton and the footman both left.

I peered around the door. No one was about. Tiptoeing across the entrance hall tiles, I made my way up the stairs to Lord Kershaw's office. If he was inside, I would once again wait. As I knocked gently, I spied a suitable place to hide where I could watch the entire corridor, but it proved unnecessary. There was no answer.

The door was locked, but I had it open within a minute. Pocketing my lockpicking tool kit, I slipped inside. I wasted no time scanning the bookshelf. It was low and not particularly wide, but it was crammed with all manner of books. They covered a variety of topics, from farming to geography, philosophy to art. Lord Kershaw had a great many intellectual interests. Or perhaps they were just for show.

I hadn't noticed what book Esmond Shepherd had been holding when I'd first met him in the office, but the leather cover had been green. I removed one leather-bound green book after another, opening them and fanning their pages, shaking them out so that loose pages would fall.

The fifth book spilled its secrets onto the carpet. There were two, each one a torn page from a parish register— Esmond's baptism and the marriage of his parents, seven months earlier. Just as I'd thought, the baptism listed Susannah's married name, Wentworth, not Shepherd. Esmond had hidden them here for safekeeping, perhaps intending to retrieve them later as proof, but not getting the chance before Lord Kershaw killed him. Lord Kershaw had desperately searched the gamekeeper's cottage for them, when they'd been under his nose the entire time.

I folded the pages and placed them in my bag, then went to slot the book back on the bookshelf. I ran my hand over the leather cover. It was a different shade of green to the stain I'd seen on Lord Kershaw's fingers. I still didn't know where the stain had come from, but it no longer mattered. It wasn't a clue after all.

I returned the book to the shelf and straightened. A document on the desk caught my eye, only because the stamped lettering across it was so bold in its finality: withdrawn.

The document was old, made from what I assumed to be parchment, not paper. Small weights held down the corners, keeping it flat. If I removed them, it would roll up into a scroll. The flourishing handwriting and old English spelling made it difficult to read, but I gathered the gist of it easily enough. It was a legal document that Lord Kershaw probably retrieved from his solicitor's office when in London. The document granted the public the right to use the bridleway on the estate. It was dated 1538. The stamped word WITH-DRAWN had the much later date accompanying it in smaller writing—1865 and the signature of the fourth Lord Kershaw. I wondered why he'd withdrawn the public's right to use the bridleway. Not that it mattered now. What mattered was that the current Lord Kershaw had proof it should have been *closed* these last thirty-five years, yet he'd opened it as soon as the threat of blackmail disappeared with the death of Esmond Shepherd. He'd wanted to return access to the villagers even though he didn't legally have to.

He was a kind man, the murder notwithstanding.

I checked the corridor was empty before slipping out of the office. I closed the door and walked quickly, my mind reeling. I couldn't decide what to do next. Inform Sergeant Honeyman? Scotland Yard? Or let Lord Kershaw remain a free man? Talking it over with Harry would help.

A door suddenly opened, wrenching me out of my thoughts. Lady Elizabeth stared at me, blinking in surprise at seeing me outside her bedchamber.

"Sorry if I startled you," I said. "I was just passing."

She glanced along the corridor, in the direction of her nephew's office. "Heading to the morning room, Miss Fox? There's a lovely Landseer in there for you to study."

"Are you referring to the pretty watercolor of a cottage? I saw it when I was staying here, although I believe it's by William Henry Hunt, not Edwin Landseer."

I smiled. She smiled back. It was clear she didn't trust me. She must suspect I wasn't there to study the artwork, but her failure to trick me meant she couldn't prove it and confront me. She had no power to stop me roaming the house.

"I'm going that way." She used her walking stick to point in the direction from which I'd just come, as she emerged fully from her room. She closed the door behind her.

But not before I'd seen something inside that made my heart thud and my mind spin.

Lady Elizabeth and I parted, each heading in different directions. Once she was out of view, I doubled back and entered her bedchamber.

I was surrounded by walls painted in soft teal green. It

was the same shade I'd noticed staining Lord Kershaw's finger in the hours after the murder. I'd thought it came from a plant, but now realized it must have been paint that he couldn't remove quickly with soap and water. There was only one reason Lord Kershaw, rather than a footman, would be painting Lady Elizabeth's room when he was hosting guests —he was covering something up.

The room was located at the front of the house, over-looking the driveway, lawn and woods beyond. Anyone who glanced out of the window would have seen the body of Esmond Shepherd lying dead on the gravel.

Anyone who opened this window would have been in the perfect position to shoot him.

A frail killer would need to rest the rifle against the sill to steady her hands, as well as be experienced at using such a weapon to hit a moving target. Lady Elizabeth had told me herself that she'd been spirited when she was younger, and it wasn't a great leap to assume that meant she was active, and that shooting was a sport she excelled at. I suspected the entire family enjoyed shooting parties. Just because Lady Elizabeth was too old to participate during our visit, didn't mean she never had.

The paint on the windowsill did indeed seem fresher than the walls. Lady Elizabeth must have enlisted her nephew's help to cover up some scuff marks she made while positioning the rifle, and possibly when it fired. He'd arrived at the body very quickly and seemed genuinely shocked to see Esmond Shepherd dead. It was likely his aunt hadn't involved him until later, at which point he painted over the scuff marks and disposed of the rifle. It was a solid theory, but proving it to the satisfaction of the police would be difficult. The only evidence I had was the paint stain I'd seen on Lord Kershaw's finger.

I scanned the room as I turned to leave and my gaze settled on the fireplace, reminding me of something Janet Browning said. Esmond Shepherd had watched her from his position in a cavity behind a wall panel beside the fireplace. Could this room have a similar hiding place?

Despite being a relatively modern house, it had been built with a Gothic aesthetic, complete with towers and battlements. Many original Gothic manors had secret passages or hiding places. Just how many of them had the architect of the new Hambledon Hall put in? As someone who'd lived through its construction, Lady Elizabeth would know every inch of the building.

I pressed on the wall panel beside the fireplace until it sprang open like a door, just as Janet described. The cavity beyond was large enough to fit a man, but the rifle didn't need as much space.

I removed it, and the box of bullets.

"I see you found it, Miss Fox." Lady Elizabeth closed the door behind her then approached me, leaning heavily on her walking stick.

"You shot him." I nodded at the window. "From there. You rested the rifle on the windowsill, scratching off some of the paint." The rifle appeared clean, but a closer inspection under a magnifying glass might yield paint flecks of the same shade as the sill. "You hid the rifle behind the wall panel then came downstairs with everyone else. Later, you informed Lord Kershaw, and he repainted the sill."

"I won't insult you by denying it. You're right about all of it."

"You're a very good shot."

"Thank you. I preferred shooting at a target with a rifle than at birds with a shotgun. It requires more skill." She crossed the room and sat on the chair at the breakfast table positioned near the window. The view was lovely. Deadly, too. "Everyone has forgotten that I used to ride and shoot as well as any man. I could swim, too, and I loved climbing trees before my mother found out and put an end to it. It wasn't ladylike, she said. Neither was having a brain, in those days."

I couldn't help my wry smile. "Not much has changed since, unfortunately."

Her smile matched mine. "At least women can attend university lectures now. Not that my parents would have allowed me to. I had to do what they wished and marry well. That's what daughters of earls do."

"Yet you didn't marry."

"They promised me they would never force me to marry a man against my wishes. I could choose my own husband, as long as they approved of him. But I never found a man I could respect who was also good enough for my parents. As time wore on, and my looks faded, it became clear I wouldn't marry. Instead, I took care of my aging parents and involved myself in charity work. That's what single women of good breeding do. They make themselves useful, until they are no longer of use to anyone." She smacked the palm of her hand on the head of the walking stick as if blaming the device for her frailty. "Once you can no longer get out and about with ease, it's as though you cease to have a purpose. That's the thing about becoming old. Everyone forgets you used to be intelligent, sporty, and fun."

"The villagers used the word dutiful to describe you," I said. "They have a lot of respect for you."

"Thank you for telling me, Miss Fox. It lifts my spirits to hear that all my hard work hasn't gone unnoticed." She sighed. "Duty is all I've had for so many years. Duty to my parents, to my position as daughter of the fourth earl of Kershaw, duty as a member of society. My brother came to realize his duty, too, although it took him longer than me. He was a little wayward when he was younger. He was a dreamer." She huffed. "I suppose he thought he was in love with Susannah and that's why he married her. You do know about that, don't you, Miss Fox? They married."

"I know. Their son, Esmond, was legitimate. You told me you learned who his father was five years ago, when your brother died, but that's not true, is it?"

"I only found out when my nephew told me, on the same day Esmond informed him. Esmond's mother, Mabel Shepherd—*grandmother*," she corrected herself, "died a month ago, but the slovenly fellow only recently got around to tidying up her things in the cottage they shared. That's when he found her letter, addressed to him. He went in search of the evidence in the parish registers and presented it to my nephew. My nephew asked me what I recollected of that time, and if I knew. Of course I hadn't known about the marriage or that my brother fathered Esmond. I only knew my brother had a brief but rather intense relationship with Susannah that ended when she died. He never mentioned they'd married, and Susannah hid her pregnancy well. Mabel Shepherd hid the entire saga well, too. I'm still in shock over the fact a woman I'd known my entire life gave no indication of the secret. Not even a hint. She didn't leave *me* a letter, just Esmond."

"If Mabel Shepherd knew Esmond was legitimate, why did she and her husband pretend he was their son? Why not force your brother to acknowledge him?"

"Apparently her letter to Esmond said that *my* father had paid them well to keep silent. They were good people, the Shepherds. Honest, hardworking people who knew Esmond would never be fully accepted by my family or society because of his mother's low birth. They decided he would have a better life if he were brought up as *their* child."

"They did their duty as employees of Lord Kershaw," I said.

"Duty," she muttered, a bitter edge to her tone.

"Your father, the fourth earl, knew the truth?"

"So it seems. Looking back, I think that's why he let the rumor about himself being Susannah's father swirl unchecked. That rumor threw everyone off the scent and distracted them from discovering the truth. Perhaps he even started the rumor. It began just after she died, when my parents were suddenly treating the Shepherds well. The cottage got renovated, they were allowed to shoot as many birds as they wanted for themselves, and my father never said a harsh word against them. Not one. I remember the first time my brother heard the rumor. He was livid. He and my father argued about it, and my father told him not to deny it. Now I know why."

"Your brother loved Susannah."

Lady Elizabeth huffed again. "Floozy that she was, yes he did. Despite his loss, he did his duty and married not long after she died. You may think it odd that he didn't claim his own son, but you must understand that my brother was under our father's control. His marriage to Susannah was the only rebellious thing he ever did, and her death seemed to stun him into dutiful complaisance. His second wife was the opposite of Susannah. Steady, not too bright, but from a good family. I suppose the haste of their marriage was our father's influence again, ensuring my brother's eye didn't fall on someone unsuitable for a second time."

"Your father sounds like an authoritarian figure."

"He was strict and mean."

"He wanted to close the bridleway to the public, even though they had a legitimate right to use it, according to a document dated 1538."

She looked surprised that I knew. "He legally withdrew that right, but never enforced it. He was quite ill by then. The villagers never found out, so when my nephew did finally close the bridleway, naturally there was uproar in Morcombe."

"Led by Mr. Faine, but only as a pretense," I went on. "He, Esmond and Mr. Browning thought a little agitation would stop the police from looking at them as suspects in the thefts from Hambledon Hall, if the thefts were reported. Which they weren't. Lord and Lady Kershaw decided not to tell Sergeant Honeyman. As long as only replaceable things were stolen, they were willing to overlook their brother-in-law's crime."

"I'm not sure either of them care about Gordon Browning that much. Esmond had informed my nephew of his legitimacy by then, so it was imperative to keep that a secret. Esmond wanted money at first, but it wasn't enough. He quickly spent it on trinkets and clothes that he thought would make him a gentleman. The closure of the bridleway became his next demand, and there would have been more. Much more."

The blackmail explained the gold pocket watch and good clothes we'd found in the cottage.

Lady Elizabeth leaned both hands on her walking stick and studied me. "I must say, Miss Fox, you have learned more than I expected you to. It's heartening to see a woman succeeding in a man's business. Well done."

"Thank you. Although part of me is sorry to have learned the truth."

"Will it help your conscience if I tell you why I did it?"

"I think I already know. At first I thought it was to keep the bloodline pure. Esmond was young enough to marry and have legitimate children, and you didn't want the Kershaw title to be tainted by the lower orders. But you lack the snobbery for that to be your motive. Now I think it's because Esmond was a horrid man and you simply wanted to keep him from destroying your lives."

"I am glad you came to exclude your original theory. It makes me sound monstrous. You are quite right about not wanting Esmond to take over. His demand to close the bridleway was only the beginning, a way of keeping Faine and Gordon happy until he was ready for the next stage. Esmond *threatened* my nephew, telling him he would demand he relinquish the title when the time was right. I couldn't allow such a despicable person to become earl, to live in this house, and *ruin* it all. My nephew and his wife don't deserve the humiliation. This is their home. It's their children's home. If Esmond didn't gamble it all away, he would have lost it through mismanagement eventually. Even if Esmond never had children, and my great-nephew inherited after him, there would be nothing left to inherit."

"You would have lost your home, too," I pointed out. "Unless Esmond was gracious enough to allow you to spend your remaining years here."

She barked a laugh. "Gracious is not a word you could associate with that man." She readjusted her grip on the head of the walking stick. "What happens now, Miss Fox? Will I be handed over to Sergeant Honeyman?"

"Would he do anything if you were?"

"If the evidence is incontrovertible, he would have to."

I studied the rifle, still in my hand. "This is a modern weapon, entirely made in a factory. It's impossible to compare a bullet fired from it to the one removed from the body. Microscopes simply aren't strong enough to detect such minor striations, if they exist. The paint smudge on Lord Kershaw's finger is circumstantial, at best, and won't hold up in court. Added to which, I doubt a jury would convict a lady of good character who is respected by villagers and peers alike."

"Or an elderly lady, which is sweet of you not to mention."

"It would come down to me recounting your confession in court, and whether a jury would believe me. I'm not sure I want to go through that. It would upset my aunt and uncle, and Aunt Lilian has enough on her plate. Also, to be quite frank, Lady Elizabeth, I don't think you're a threat to society."

She nodded. "Not to mention Esmond wasn't worth the trouble. No one is mourning him."

"Not even Mrs. Browning?"

"He spied on her daughter in the privacy of her bedroom. Not even Cicely could love him after that. Besides which, a court case would lead to the truth about Esmond's birth and I don't think Cicely could cope if she found out her lover was her half-brother. I suspect that might send her down the same path your aunt has taken."

I returned the rifle and bullets to their hiding place and closed the panel. Once shut, it was impossible to tell it was a door. I then handed over the two torn pages of church records. "I believe you've been looking for these."

"Ah, yes. Thank you." She held them at arm's length and squinted to read them. "My nephew searched the gamekeeper's cottage after Esmond's death but couldn't locate them."

So it was Lord Kershaw who'd been in the cottage before Harry and me, leaving behind evidence of his search. I suspected it was Esmond himself who'd moved the photo of Susanna after he read Mabel's letter.

"There's a price for my silence," I said.

She arched her brows. "How much do you want?"

"It's not for me. It's for Miss Crippen. She's going to have Esmond's baby soon, and as an unwed mother, the road ahead will be difficult for her. I'd like you to pay for the child's upbringing." I'd promised Miss Crippen I wouldn't divulge her secret to anyone, but I felt an exception needed to be made, for the baby's sake.

Lady Elizabeth nodded without hesitation.

I gave her Miss Crippen's address. "Goodbye for now. I'll see you at Janet's wedding."

"Goodbye, Miss Fox. Close the door on your way out." She turned to the window, her palm resting on the torn pages, and stared up at the sky, as clear and cloudless as her eyes. The white hair, deep wrinkles, and heavy reliance on the walking stick were testament to her age, but there was a defiant, inner strength and sharp intelligence that rejected pity and sympathy. She regretted nothing.

Would she have murdered Esmond if she'd been younger, with her future ahead of her and more to lose? It was impossible to say. All I knew was that she was a complex woman who was no less complex now than she had been decades ago with her whole life to look forward to. Age didn't change that.

I sought out Lord and Lady Kershaw and informed them that I'd finished my study of their masterpieces. Lady Kershaw expressed her surprise. Lord Kershaw's gaze flew to the staircase. I suspected the moment I was gone, he'd check on his aunt.

I left the house, only to stop on the drive on the spot where Esmond died. I glanced back at Hambledon Hall, a commanding and stoic structure that wouldn't look out of place in Medieval times. Its appearance was all pretense, however, a lie created by Lady Elizabeth's father to make it seem as though the family's wealth and power stretched back many centuries, not just one or two. He'd continued the lies by excluding his firstborn grandson, Esmond, from the line of inheritance. The lie wouldn't die completely, not until everyone who knew the truth was gone. I was quite sure the only three people who knew Esmond should have been the sixth earl instead of his younger half-brother would never tell. Lord Kershaw and Lady Elizabeth would take it to their graves. I doubted he would even tell his wife or children. And I wouldn't tell anyone either, after I informed Harry, of course. That would make four people to know the truth, not three. None of us would speak of it again.

Something moving in one of the windows on the first floor caught my eye. I wasn't precisely sure which window belonged to Lady Elizabeth's bedchamber, but I suspected she was sitting there watching me. I lifted a hand in a wave, then turned away. My steps quickened without me realizing it at first. It wasn't until I found myself at the edge of the village, out of breath, that I realized I'd maintained a fast pace because I was eager to see Harry again.

CHAPTER 19

"*K*eeping secrets does more harm than good," I told Uncle Ronald. "Secrets have a way of exploding at the worst possible time, causing havoc."

We sat in his office in the late afternoon. Clouds had crowded into the sky and darkened the room. He worked by strong lamplight that fell across his face, creating shadows below the bulges and making him look exhausted. Perhaps he was exhausted. Aunt Lilian's health must be weighing on his mind.

He'd greeted me amiably, if somewhat cautiously, knowing I'd just come from Hambledon Hall. He must be expecting me to announce I'd found the killer. He must also be worried the killer was one of Lord Kershaw's family.

"Mrs. Short's new rule of no fraternizing is forcing the staff to conduct their relationships in secret," I went on. "It has done nothing to stop them."

He stared at me, frowning. "I am aware of that."

"Nor do I think we should try to stop them," I went on. "For one thing, it's not our place to interfere in the staff's private lives. They're all adults, after all, and some of those relationships are genuine. For another, by dismissing those who are caught breaking the rule, we dismiss perfectly good employees. Also, Mrs. Short claims her rule is protecting the maids, but it isn't. If one of the male staff is taking advantage of a maid, dismissing them may not stop him. It would simply stop it from happening at the hotel or residence hall. All her rule does is remove the problem from being *her* responsibility."

"Cleopatra—"

"If the rule is going to be applied at all, then is should be on a case-by-case basis, not with an indiscriminate sweep. For example, *was* Mary's footman taking advantage of her? Was he going to abandon her? We simply don't know. What if their relationship was genuine? What if they were going to marry? We have just taken away the livelihoods of both, making the start of their life together very difficult. We ought to be ashamed, Uncle. We're forcing the couples to become secretive and, as I said, no good comes from secrets."

I was well aware how hypocritical I was being, after promising to keep Lady Elizabeth's secret and planning on keeping a rather large one of my own, at least for a while. Even so, I felt keenly about getting my point across.

"Cleopatra," Uncle Ronald boomed. Realizing I wasn't going to talk over him, he cleared his throat and lowered his voice. "Cleopatra, there's no need to concern yourself about Mrs. Short's rule. It's no more."

"You overturned it?"

"She came to see me today and revoked it herself, using the same arguments you just laid out so concisely for me. She has also re-employed Mary and the footman."

"I didn't think she was capable of seeing a different point of view, but I'm glad she has."

His chins wobbled with his throaty chuckle. "I'm reasonably sure Hobart pointed it out to her, although neither has admitted it to me."

I started to laugh. Mr. Hobart told me he'd reminded Mrs. Short that he was her superior. It was his way of laying the groundwork before he tackled her over her new rule. A rule he couldn't personally support. He'd not gone over her head to Uncle Ronald, but he'd subtly reminded the housekeeper that he could. It allowed her to retract the rule without losing too much respect with her employer.

Well played, Mr. Hobart.

I stood and made to leave.

"Cleopatra, one moment. I have something to ask you."

"You don't have to worry, Uncle. My investigation into the gamekeeper's murder has come to an end. There'll be no arrest."

"I'm glad to hear it, but it's not about that." He leaned forward and clasped his hands on the desk surface in front of him. "It's about your acquaintance with Harry Armitage."

Oh no. It would seem I was going to be forced to reveal my secret sooner than I expected.

"Do you think you could use your influence with him to gauge whether he would return to the hotel?" When I didn't respond, he added, "As manager-in-waiting. Hobart can't last forever, sadly, and Peter Leyland isn't up to it yet. A new role could be made for Armitage, something between Hobart and Leyland, so that Hobart could move into semi-retirement, if he felt so inclined."

"I don't think he does feel that way inclined."

"Even so, it's best to be prepared. Could you sound out Armitage?"

"No, I won't. I don't think he would return to work here under any circumstances. You weren't fair to him when you dismissed him. Anyway, his business is doing too well for him to consider walking away from it."

Uncle Ronald's lips flattened. "No, I doubt that's it. Perhaps his relationship is holding him back."

My mouth went dry. "His relationship?"

He stroked his moustache. "What's her name again? Miss Morris, I think. Yes, that's it. Miss Morris."

I blew out a long, measured breath. This was one secret it was time to end. "Harry and Miss Morris have ended their relationship."

Slowly, slowly, he pushed himself to his feet. "Then I'm afraid I have to forbid you from seeing him anymore, Cleopatra. Without another woman in the picture, your acquaintance sends the wrong message."

I squared up to him and lifted my chin. "I am sorry to go against your wishes, but I *will* see Harry again. Speaking of your wishes, it was you who wanted me to investigate the murder of Esmond Shepherd."

He sniffed, as if trying to sniff out the meaning behind my sudden reminder. "What of it?"

"He was shot by a member of Lord Kershaw's family. I'd rather not say who or why they shot him, but I will if you force my hand."

Uncle Ronald leaned his fists on the desk and lowered his head. "I see. Well. You are more ruthless than I've given you credit for, Cleopatra."

"I wish it weren't necessary."

He straightened, but still did not look at me. He concentrated on some papers on his desk, or pretended to. He seemed to be moving them about with no real purpose. "You may see Armitage for the purposes of your mutual interest in criminal investigation. That's all."

I left his office without responding. Having him agree that I could see Harry after he'd learned that Miss Morris was no longer Harry's sweetheart was a good first step. More steps were still required, but they would be made when the time was right. Now was not that time.

I was passing my aunt and uncle's suite when the door opened and Aunt Lilian emerged. "Cleopatra. I was just on my way to speak to you. May I have a word?"

Blackmailing my uncle into letting me continue to see Harry was nowhere near as anxiety-inducing as facing my aunt again. I steeled myself. "Is there something you need, Aunt?"

"Yes." Her voice quavered and her lip quivered. "I need to apologize to you."

I took her hands in mine. They were ice-cold and trembling. "It's all right."

"It's not. I was beastly. Please forgive me, dearest girl."

"There's nothing to forgive because it wasn't you who said it. It was the cocaine's effects."

She flinched before giving the smallest nod, as if a larger movement would pain her. "You're right. I haven't been myself. I am not *this* person." Her face crumpled. "I don't want to be this person. But I don't know how to stop."

"I know, Aunt. I know."

"I *want* to stop. I *want* to be myself again."

It was the most heartening thing to hear. I squeezed her hands and smiled in encouragement. "I am here. You are not alone."

For the first time in a long time, she smiled. "I will need your help. I don't know how to begin, or where."

"The first step is to throw away your tonic."

"I tipped it out this morning."

That was an encouraging sign that she genuinely wanted to get better and wasn't simply saying what she knew I wanted to hear. "Good. The second step is finding a new doctor. I'll do that for you. We can visit him together."

She drew me into another hug with more force than I expected from her frail figure. I hugged her, too, squeezing a little too hard, perhaps, out of sheer relief and joy at having my sweet aunt back.

* * *

THE FOLLOWING MORNING, Harmony was full of questions at breakfast. Not a single one of them was about the murder, after I told her I knew who committed it but couldn't tell her any more.

"So? How did it happen? Did you spontaneously kiss in the heat of the moment or was it a decision you took with a clear head?"

"I see Victor has told you."

"As much as he knows, which is not enough." She tapped my arm. "Go on. Tell me how it happened."

"We kissed on the threshold of his flat."

"His flat!" Her eyes flashed with mischief. "I never thought you'd be that unconventional and daring."

"It was a kiss, Harmony, nothing more. But it was a very good kiss. Wonderful, in fact." I clutched my coffee cup to my chest and smiled. "So good that I lost track of time."

"Those are the best sort. What happens now?"

"I call on him at his office after breakfast. I need to ask him some medical questions."

"How romantic," she said with a laugh.

I giggled, too. Indeed, I couldn't stop my giggles. Despite knowing there would be headwinds ahead when it came to talking to my family about Harry, I felt utterly, ridiculously happy.

* * *

I FOUND Harry drinking coffee and reading the newspaper in the Roma Café. He wasn't due to open his office for another half hour, but I couldn't wait. I wanted to see him, and knowing he often stopped at the café, I'd hoped to find him there.

Luigi spotted me entering before Harry did. He greeted me with a nod that wasn't a simple nod, but more of a knowing one. The two elderly men on the stools at the counter both swiveled to follow the direction of Luigi's gaze. They broke into twin grins then winked, one after the other.

I peered over Harry's newspaper. "You told them?"

He looked past me to Luigi and the two regulars. "No. I must have given it away."

"How?"

"I haven't been able to wipe the smile off my face since you kissed me."

"*You* kissed *me*."

"Will you come up to my office so we can…discuss it?"

"All right."

He didn't bother to fold the newspaper. He simply left it on the table where it slid onto the floor in a jumble of loose pages. He tossed an apology over his shoulder to Luigi before ushering me out of the café.

Once we were alone in his office, he closed the door. Before I'd had a chance to remove my coat and deposit my umbrella in the stand, he gently pushed me back against the door and kissed me.

I dropped the umbrella and clutched his impressive shoulders, before stroking my hands up the back of his head into his hair. Touching him like that, holding him and being held by him in return, was more thrilling than the first time. More thrilling than I'd expected it to be, and far more satisfying.

When the kiss came to an end, he helped me out of my coat. "Is this business or pleasure?"

"Neither." I picked up the umbrella and speared it into the stand while he hung up my coat and removed his hat. "I want to ask you if we can call on Dr. Garside as soon as possible. Aunt Lilian is ready to accept help."

He took my hand and rubbed his thumb along mine. "That's good news. We can see him this morning. Does this mean you told her about us?"

"Not yet. She's delicate, and I don't want to trouble her. Also, my uncle needs careful management if he's to accept you. Our news has the potential to upset my relationship with them. We need to keep it secret a while longer." I was well aware that I'd just lectured my uncle on the very topic of keeping secrets. In that case, the secrets would cause an explosion if discovered. This situation was different, however. In our case, it would prevent one.

"Very well, if that's the way it has to be for now, then so be it."

Harry was more accepting than I thought he'd be. He must have already come to the same conclusion.

"Thank you. My family is important to me, but not as important as you are. If I have to distance myself from them over this, then I will, without hesitation. But not yet."

He tucked a loose strand of my hair behind my ear then traced his thumb along my jaw. "You won't have to, Cleo. I promise. I'm going to charm Lady Bainbridge into wanting me for her nephew-in-law, and I'm going to manage Sir Ronald with such skill he won't remember ever having rejected me as your suitor."

I grinned. "I know you will. Thank you for understanding, Harry."

He stroked his thumb along my jaw again, all the way to my lower lip. His smoky gaze followed the trail. "As long as this isn't your way of saying you've changed your mind and no longer want to move forward."

"No! Not at all."

One of his dimples appeared with his lopsided smile. "Then I accept the delay on one condition."

"Name it. I'll even share my next investigation with you."

The second dimple appeared. "Nothing as drastic as that. My only condition is that I can kiss you in the meantime, when we're alone."

"That's a condition I willingly accept."

He circled his arms around my waist and proved exactly

how much he appreciated our agreement with another heart-pounding, breath-stealing kiss.

Available 2nd December 2025 :
MURDER ON HARLEY STREET
The 11th Cleopatra Fox Mystery

Cleo and Harry investigate the electrocution of a patient by a medical therapy device. Read on for a description of MURDER ON HARLEY STREET by C.J. Archer.

Wentworth Family Tree

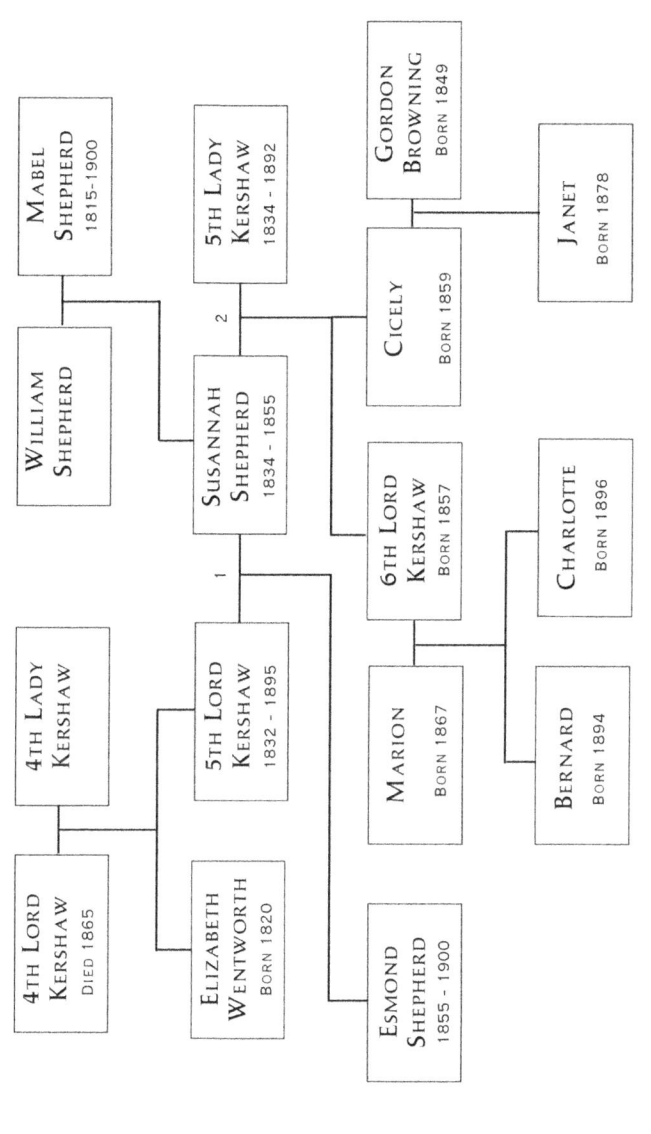

MABEL SHEPHERD
1815-1900

WILLIAM SHEPHERD

4TH LADY KERSHAW

4TH LORD KERSHAW
DIED 1865

5TH LADY KERSHAW
1834 - 1892

SUSANNAH SHEPHERD
1834 - 1855

2

5TH LORD KERSHAW
1832 - 1895

ELIZABETH WENTWORTH
BORN 1820

1

GORDON BROWNING
BORN 1849

CICELY
BORN 1859

JANET
BORN 1878

6TH LORD KERSHAW
BORN 1857

MARION
BORN 1867

CHARLOTTE
BORN 1896

BERNARD
BORN 1894

ESMOND SHEPHERD
1855 - 1900

ABOUT: MURDER ON HARLEY STREET

When a patient is electrocuted by a medical therapy device, the manufacturer proves it was tampered with. Who killed her? And what grudge did they hold against her doctor, whose reputation now lies in tatters?

The medical profession's faith in electric shock therapies for treating female nervous conditions is shaken after a patient dies while connected to one such device. Harry Armitage is hired by the doctor arrested for her murder, and he invites Cleo to help him uncover the truth. After all, the doctor is the same one who tried—and failed—to treat Cleo's aunt. As they dig deeper, it becomes apparent the doctor has failed other patients too, and those patients' loved ones want revenge.

Did that desire for revenge lead to the death of an innocent patient? Or did the victim have enemies of her own? As Cleo and Harry unravel the multi-layered mystery, they realize not everyone is who they seem. Suspects are hiding secrets that, if exposed, could shatter reputations and relationships.

Meanwhile, the manufacturer of a popular but highly addictive medicine has booked the Mayfair Hotel for a major presentation to important clients. As the day of the event looms, Cleo and Harry learn of a plot to sabotage it.

Can they solve the mystery and save the presentation? Or will it be ruined? And will someone get away with murder?

Available December 2025 :
MURDER ON HARLEY STREET
The 11th Cleopatra Fox Mystery

A MESSAGE FROM THE AUTHOR

I hope you enjoyed reading MURDER AT HAMBLEDON HALL as much as I enjoyed writing it. As an independent author, getting the word out about my book is vital to its success, so if you liked this book please consider telling your friends and writing a review at the store where you purchased it. If you would like to be contacted when I release a new book, subscribe to my newsletter at http://cjarcher.com/contact-cj/newsletter/. You will only be contacted when I have a new book out.

ALSO BY C.J. ARCHER

SERIES WITH 2 OR MORE BOOKS

The Glass Library

Cleopatra Fox Mysteries

After The Rift

Glass and Steele

The Ministry of Curiosities Series

The Emily Chambers Spirit Medium Trilogy

The 1st Freak House Trilogy

The 2nd Freak House Trilogy

The 3rd Freak House Trilogy

The Assassins Guild Series

Lord Hawkesbury's Players Series

Witch Born

SINGLE TITLES NOT IN A SERIES

The Warrior Priest

Courting His Countess

Surrender

Redemption

The Mercenary's Price

ABOUT THE AUTHOR

C.J. Archer has loved history and books for as long as she can remember and feels fortunate that she found a way to combine the two. She spent her early childhood in the dramatic beauty of outback Queensland, Australia, but now lives in suburban Melbourne with her husband, two children and a mischievous black & white cat named Coco.

Subscribe to C.J.'s newsletter through her website to be notified when she releases a new book, as well as get access to exclusive content and subscriber-only giveaways. Her website also contains up to date details on all her books: http://cjarcher.com She loves to hear from readers. You can contact her through email cj@cjarcher.com or follow her on social media to get the latest updates on her books:

facebook.com/CJArcherAuthorPage

instagram.com/authorcjarcher

Printed in Great Britain
by Amazon

63045346R00150